Wyatt couldn't keep his eyes from straying to Sadie.

She'd about taken his breath away when he'd walked into the kitchen. She wore a sundress, exposing her arms and legs. And they were mighty fine arms. And the legs, well, he couldn't continue those thoughts while a guest at her table. She had her hair piled up in a haphazard bun at the back of her head. Several of the curls had escaped and one swayed against the nape of her neck, taunting him. He wanted to brush it aside and press his lips to the tender skin below it.

He looked down at his plate and sopped up sauce with a bit of bread. *And you are a lying, deceitful spy who has no right to even think about her.* Pretty soon, he'd "quit" and move on. She'd never know.

The idea of hurting her made him feel like an even bigger jerk.

Dear Reader,

It was just me and a few friends, chatting on Twitter about cute guys. "You should have seen the hot guy my cleaning company sent over," she said.

"Hot? What? *Please* send us a picture!"

She didn't send the picture, but later that day, when my partner came home from work, I said, "You know what I should do? Start a cleaning company. Hot guys cleaning houses."

"I don't know about starting a business," he said. "You're a writer. How about a book?"

That's how all of this started.

Sadie, Wyatt and I have been on a long journey together. At one point, I even thought their story would end up under the bed, in a trunk of discarded papers, never to be seen again. Then I got the call from Harlequin through its SYTYCW (So You Think You Can Write) contest.

It's always when it seems darkest that the light breaks through, isn't it?

I hope you love Sadie and Wyatt as much as I do.

Thank you,

Janet Lee Nye

JANET LEE NYE

Spying on the Boss

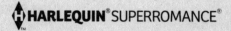

HARLEQUIN® SUPERROMANCE®

Recycling programs
for this product may
not exist in your area.

ISBN-13: 978-0-373-60943-7

Spying on the Boss

Copyright © 2016 by Janet Lee Nye

All rights reserved. Except for use in any review, the reproduction or utilization of this work in whole or in part in any form by any electronic, mechanical or other means, now known or hereinafter invented, including xerography, photocopying and recording, or in any information storage or retrieval system, is forbidden without the written permission of the publisher, Harlequin Enterprises Limited, 225 Duncan Mill Road, Don Mills, Ontario M3B 3K9, Canada.

This is a work of fiction. Names, characters, places and incidents are either the product of the author's imagination or are used fictitiously, and any resemblance to actual persons, living or dead, business establishments, events or locales is entirely coincidental.

This edition published by arrangement with Harlequin Books S.A.

For questions and comments about the quality of this book, please contact us at CustomerService@Harlequin.com.

® and TM are trademarks of Harlequin Enterprises Limited or its corporate affiliates. Trademarks indicated with ® are registered in the United States Patent and Trademark Office, the Canadian Intellectual Property Office and in other countries.

Printed in U.S.A.

® www.Harlequin.com

Janet Lee Nye is a writer by day and a neonatal nurse by night. She lives in Charleston, South Carolina, with her fella and her felines.

She discovered romance with books she "borrowed" from her grandmother and renewed her love affair with the genre after stumbling upon Robyn Carr's Virgin River series.

Rumors of her jelly bean addiction are completely exaggerated.

For Danny. Thanks for letting me be your mom.

CHAPTER ONE

FRIDAY SHOULD NOT start with a dead cat. That seemed more of a Monday sort of problem. Sadie ended the call and slumped back in her desk chair. Her black-and-white mutt, Jack, came over to sniff the phone dangling from her hand. "Seriously?" she asked the ceiling. "For real? This is happening?"

The ceiling didn't answer and when Jack found no treat in her hand, he went back to his doggy bed with an aggrieved sigh. Sadie hauled herself out of the chair with her own sigh. *Dead cat.* Even worse, it was a client's. She picked up her purse and pointed at Jack.

"Stay!"

He obeyed. Probably because he was already back to sleep. Sadie shook her head as she headed down the hall, digging in her purse for her keys. *Dog never listens to a word I say anyway.*

"Hey, Molly?" she called. "Rosie's dead, and Heidi is flipping out so I've got to get over there and…"

The words stuttered to a stop as her mouth

fell open. There was a man sitting in the small reception area. She glanced in the direction of her receptionist's desk but it was empty. "Who are you?"

The man stood. "Wyatt Anderson. I have a nine-thirty interview."

"Sorry. Hold on. I've got a bit of a situation."

She turned and backtracked to the kitchen where she spotted Molly coming out of the supply room with a package of copy paper. "There's a man out there." Sadie whispered.

"Must be your interview. Is he cute?"

"No, he is not *cute*. He's freaking gorgeous."

Good-looking guys hanging out in her lobby was nothing new. Her entire company was built on them. The Cleaning Crew's business model was simple: hot guys cleaned your house or business. But her guys were only that—guys. Young guys who were hot, just in the abstract. They were like her little brothers or something. But this guy was a blond, tanned, full-grown hunk of a man.

She and Molly returned to the reception area. The small space with the two wingback chairs and Molly's desk seemed even smaller with him standing there. He was smiling somewhat uncertainly, laugh lines bracketing his eyes as twin dimples appeared in his cheeks. Sadie knew she should say something, but those dimples rendered her incapable of coherent thought. She'd never found blond men very attractive. They seemed too pretty. This man was not pretty. No, he was ruggedly handsome. His dark blond hair was wavy and a tad shaggy. Brown eyebrows arched over hazel eyes. His nose looked as if it had been broken in the past and his lips made a woman wonder how they might feel against hers.

Molly let out a quivering little sigh. That broke the spell and Sadie frowned at her. Molly was sixty years old. She'd been the second person Sadie had ever hired. She was a tiny, round woman with red hair fading to white and green eyes that missed nothing. She kept all the guys—and Sadie, too—in line with either grandmotherly love or sternness, whichever the situation required. But she could hardly blame Molly when her own mouth wouldn't stay shut. She snapped to attention and took a step forward, shook his hand and managed to choke out, "Sadie Martin, nice to meet you." A thrill raced from her palm up her arm at the touch. *Holy cow.*

She retrieved her hand. He'd followed the interview request to wear jeans and a white T-shirt. It was the Cleaning Crew uniform, although the official T-shirt had the logo on the breast pocket. She forced herself to focus. *This is a job interview.* He had the face. Her eyes swept over him. And he most definitely had the body.

She sucked at guessing people's height, but she had to tilt her head up to look him in the eye and she was five-nine. The shirt was snug over broad shoulders and a solid chest, the sleeves tight around his biceps. It fell loose over his abdomen and she would bet the stash of jelly beans in the bottom drawer of her desk there was a nice six-pack under there.

And... *Oh, shit! The cat.* She turned to Molly. "I have to go. Josh needs help with Heidi Klingman. Rosie's dead. She's upset and Josh made it worse. It's a mess. I've got to get over there and play St. Gertrude. Make a note to send her flowers and a card tomorrow."

She turned and once again froze at the sight of Wyatt standing there with his arms crossed, all sexy forearms and bulging muscles. Oh, heck, the interview. She needed to get him on board. The clients would be fighting over him. If he passed the testing. *Please, God in heaven, let him pass the testing, pretty please with jelly beans on top.*

"Want to take a ride? We can do the interview on the way."

"Sure."

It seemed like a good idea until she was in the car with him. Strapped into the passenger seat, he made her Explorer feel claustrophobic. Her employees were college kids who needed the flexible hours of the job. He was her age, maybe a little older. She was unusually aware of his presence. Big and male and, damn, he smelled good. Like sunshine and salt water and man.

"It's not far," she said as she pulled out onto Savannah Highway. "Hopefully, I can get the situation under control quickly."

"Who's dead?"

He sounded serious and she remembered from his application that he'd been a cop. *Yeah, that was interesting.* A cop, then in the National Guard, and his last job was as a house painter. Not the typical career path. "A cat."

"And St. Gertrude?"

Sadie laughed. "Patron saint of cats. I only know this because Heidi has an altar with her picture and the pictures of every cat she's owned since she was, like, ten. There are a lot."

She cleared her throat, trying to find her inner boss. Make this gooey girl melting over a man go away. *Get it together. You can't hire a man if he's going to make you violate your number one rule. No fooling around, ever. Not in word, jest or deed. Interview.* His hand was resting lightly on his thigh and she remembered the pleasant shock of his skin touching hers. She'd never felt that before. *Stop it. Focus. You're not picking him up in a bar.*

"You were a police officer?"

He shifted in his seat so he was facing her. This was unfair. She could only steal glances while navigating traffic. He was looking right at her. She couldn't remember if she'd bothered with makeup that morning. She glanced in the rearview, pretending to check traffic. Not too bad. Nothing hanging from her nose at least.

"That's right."

"Why'd you quit?"

"Did two tours in Afghanistan with the National Guard. After I got home, the whole law-and-order, stress-and-danger thing didn't appeal to me."

At the red light, she watched him carefully for a long moment. His body language and facial expression were relaxed. His tone of voice hadn't changed. She nodded. "Here's where I say thank you for your service and mean it but feel sort of dorky saying it."

His laugh took her by surprise. It was lush and without restraint. "Here's where I say thank you and feel slightly embarrassed about it for no particular reason."

She smiled and some of her awkwardness slipped away. "So you started painting houses?"

"A guy I knew in the guard was kind enough to hire me."

"Why are you applying with us?"

"With the economy, painting jobs are scarce.

If we get a job, we're there evenings, weekends. Whatever's needed to finish. On the flip side, if the weather's bad, no work. I need steadier hours."

"That's why you need a job. Why us?"

He held up a hand as he ticked off items. "Your reputation. Your salary. Your growing customer base."

"And what can you offer us?"

"Strong back. Strong work ethic. Good organizational skills. Eye for detail. And I know how to handle a hysterical woman."

She grinned. *I'll bet you do know how to handle a woman, hysterical or not.* She forced those thoughts from her mind. *Employee. Employee. If he passes the testing, he's going to be an employee.* Her brain was with the program. Parts south, not so much.

CHAPTER TWO

AS THEY PULLED into a parking space in the up-scale apartment community, Wyatt saw a guy sitting on the stairs. He wore the Cleaning Crew uniform of jeans and white T-shirt and when he stood, Wyatt noted he was about his own age. Since most of the employees seemed to be college age, this made him feel as if he might actually fit in. The man walked toward them as Sadie climbed from the car. Josh, he remembered she'd said.

"I haven't even finished. She kicked me out. I left everything."

Sadie put a hand on his arm. "It's okay. Is she still crying?"

"No. She's sitting in the living room and holding it. It's creepy."

"What did you say to her?"

"Nothing. I told her I thought something was wrong with the cat. She came in and starting screaming. I asked her if she wanted me to bury it or something."

"Or something?"

Josh shrugged. "It's a cat. The hell do I know what to do with a dead cat?"

"And I'm supposed to know?"

"You're the boss."

"Oh, for Pete's sake." She glanced up at an apartment door on the second floor. Frowned. She looked at Wyatt. "Do you know what you're supposed to do with a dead cat?"

"Bury it or something," he said. He kept a straight face but put a humorous tone to his words. It was a risk, but the chance to get on the good side of one of Sadie's guys couldn't be missed. Josh snorted out a laugh. Her frown deepened and he felt a stab of worry.

"I see now why you left out problem-solving skills on that list you gave me."

His worry subsided at the sarcasm in her voice and the exasperated roll of her eyes. It disappeared when Josh hooked an arm around her shoulders. "Come on, Sadie. That's what everyone thinks you do with a dead cat. Bury it."

Wyatt watched as Sadie's expression changed to a careful neutral. *Putting on her game face.* She drew in a deep breath and let it out. He wasn't sure what he'd been expecting to find, but Sadie Martin wasn't it. She was younger than he'd expected. And pretty. Her hair was tangle of black curls, barely contained in the ponytail spilling half way down her back. Her skin was a delicate shade of white that was rare in this southern climate and showed off her dark blue eyes and full lips. He'd heard the term Cupid's bow before, but now recognized it in the shape of her mouth. He liked it.

"Wyatt?"

Come on. Pay attention. You're here to get a job, not get laid. "Yeah?"

"Come on upstairs with us. I'll talk to Heidi while you and Josh collect his stuff. If it seems like I'm going to be tied up awhile, I'll have Josh take you back."

"Sounds like a plan."

She shook her head while staring up at the apartment door. "I hate this."

"Dead cats?" Josh teased.

"Pain."

Wyatt followed her up the stairs. She paused at the door, her head lowered. With a deep breath, she squared her shoulders and went inside. She crossed the room to sit beside the woman cradling the body of an orange-and-white cat. "Oh, Heidi, honey," she crooned. She hugged the woman who burst into a fresh torrent of tears. "Poor Rosie."

Clearly, whatever reservations she'd had about dealing with the situation were gone. Her compassion was real. He'd seen enough fake compassion, doled out some of it himself when he wore a badge, to recognize the real thing. Sadie's hand reached out to pet the cat and Josh turned away with a jerk. Wyatt followed him into the back room where he helped him gather the various supplies he'd left behind.

Heidi told Sadie how Josh found the cat and came to get her. Sadie's voice was warm and sad. "She just slipped away from us."

He was crossing the living room when Sadie let out a small laugh. "Remember when I first started cleaning for you? How she would follow me from room to room and we started calling her Inspector Rosie?"

He slowed his steps to look at the two women. Sadie had one hand on Heidi's shoulder and the thumb of the other stroked over the cat's cheek and ear. And damn if Heidi didn't laugh, too. "Oh! And remember the time she hid in the closet and you thought she'd gotten outside and we spent an hour searching for her and when we came back in, she was sitting on the couch staring at us like we were crazy?"

Back in the parking lot, he helped Josh load the equipment into his car. Josh closed the trunk and leaned against the car. Wyatt pegged him to be late twenties. Dark hair and a strong build.

"You a new guy?" Josh asked.

"Don't know. I was there for my interview when she got your call."

"Sadie's good people. You could do worse for a boss."

"What about the clients?"

"Pretty cool. I mean, I know it seems weird. People think they hire us like we're strippers or something. But it isn't like that. Sadie screens the clients pretty well. Most of them know we do a good job. Having a guy clean your house is something to brag to their friends about."

"So, no, uh, problems?"

Josh shook his head. "She's got strict rules for us and the clients. It's the one thing that will make her go ballistic. Instant termination if you break the rules."

"That's good to hear. I don't need a hassle. Just a paycheck."

He'd done some digging and what Josh was saying was consistent with everything he'd heard about the Cleaning Crew. They both looked up as Sadie came out of the apartment. She hurried down the stairs. Those luscious lips were pressed together in a tight line and he could see the tension in her shoulders. He wanted to touch her. "You were doing great up there," he said.

"Thanks. Do you want the job?"

"Yes. Unless I have to bury the cat. I'd have to negotiate a bonus."

He smiled when she laughed and her shoulders relaxed. Yes, those lips looked much better loose and smiling.

"There's still testing to do before a final offer." She turned to Josh. "Take him back and tell Molly to get started on the paperwork. I'm taking the cat to her vet so they can arrange a cremation. Oh, and have someone take Jack out."

She held out a hand and smiled up at him. He shook her hand. His fingers tightened against hers for a second at the pleasant jolt of the touch.

"Welcome aboard," she said.

"Thanks. I appreciate it."

If only he wasn't lying about everything. He was starting to feel bad about it.

SADIE PULLED INTO the parking lot and rested her head on the steering wheel for a moment. She'd delivered the cat to the vet. Freaking out the whole way, worried she'd get a ticket and have to explain why she had a dead cat in the car. She'd never had a pet until Jack, and it had taken everything she had to touch the too-still body of poor little Rosie. But one thing she understood quite well was the pain of being left alone. She had gone back to check on Heidi afterward. Found her tearful but coping. She wouldn't go long without a cat. By tomorrow, she'd be looking at adoptable cats on the SPCA website.

She climbed out of the car and as she did, her

eyes passed over the brick facade of the building. She still had trouble believing she owned the place. It wasn't fancy, just a cracker box–style brick house, but it was hers. She'd bought the house six years ago after running the business out of her apartment for three years. The two-story brick building had been empty and neglected for several years. The stretch of Savannah Highway it sat upon was a short ride to downtown Charleston and the location—and price—had been perfect. She'd converted the second floor into an apartment where she lived and the downstairs was the Crew's office.

A warm sense of pride and accomplishment filled her. She'd built this. Starting with her first job as a housekeeper, she'd put aside money and cultivated a customer base, hoping to one day work for herself. To be running the most successful, most sought-after maid service in Charleston blew her mind. And terrified her. Didn't they know that every day she was winging it?

Jack barked happily when she let herself in the front door. He skidded down the hall and crashed into her. Eighty pounds of shaggy fur, lolling tongue and stupid. She grabbed his head between her hands. "Who's a good boy? Who's the best boy?"

His entire body wagged out his answer. Molly laughed from her desk. "And you wonder why he won't behave for you. You encourage bad behavior. Jack. Sit."

And he sat, his tongue hanging out the side of his mouth and his tail swishing across the floor. Sadie leaned down and kissed the top of his head. "I think you're the best boy," she told him. "Granny Molly is just a meanie."

"Your new hire is still in the back, taking the personality tests. I called his references, they check out. Told them to expect a call from you."

Sadie took the handful of mail Molly held out to her. "Anything else?"

"Deanna Carter—"

"No."

"—asked if you'd reconsider."

"No."

"Says she was under stress and is—"

"No."

"—taking medication and has her issues under control."

"Don't care if God Himself writes her an excuse. She groped one of my guys. No."

Molly held up her hands in surrender. "Only relaying the message. Don't get mad at me."

"I'm not mad at you. I'm still mad at her."

She bit back several colorful words. There was a new hire in the back. A new hire she wasn't sure she should hire. He was too…*too much*. She went to her office and tossed the mail on the desk. *Get it together. You can't deny a man a job because he makes you remember you're a woman. You're an adult. You're a professional. Deal with it.* She pulled the band out of her hair and shook out the curls, running her fingers over her scalp, trying to ease the brewing headache. An unfamiliar creak on a hallway floorboard was the only warning she got before Wyatt appeared in her open doorway. He stood with an easy, relaxed confidence and it made her wonder what it would take to rile him up a bit. And the thought sent a delicious little wave of pleasure through her. She tossed the hair band on her desk and squared her shoulders. "All done?"

"I think so. Hope so. My eyes are about to fall out of my skull. Not used to staring at a computer for so long."

He turned as she approached the door so she brushed lightly against his arm when she passed. Apparently all he had to do was stand there to rile her up. She shook her head as she walked down the hall. He followed and she swore she could feel his gaze on her back. She did what she always did when flustered—reverted to business mode.

"Have a seat," she said, waving at one of the tables set up as desks. She remained standing until he sat. Only then did she sit across from him. "There's a reason we do so much testing.

The results will be calculated and I'll get a report."

"Seems to be pretty standard with any job application these days," he said.

"True. It's for everyone's protection. My business model is a bit odd, some might say. So I make sure everyone, employees and customers alike, are on the same page about the services provided."

He leaned forward, crossing his arms on the table and distracting her with those tanned, muscled forearms, lightly dusted with sun-bleached blond hair. "And those services are?"

She snapped her eyes back to his. "We clean. Period. The end."

"I understand you perfectly. Do the customers? I recently got custody of my eight-year-old niece. I'm her only living relative. I can't afford any kind of accusation."

It took a moment for her to answer. Eight years old. Only living relative. Her heart raced and she drew in a slow breath. She clasped her hands together, staring down at her fingers. She cleared her throat and forced the corners of her mouth up into a smile.

"A lot of our clients have been with me since before the Cleaning Crew existed. New customers come primarily from referrals. All new clients have a sit-down interview with me and they have to sign a behavior agreement as part of their contract. Employees sign one also."

He rocked back in his seat. "That's pretty thorough."

"When we were first starting out, a woman made accusations. She fairly quickly confessed she'd made up the entire incident. She'd developed a crush on one of our guys, and when he did not reciprocate, she tried to get him fired by lying."

She stopped there. It still made her furious. She took a few deep breaths so she could talk without her volume climbing to shouting range. "Even though it was straightened out right away, it scared me. Max was a college kid majoring in education. If there had been some sort of crime reported against him, it could have landed him on the sex offenders list and he would never have been able to get a job as a teacher. It could have ruined his entire life. So I take this very seriously."

"Good. Exactly what I want to hear. I need a job and a paycheck. I don't need to risk my future and my niece's future."

She stood and he followed suit. "I think you'll be fine. I'll get the results and call you tomorrow."

CHAPTER THREE

THE DAY WAS pleasant and Wyatt would have chosen the outdoor seating, but Marcus Canard had already taken up residence in a corner booth at the Citadel Mall location of Sesame Burgers & Beer. The lunch crowd was beginning to thin out which troubled him a little. People in large noisy crowds were less likely to eavesdrop.

Wyatt hesitated, studying Marcus for a moment. He wore the Southern gentleman's casual uniform of khakis and a polo shirt. But everything was a bit off. The shirt stretched over a too-large gut and one collar was frayed. The fabric of the khakis was stiff and shiny. By his appearance, he wouldn't seem to fit with the business elite of Charleston, but he did.

He'd first noticed it when he'd been summoned to the office of Henry Moody to meet Marcus. The contrast between Henry's Old World grace and Marcus's crude appearance and speech was almost comical. Until you realized they were both rich and powerful men. And in the business world, money and power were all that really mattered.

Wyatt had taken this assignment when he really didn't want to. The work he did for Henry's insurance company was his main source of income. He couldn't jeopardize that relationship. Not with Jules's welfare to consider. So he was stuck with Marcus Canard. He crossed the room, pulling on his bland cop face.

"Did you get the job?" Marcus asked around a mouthful of fries as Wyatt sat across from him.

"Start on Monday. It'd be helpful if you told me exactly what it is you're looking for."

"Anything. I know that gal isn't running a legitimate business over there. And what's with the guy thing? Is that a gimmick or are those boys doing more than mopping?"

Wyatt corralled his irritation while he gave the waitress his order. Clients usually knew exactly what they wanted him to find. When he turned back to Marcus, he had it mostly under control. "You think there's something illegal going on, then?"

"All I know is she charges twice what I do, and for what? So a good-looking guy can clean your house? Who cares what he looks like?"

A spark of interest flared at that and Wyatt leaned forward. "You think she's running a male-prostitute service?"

"Why not? Women can pay for it now, too, right?"

"My preliminary investigation hasn't turned up anything. Not even a rumor."

"Find a rumor. Find something. Find anything. I want her out of business."

"Why?"

"That's nothing you need to know to do your job. Just do it."

Marcus had barked out the order, but his eyes had slid away from Wyatt's and lingered on the shoppers passing the window. His hands clenched into fists on the table. The man was angry. Anger was usually personal.

"You said she couldn't run a legitimate business. How do you know that?"

Marcus looked back at Wyatt and the silverware clanged on the table as he slammed his fist down. "There is something going on. She's nothing. A minimum-wage trailer-park maid. Thinks she's something now." He leaned forward and pointed his index finger at Wyatt. "I won that ridiculous *City Paper* award five years in a row. She took it from me. Now I'm losing customers. Find me something. Anything."

And there it was. She was hurting him financially and now she'd publicly beaten him. The *City Paper*'s Best of Charleston Award may have been the catalyst for Marcus seeking revenge, but money was always the motivation for men like him. He shrugged. "I don't think there's anything going on, but if you want to continue the investigation, it's your money."

"Damn right, it's my money. You find something. Anything. Be a shame if I had to tell Henry you let me down."

Wyatt pressed his lips together. His first impulse was to get up and walk out. But there was Julietta to consider now. He couldn't do anything to risk the stability he was trying to give her. If his relationship with Henry was damaged, he'd lose his biggest source of income.

He shrugged as he squeezed lime over his fish taco. "It's your money."

"And you'll have a report for me next week."

Marcus wiped his mouth and threw the napkin on his plate. He reached into his wallet and left a twenty on the table before lumbering away.

Asshole. Wyatt tried to finish his lunch, but the food tasted like sawdust and his stomach burned with frustrated anger. He shoved the plate away and smiled at the waitress to let her know he was ready.

He should probably try to dig a little deeper into the story of the woman who made the false allegation. *Most likely a waste of time.* He'd heard the passion and the fierce protectiveness in Sadie's voice when she'd told him the story this morning. She wasn't lying. She wasn't stupid, either. There was more going on here than Marcus was telling him. His phone buzzed in his shirt pocket. The display read Springfield Elementary and everything else was forgotten in a wave of concern. Julietta.

"Mr. Anderson? This is Mrs. Rigby, the principal at Springfield."

"Yes, ma'am. Is Julietta all right?"

"She's having a bit of a rough time today. Would you be able to come to the school?"

"On my way."

A bit of a rough time today. Poor kid had had a rough time the past six months. Her mother, Maddie, his baby sister, had been filling in for another flight nurse when the helicopter she was in went down in the Smoky Mountains. There had been no survivors. Julietta had been dropped off for school and had never seen her mother alive again.

He found her sitting in a chair in the school office, clutching her book bag to her chest. She sat perfectly still. No fidgeting, no swinging of the legs or tapping of feet. None of the constant motion you would expect from an eight-year-old. She didn't smile at him, only turned those big, dark eyes in his direction. He squatted beside her and ruffled the black hair falling in a messy sheet down her back.

"Hey, Jujube. What's up?"

She lowered her head to the book bag but her eyes, so full of a sadness he'd give anything to know how to relieve, never left his. "I want to go."

She didn't say she wanted to go home. In her mind, home was still in Asheville. Home was as dead and gone as her mother. He brushed back a lock of hair from her face.

"Okay, we'll go. Let me talk to Mrs. Rigby first."

"I'm sorry to have called you," Mrs. Rigby said as he sat across from her. "Usually, if we give her a little quiet time in the library or here, she can regroup and go on with her day."

"No, call me whenever you think it's necessary. She's my primary concern. Do you have any idea what may have upset her?"

"I think it was a geography lesson. Her teacher was talking about plains and mountains."

Wyatt took in a deep breath. Mountains. Asheville. Home. Her mother. The child psychologist said it was normal. Anything could trigger a memory reminding her of the loss and all he could do was be supportive.

He'd spent hours on the phone with Maddie's best friends trying to learn their rituals and habits and the things they celebrated so he could be prepared. That's how he'd known Julietta got a new stuffed bunny rabbit for Easter every year, not candy. He'd worried it had been a mistake to try to replicate a gift from her mother when Julietta had stared silently at the bunny. After what had seemed like forever, she'd stroked the soft, plush fabric and given her uncle a hug. Wyatt had never had a better hug in his life.

"I'm going to take her home, then. School's almost over for the day."

"Is she still getting help?"

"Yes. We're seeing the counselor twice a week. She's making good progress. It's slow, but steady. Due for some sort of breakthrough, the counselor thinks."

"Good. If there's anything we can do to help, please schedule a meeting with her teacher and me."

He stood and shook her hand, thanking her. As he left, he held out a hand to his niece. "Come on, Jules, let's hit the road."

She stood and carefully, deliberately settled the book bag around her shoulders. After a moment she placed her little hand in his. He closed his fingers gently around hers and let out a breath as sadness washed over him. He wanted to see her have some sort of normal childhood. He simply had no idea how to get her there.

CHAPTER FOUR

A SLENDER HAND with golden-brown skin and a perfect manicure reached over Sadie's shoulder and snatched the phone out of her hands. She reached to grab it back and noticed the jagged nail she'd forgotten to fix after breaking it while opening a box of mop tops.

"Magdalena!"

Her best friend slid into the booth across from her with a flounce of heavy dark hair and pinned her with nearly black eyes. She held the phone up. "Don't try to piss me off by calling me that. You can't distract me. Why were you looking at it?"

Sadie ignored the flare of guilt and gestured to the glasses of wine on the table. "I already got your chardonnay. And I ordered the hummus."

Lena lifted the wineglass and took a healthy sip. "Thank you. Why do you keep looking when you know it only makes you feel bad?"

Sadie took her phone back. Setting it aside, she took a long sip of her own wine. She knew she should stop checking her mother's Facebook page. It stirred up pain and anger she should have left behind years ago. It wasn't healthy, she knew, to read the accomplishments of her half brother and sisters and feel the need to shout, "Hey, I still exist! I'm accomplishing things, too!" Her jealousy of mere children made her sick with shame. But she couldn't stop. A part of her wondered if her mother had wanted her to find it. There were no privacy settings on the account. All she had to do was send a friend request.

She didn't need to say these things to Lena. She knew. The waiter brought the hummus and, as Sadie reached for a wedge of bread, Lena put her hand over Sadie's.

"I'm sorry, Sades. I didn't say that to hurt you."

Sadie shrugged and pulled her hand away. She kept her eyes on the bowl of hummus. She was capable of hurting herself without any help. "I know. You're right. It's like picking at a scab."

She sat back in the booth of the Avondale Mellow Mushroom restaurant. Avondale was a booming little microcosm about a mile over the Ashley River from downtown Charleston. While Sadie's home wasn't quite in the Avondale neighborhood, it was close enough to walk. In the past few years, the intersection where Magnolia met Savannah Highway had become a hot spot for local restaurants, artisan shops and amazing mural art. The revitalization was the reason her property values had skyrocketed, and she tried to repay the community by frequenting the shops and restaurants.

"Congrats on winning the *City Paper*'s Best of Charleston Award. Are you going to the big party to accept it?"

"No. A couple of the guys will. They're the reason we won."

"You should go, too. Come on, you built the company. Take some credit."

"I take credit. I don't need to go to a party. I do the important stuff."

She belonged to all the proper business groups. Lena, who owned her own financial management agency, had dragged Sadie to the meetings and forced her to join. She still felt uncomfortable. The professional women with their cool grace, beautiful suits and master's degrees made Sadie feel uncouth, sloppy and stupid. She eyed her gorgeous friend as she flirted with the waiter while giving her order.

She and Lena had begun working as maids twelve years ago when they were both fresh out of high school. Lena had graduated and Sadie had been forced to leave school. Lena had been focused and beautiful even then. She came from a huge family, and they were determined she was going to be their first college graduate. Her parents, grandparents, aunts, uncles and cousins came together to fund her education. She earned scholarships and qualified for grants. With her hard work and her family's help, Lena had graduated with a master's degree and not one penny of debt. The commitment and sacrifice of her family took Sadie's breath away.

"How's Paul?" she asked after she'd ordered.

Lena made a face and took a sip of wine. "Your attempts at distraction are pathetic. But since you asked, I'm going to break up with him."

"Why? I thought he was perfect."

"He is, on paper. In real life, he's boring. Don't get me started on the sex."

"Don't want to know."

"On. Off. Back to the computer. There should be no reason to self-induce when you have a man in the house."

Sadie stuck her fingers in her ears. "La la la la la, not listening." She did not want to hear this. Especially since the last time she'd had a man in the house or otherwise was… *Two years ago?* No wonder random men were making her horny. She took a sip of wine. *Be honest. One man was doing that. Only one.* She turned her attention back to Lena.

"Well, hell. You've sworn off bad boys. Now the nice young executives on the rise are boring? You're narrowing your options."

"There has to be a hybrid. I need a beta in the living room and an alpha in the bedroom. Do they exist?"

"You're asking me? I've given up."

"You're too young to give up."

"I can't do it. All the dating and getting to know someone and explaining…"

"You have nothing to explain. Nothing to be ashamed of, do you hear me?"

"Sure, right. Until he takes me home to meet his family. And wants to meet mine."

"So, bring him home to meet mine."

She smiled as she said it, a wicked little gleam lighting up her eyes. It made Sadie laugh. That would be a sight. Lena had paid her family back after her success by building her parents a huge home south of Charleston near the Edisto River. It had six bedrooms, six bathrooms, a huge kitchen and large yard. It was full to the roof with the same extended family that had helped her through college. They were loud and boisterous and nothing went unsaid—good, bad or ugly. You could feel the love crackling in the very air.

"It would certainly show us what he's made of."

Their pizzas arrived and Lena ordered another round of wine. They ate in silence for a few minutes.

"So, the new guy you hired seems interesting," Lena said.

Sadie, concentrating on her never-ending indecision of whether or not to use a fork and knife for the pizza, glanced at her friend. Lena was her accountant and Molly would have sent over the information to put him on the payroll.

"Whoa! What was that look all about?"

"What look?" Sadie said.

"That look. Last time I saw that look, it was from a dog growling over a bone. What's up with Mr. New Guy?"

"Nothing."

Lena laughed. "You're actually blushing, Sadie. Spill it. Is he hot?"

"Of course he's hot. He works for me. It's my business. Hot guys."

"True, but there's something about this one. Is he giving you the flusters?"

Taking a long sip—or three—from her wineglass, Sadie mulled over those words. Lena had gotten closer to the truth than she'd like to admit. Wyatt Anderson turned her into a nervous, giggling girl. Her mind offered up the memory of his hand, strong, tanned and calloused, clasping hers for a brief moment. The lust his touch had sent rocketing through her body wasn't girlish, though. Those had been the feelings of a woman who hadn't had a boyfriend in a very long time and led to thoughts of his hands on other parts of her body. *Sigh.*

"He has a certain appeal," she said. She tried to downplay it with a detached tone, but Lena didn't fall for it.

"Oh. *Dios. Mio.* It's a miracle! The ice is melting. *Digame.*"

"There's nothing to tell. He's an employee. Doesn't matter."

"It matters. Is he starting orientation Monday? Can I bring the paperwork over for him to sign? Get a peek at the man who made the mighty Sadie Martin feel like a woman?"

"No, you can't. Employee. Period. End of story."

"Who says you can't have a couple of thrills with an employee?"

"Have you lost your mind?"

"You know what I mean. Plenty of people meet on the job and figure out how to make it work."

Sadie swirled the last of the wine before downing it in a gulp. She shook her head. "Stop it. The guy's gorgeous. I looked. That's as far as it's going to go."

Lena held her hands up in surrender. "Fine. But we're getting to the age where we need to take advantage of every opportunity."

"There's the difference between us. You want

the whole deal. Marriage, kids, happily-ever-after. I really don't care about all that."

The understanding and touch of pity in Lena's eyes irritated her. She didn't know what made her madder: the look or Lena continuing to poke at this sore spot.

"Yes, you do. You're afraid."

Sadie raised her glass in a signal to the waiter to bring another. To hell with it—she wasn't driving. She pressed her lips together in a tight line. *Breathe.* She hated when Lena hit the truth dead-on. She *was* afraid, but Lena didn't have it quite right. Lena thought she was afraid of trust, of love. But that wasn't everything. She was afraid to let someone close enough for love because he would discover there was something wrong with her. She didn't know how to love.

She pushed those thoughts away. "How's Lito doing?"

Lena slumped back and Sadie felt her heart slump, too. A small frisson of fear bloomed in her belly. Lito, Abuelito, was Lena's grandfather. He had taken Sadie under his arm when she'd been introduced to the family. He was the closest she had to a father figure in her life. His diagnosis of pancreatic cancer several months ago had sent her on a roller coaster of fear, denial and hope. She'd stuffed all her messy emotions in a box, labeled it "doctors can cure anything these days" and begun a highly successful effort to pretend the entire thing wasn't happening.

"It's not good, Sades. It's too advanced for surgery. He hates the chemo and radiation therapy."

"But he's going to keep doing it, right? I mean, isn't that normal? The chemo and stuff is bad, but it helps eventually, right?"

Lena shook her head. "I don't know. He's eighty-three, Sades."

Tears clogged her throat. Selfish tears, she realized. She wanted him to keep fighting because she didn't want to lose him. "I know."

"He's questioning whether it's all worth it."

"Of course it's worth it! What's the alternative? To just die?"

Lena's dark eyes met hers and Sadie felt everything in her grow cold. The laughter and conversation around them dimmed to a distant buzz. She felt her head begin to move from side to side. *No.*

"It's his choice to make, Sadie. Only he can say what he wants his quality of life to be."

"I know."

The words were weak and wavering. She did know. But she felt like a child in her fear. Lito was going to leave her. Just like everyone else. She shook her head. *You are being selfish and childish. Stop it.* Her brain knew this. Her heart would accept it eventually.

CHAPTER FIVE

SADIE TRIED TO keep on the shady side of the path, but Jack had other ideas. He pulled on the harness with such strength she had no doubt that if she fell, he'd drag her along behind him. He'd been a rampaging whirl of doggie ecstasy ever since she'd put his halter on. Dog park day. Oh boy oh boy oh boy. The little park wasn't really a dog park, but no one had complained about her tossing tennis balls to Jack along a grassy stretch off the bike path, so she kept going there.

She'd slathered herself with eighty SPF and wore lightweight cotton pants to cover her legs, but a long-sleeve shirt was impossible in Charleston's May weather. Today the humidity was relatively low, so the temperature in the mideighties was pleasant. Her fair skin burnt to a crisp with ease and she'd long ago given up trying to get any sort of tan.

"Hold up, Jack. You're going to pull my arm out of its socket."

Of course he didn't listen. If Molly were here, he would trot obediently at her side. All he knew was they were approaching the stretch of grass where he could run until he collapsed or Sadie's throwing arm gave out, whichever came first. It was their Saturday ritual. A late-morning run in the park, then a bath. She'd discovered bathing an exhausted dog was much easier.

They reached the edge of the grass and Jack sat panting over his shoulder at her, his silly tongue lolling out. He let out a happy bark and tried to wag his tail through the grass. She took his head between her hands and squatted to look him in the eye. "You're such a goofball, Jack. Do you know this? Do you know you're a goofball?"

He barked again and quivered in anticipation. She led him to the shade of a large oak tree and undid the leash. As she shook a tennis ball out of the tube, he began to run in circles at her feet, making her laugh. Adopting him had been the best idea she'd ever had.

"Okay, you ready?"

She threw the ball as hard as she could, but honestly, not very far. Jack didn't care. He took off like a bullet, outpacing her throw and catching it neatly. He ran back to her and pretended to tussle over the ball. She threw the next one almost straight up. This allowed Jack to jump a fairly impressive distance into the air. As he did, she heard a little girl call out.

"Did you see that doggie jump?"

Sadie smiled at the little girl who had stopped her bike and was straddling it, pointing at Jack while looking back over her shoulder. Her hair was a shining wave of pure black falling half-way down her back. A man approached the girl. Her heart tripped over itself. *Oh, great.* It was Wyatt Anderson. He watched Jack run back and his gaze met hers the same instant Jack dropped the ball at her feet.

Oh, Jesus. Maybe he wouldn't recognize her. Maybe he'd keep on going. *Please, because dear God.* Because he was wearing shorts and a sleeveless T-shirt and he'd been running and was all muscle and sweat and devilish goodness. He raised his hand in a wave and smiled and even from this distance, she could see those dimples. Jack yipped impatiently at the delay. She waved back. *Perfect. Here he comes.* Without business matters to hide behind, she was going to make a fool of herself. Because those hazel eyes made every brain cell she had melt into a useless pile of goop. And she wanted to press her lips to one— or both—of those dimples.

"Hey," he said as they approached. The little girl left the bike on the side of the path and trailed behind him shyly. Must be the niece he'd mentioned.

"Oh, hi." *Going for casual, coming across as stupid. Brilliant.* Jack was having his own meltdown and gave her an excuse to look away for a moment so she could throw the tennis ball. The little girl stopped to watch him run.

"Wow," Wyatt said. "He's fast."

He turned his attention back to Sadie. She smiled up at him. He seemed taller. Wider. Her gaze slid along the curves and dips of the muscles of his arm. The man was cut. She eyed the front of his shirt. *Wonder what's under there.*

Come on! Stop staring.

She looked back at him, and the faint smile on his lips made her cheeks burn. Jack ran back, dropping the ball and letting out a yip. She threw it again.

"It's his favorite thing to do. He'd chase it until he collapsed if my arm could hold out long enough."

The girl inched closer and he reached around to put a hand on her shoulder, pulling her forward. She pressed close to Wyatt and peeked up at Sadie with solemn dark brown eyes. She didn't smile. A ping of sorrow ran through Sadie. She recognized that expression. It was the look of a child who has learned that the world isn't always a safe place. Who was always waiting to see what was going to happen next. Wyatt had said he recently got custody, so something had happened to her. To her world. She squatted to be eye to eye with the girl.

"Hi. I'm Sadie. What's your name?"

"Julietta," the girl whispered.

"That's very pretty."

Jack came back and did something remarkable. Instead of another doggie meltdown because the ball throwing stopped, he sat quietly. Sadie put an arm around him. "This is Jack. Jack, this is Julietta. Can you shake?"

For the first time, Jack did what Sadie asked at once. His paw went up and Julietta turned her serious little face up to Wyatt. He squatted also.

"If you want to."

Julietta took the offered paw and gently shook it. "Hello, Jack. It is very nice to meet you."

Sadie smothered a smile. Her eyes met Wyatt's and saw the same amusement there. She stood. Her knees would only take so much abuse. "Do you want to throw the ball for him, Julietta?"

The girl looked at Sadie in wonder. Her mouth fell open and she drew in a breath of air. "Can I?"

Her little voice, so carefully hopeful, sparked a wave of tenderness. "Of course you can, honey."

Sadie got a dry ball and showed her how to throw it. Jack joyfully scooped up ground balls and ran them back to her in a black-and-white blur. Sadie sat under the oak tree with Wyatt and watched.

His fingers closed on her forearm in a brief, gentle squeeze. "Thank you."

"For what? Letting her play? Saves my arm some wear and tear."

He pointed at Julietta. The game of toss had morphed into a game of toss and tag. "This is the first time she's played."

She turned to look at him. He sat with his elbows braced on his knees. His gaze, full of relief, was on Julietta. He turned to her and grinned, shaking his head. "If she laughs, I may kiss you."

A slow heat boiled up out of her belly and her breath hitched in her throat. Her eyes lingered on his lips. *What would they feel like? Taste like?*

Stop it, Sadie. He is an employee. Stop it now. She forced a return grin.

"Maybe you should kiss Jack. He's the reason she's playing."

"I'd do it. God, you don't even know what this means. She's playing. Playing!"

Sadie watched the two romping figures. Julietta threw the ball and raced with Jack to retrieve it. The heat stirred by his casual remark about kissing cooled while she watched. Yes, she was playing. But she wasn't laughing or shrieking like little girls did. She was calling out to Jack, but that was all. Her pretty face wasn't as guarded, but her expression was still serious. Sadie laced her hands together to hide the tremble.

"What happened?"

Wyatt rocked back, his feet leaving the ground

as he balanced for a moment, glancing up into the branches of the oak. He settled back, cross-legged. His eyes remained on Julietta.

"Her mother, Maddie, was a nurse in the emergency room. She'd done helicopter flight nursing but stopped when Julietta got older. But she loved it and still filled in from time to time."

Sadie couldn't stop the little gasp that tore from her throat. "The crash outside of Asheville a few months back?"

"Yeah. No survivors. Jules's whole world was taken away. Her mom gone. New home, new school, new everything. It's amazing, when you think about it, how well she's coping. She's not acting out. She's not having bad dreams. She's doing well in school. She's just still…flat."

Sadie couldn't answer. Her throat clogged with suppressed tears and memories. Her breath sounded ragged when she drew it in, slowly. She blinked hard. *This wasn't about her.*

"Her mother was your sister?"

"Yes."

"What about her father?"

Wyatt shrugged. "Maddie never said who he was. She went on a postcollege trip with some of her friends. Italy, Spain, Greece. Came home pregnant." He let out a small laugh. "Maddie was as blonde as I am. I'm suspecting Julietta is half-Italian."

"She's lucky to have you."

"I hope so. I'm trying. My immediate goal is to not make things worse."

"No. I think you're doing great."

He turned to face her. "Based on what?"

She leaned back and braced her hands on the ground behind her. Seeing his serious expression, she paused to consider her words. Single guy suddenly saddled with a grieving child. A girl child, no less. And he was stepping up to the plate. Had to give him credit.

"One, you took her in. Two, you know she needs time, and you are showing her the respect of allowing her to mourn. Three, I saw the way she clung close to you as you walked up to me. She trusts you to protect her. Four, the look on your face when she asked to play with Jack."

His eyes darkened and he turned away from her. When he turned back, his voice was thick. "Thank you. That means a lot to me."

Her heart melted a little and she fought against it. *Yes, a gut-wrenching Lifetime movie moment. Don't get sucked in. It's their life, not yours.* Jack trotted up to her and collapsed on the ground. Julietta trailed behind him.

"He won't play anymore."

"I think you wore him out, honey. And he's thirsty."

Sadie reached into her backpack and pulled

out a water bottle and bowl. Julietta knelt beside Jack and petted his back while he noisily slurped up water. She looked at Sadie and her lips turned up at the corners. An almost smile that was gone as quickly as it had appeared.

"I like your hair," she said.

Sadie touched the tangled mass of black curls. She'd put it up in a ponytail, but some tendrils had escaped. "Thank you. I like yours. I wish mine was so straight."

Julietta reached out and touched one of the tendrils. Sadie had the sudden and unexpected urge to grab her little hand and kiss it. To tell her it would be okay one day.

Julietta moved her gaze from the curl to Sadie's eyes. Her mouth opened. Closed. Opened again. "My mom used to curl my hair," she whispered.

From the corner of her eye, Sadie saw Wyatt's entire body jerk as if he'd been touched by electricity. Everything else faded away and a buzz filled her ears. She kept her eyes on Julietta's. This was something. This was important. Tension radiated from Wyatt. Was this the first time Julietta had mentioned her mother? *Probably.* She was going to completely mess this up. She always said the wrong thing. She took a deep breath.

"Did she curl all of it?"

Julietta looked relieved, which only increased Sadie's anxiety. It had been a test. She'd mentioned her mother in front of a stranger to see what would happen. She didn't know whether to acknowledge it or keep talking about curls.

"No." She touched her temple. "One. Right here. When she was curling her hair in the morning, sometimes she'd give me a curl, too."

"I bet it was very pretty."

Julietta's gaze remained on Sadie's. The girl wanted her to say something. *But what?* She was no good at this. What if she said the wrong thing and made her cry? Ruined the progress Wyatt had made? She moved her eyes in a quick glance at him. He dipped his chin in the barest of nods. *Keep going*, the nod said.

Uh...

"Did you like having the curl?"

Oh, now, what a stupid question. Come on, Sadie. Think.

Julietta nodded. "I miss it sometimes."

Oh, dear God. She misses her mother. She blinked away the tears stinging her eyes. *Think.* Her mouth went dry.

"I'll bet your Uncle Wyatt would be happy to curl it for you if you wanted."

Jack picked up on her anxiety and leaned against her. His warmth steadied her. Julietta glanced over at Wyatt and back at Sadie as a frown crossed her features. She'd said the wrong thing.

Julietta leaned in closer. "But he's a boy," she whispered.

Sadie managed not to laugh, but she couldn't stop the smile. She caught the girl's hand in hers. "I know. But you know what I think?"

"What?"

"I think he loves you very much. And I think he'd be willing to learn how to do the curl if it would make you happy. That's what I think."

Wyatt took Julietta's other hand. "This is true, Jujube."

Julietta glanced between the two of them, her little face serious. "Would you show him how?"

"Sure. Anytime."

"Then it's settled. I'll learn curls." Wyatt climbed to his feet. "Come on, Jules. It's way past lunchtime. Tell Ms. Sadie thank-you for letting you play with Jack, and go get your bike."

"Thank you, Ms. Sadie." She bent to hug Jack's neck. "Thank you, Jack."

As she ran to her bike, Wyatt let out a breath. "Wow. Thank you. That was the first time she's mentioned her mother."

"I thought so. Scared the heck out of me. I hope I did all right."

He took her hand and squeezed. "Perfect. Honestly, thank you."

A pang of regret plucked at her as he let go of her hand. It had felt good. "Anytime."

"Come on, Uncle Wyatt. I'm starving!"

"Hold on," he called back to her. He turned and his gaze met hers. A moment of super-charged heat flared in Sadie. His hand reached out before falling back to his side. A rueful smile turned up one corner of his mouth. "Guess I'll see you Monday, huh?"

Reality slammed back to her. "Y'all have a great weekend."

She returned Julietta's wave and sank back on the ground. She looped an arm around Jack. "Why's he gotta be so damned nice on top of all that gorgeous, huh, Jackie Boy?"

NORMALLY, WYATT WOULD pick a spot where he could see the entire room. But the seating had been decided for him. Molly directed him to the same small classroom where he'd taken the per-sonality tests. The building had obviously been a private residence, and Sadie had kept much of the layout intact. Her office and this room had once been bedrooms. There was another room down the same hall and a bathroom between them. A young man sat at the round table in the center of the room, sifting through a folder. There was another folder on the table with his name on the front. The guy looked up as he approached.

"Morning," Wyatt said as he took his seat.

"Hey. You starting today, too?"

He held out a hand. "Wyatt."

"Aaron."

He shook the kid's hand and opened his own folder. More forms. *Great.*

"You don't seem the type."

Wyatt met his eyes. The kid looked to be all of eighteen. If he was twenty, Wyatt would eat the candles off his next birthday cake. "What do you mean?"

The kid shrugged. "You're a little older, I guess."

Wyatt stared at him until the kid's cheeks showed a little color. He was only thirty-one. Not exactly ready for the nursing home. He gave his own shrug. "I guess."

"It's a great gig, though. A couple of my buddies work here."

"What's great about it?"

"It's better than flipping burgers. Pay's decent. Work's not bad. And you can rack up some serious tips."

"Tips?"

That was interesting. He'd have guessed a tip at Christmas would be normal. But tips, plural? What would earn a tip and how often? Was there something going on behind Sadie's back? Boys would be boys, after all. And a college kid turning down strings-free sex seemed a little much to believe.

"My buddy Noah, he gets tons of tips."

"What's he gotta—"

There was a clatter on the hardwood floor and flash of black-and-white fur streaking through the room. The dog jumped to put its paws on the table across from them, tongue falling out of a doggy grin. Wyatt had to smile back.

"This our teacher?" Aaron asked.

The dog let out a playful yip.

"Jack!"

The dog dropped to all fours as Sadie came in. She frowned at Jack, whose tail wagged hard enough to shake the entire back end of his body. Sadie pointed out the door.

"Bed!"

Wyatt brought a hand up to cover his smile. She was sexy as sin. She wore that wildly curly black hair loose this morning, and he wondered how it would feel in his hands. Those full pink lips formed an irritated pout and made him want to make them smile again. She'd never have to order *him* to bed, that was a fact. She was dressed in jeans and a white Cleaning Crew T-shirt. The uniform looked much better on her. *Especially the jeans. Especially her ass in those jeans.* He shifted in the chair and dropped his gaze to the dog. Walking slowly out of the room with his nose pointed at the floor, he was a canine con artist of the finest sort.

"Good morning. Sorry about that," she said. She took the seat across from them.

While she seemed perfectly composed with a smile lingering on her lips and her hands folded on the table, Wyatt could see the pulse point at the base of her throat fluttering. *Why the nerves?* Her hands were clasped tightly and her entire body was taut. Her gaze met his and a faint pink stain touched her cheeks, so he concentrated on the folder in front of him. *Was* he *making her nervous? Why? Did she suspect something? Was he not acting his part well enough?*

Maybe you should stop drooling over her. That might be what she's picking up on.

"Today, we'll go over the information in the packets. Most of it has to do with policy and procedures. Pretty dry stuff. Since there's only the two of you, I hope we can get through it quickly. I'll give you a tour. Then I'll introduce you to your preceptors. You'll spend at least two weeks with them—more if you or your preceptor thinks you need it—then you'll be assigned to a partner. You'll be on probation for three months."

She rolled her eyes in Aaron's direction and gave him a skeptical look. "But since Noah recommended you, I should keep you on probation for a year or so."

Aaron laughed and so Wyatt did, making note of the name. *Was Noah actually a troublemaker?* As much as he disliked Marcus, he was a professional. He'd do a thorough investigation. Even if he was sure Sadie wasn't the madam of a male prostitution ring, he had to make sure the guys weren't supplementing their incomes with some hanky-panky. Which meant he was going to be hanging around for a while.

The morning passed slowly. There was no way to make going over policy and procedure interesting. Wyatt amused himself by watching Sadie. She had a snarky, sarcastic sense of humor she tried to keep hidden, but it slipped out in unguarded moments. Several times he'd made her laugh and had been rewarded with a conspiratorial smile. He found himself looking for ways to earn more of them.

"Okay," Sadie said after they'd gone over how to sign up for their free Planet Fitness membership. She tilted her phone to look at the time. "I'm getting hoarse, and it's close enough to lunch. Let's take a break. Meet back here at twelve-thirty."

Wyatt walked the few blocks and risked his life crossing Savannah Highway to have lunch at Gene's Haufbrau. The Avondale burger with bacon, pimento cheese and a fried green tomato was worth the risk. While eating, he tried to de-

vise a game plan. Whoever he was put with for
initial training would most likely be someone
who'd been there a long time. And he was sure
the partner he'd be assigned to would be experienced, also. He'd have to gain their trust enough
for them to talk freely around him. The age thing
might be a problem. While it wasn't a problem
for Sadie, these college kids were looking at him
like some sort of relic and it might make them
reluctant to let him in on their secrets. *If there
are any.* He dumped his trash and headed back.

The door was unlocked but Molly wasn't at
the receptionist's desk when he let himself in. He
almost called out when a small sound stopped
him. He took a few quiet steps toward the hall.
Funny how quickly the stealth came back. How
familiar the feeling of adrenaline flooding the
system, enhancing sight and hearing. A sense of
dread drifted through him when he saw Jack sitting quietly in the hall. The dog turned his head
toward Wyatt and let out a low whine. Before he
could say anything, the dog stood and padded
quietly into the room.

Wyatt froze and listened. Another whine from
Jack, then the shuffle of feet and a sniff. Then
Sadie's voice.

"No, Lena. I'm okay. It's just that I was hoping
for…" A sigh drifted through the room. "I don't
know what I was hoping for. Not this."

Silence again. She must be on the phone. He stepped into the hallway.

"I understand. I know it's the right thing. I wish there was another way."

More silence. Wyatt frowned, trying to put together the pieces of conversation. It certainly didn't sound like anything criminal.

"I'm okay. Yes. That sounds good. Tell everyone I love them."

Personal call. *What did you expect? To overhear her booking one of the guys for a sex act? Plans for a drug buy?* "Hello?" He stepped into the kitchen and spotted her leaning against the counter. He was suddenly, absurdly unsure of what to call her. *Sadie?* She was about his age, but also was now his boss. *Miss Martin? Ms. Martin?* "Hey, you okay?"

She spun around, clearly startled. Her hands wiped across her face and she cleared her throat. "Sure. Wow. It's been an hour already?" She turned to the sink, filled a glass of water and took a long sip.

"Bad habit I picked up in the military. Being early."

He leaned against the counter and crossed his arms. Her eyes were pink rimmed and her lower lip still wanted to quiver. He had no idea what to do. She was ignoring the tears. Should he?

Maybe it was nothing. The call was clearly personal. But he was here for a reason.

CRAP. SADIE PUT the glass in the sink and turned away from Wyatt's appraising eyes. *I can't believe I let him walk up on me.*

Losing your touch, Sadie girl. Getting soft and stupid.

"Are you okay?" he asked. Again.

"Sure. Got some news I didn't want to hear. It's fine. I'm fine."

She walked out of the kitchen. *Fine, ha.* What was that old saying? *Fine* meant *fucked-up, insecure, neurotic and emotional.* Sounded about right. He followed her. She could sense his gaze on her back and she purposefully straightened her spine and lengthened her stride. *Show no weakness.* She'd learned the lesson hard and young. By the time she was six, she knew tears and pain were invitations to predators and bullies. In the classroom, she pretended to look for something in a filing cabinet. He perched on the edge of the table, still watching, which was starting to get annoying. *Oh, it didn't bother you this morning when he was getting your jokes and Aaron wasn't.* All that eye contact was causing some serious non-boss-like feelings. She slammed the file shut in disgust.

"Anything I can help with?"

She looked at him. There was a faint look of concerned puzzlement in his expression. Proved how little he knew. She didn't need help. Ever. "No. I'm going to take Jack for a walk before we get started again."

Thank God he didn't follow her this time. She and Jack circled the block and she struggled to get her emotions under control while he watered his favorite plants and sign posts. Lena's phone call had not been unexpected. She wished it weren't so soon.

When she and Lena became friends and her family learned Sadie was essentially alone in the world, it had horrified them. So they took her in. They'd reduced her to tears with a surprise birthday party once and refused to let her pull away when their love frightened her. Lena's grandfather was especially concerned about her and she often found ten- or twenty-dollar bills tucked into her jacket or purse after leaving their home. He was the one she'd let get the closest to her heart.

He had decided to end treatment for his cancer and was going into hospice care. While she knew it was probably for the best—an eighty-three-year-old man should have a peaceful exit from life surrounded by his loved ones, not medical procedure after medical procedure—she didn't know how to deal with the impending loss. The tools of self-preservation learned in childhood would do her no good now.

Jack bumped his head into her hand as they reached the backyard. She squatted and hugged his stupid, furry neck. He wiggled around and licked at her tears.

"I know, Jackie Boy. I'm a hot mess, huh?"

His doggy grin seemed to agree. But he loved her anyway. She buried her face in his fur. *Time to suck it up. We'll cry about this later. We'll figure out what to do later. For now, you've got a business to run.*

She found Wyatt sitting alone in the classroom. He looked up at her entrance and dropped his gaze immediately. Her stomach dropped almost as suddenly. She could feel the awkwardness in the air. *He was being nice. Like a normal person. And you messed up. As usual.* She took a deep breath. "Hey. I'm sorry. I got some bad news about someone I'm very close to and was trying to process it."

"It's okay. Sorry I intruded on a private moment."

She sat on the edge of the table and rubbed her hands against the backs of her arms. He tilted his head to look up at her and she got caught up in those warm hazel eyes. The concern was still there. *But why? Why would he care?* A small frown crinkled the corners of his eyes and the urge to spill out the whole story bubbled up inside her. How she used to pretend Abuelito was her real grandfather and how that little fantasy gave her something to hold on to in the seemingly bottomless free fall of her life. How she was terrified to watch him slip away. She was afraid she'd run away and shame herself in front of the family who had done so much for her. Pain and anger and fear rose from her gut to clog her throat with unshed tears.

"Hey," Wyatt said, reaching for her arm. The frown deepened and his voice was soft, so soft and tender.

She leaped away. *Pity.* No. Horror at the idea of him feeling sorry for her drowned the pain, at least momentarily. Confusion showed clearly on his face and remorse stung her again. *Would she never get this right? Could she not let her walls down?*

"Dudes. Sorry I'm late. Traffic is a bear."

She turned to Aaron with relief. Normally, she would lecture him on punctuality, but he'd saved her from making an even bigger fool of herself, so she forgave him. This time.

CHAPTER SIX

A RUMBLE OF voices greeted Sadie as she stomped down the back stairs from her apartment to the first-floor kitchen. She had enlarged the pantry and turned it into a supply room but had left most of the kitchen intact. It had a stove, sink, fridge. She and Molly had filled the cabinets with garage-sale finds. It was large enough for her to cook up a company dinner every month. She kept the fridge stocked with lunch foods and snacks for the guys. College kids ate constantly, it seemed. All that learning must burn calories. Several of the crew were grouped around the coffeemaker, filling up cups for the Tuesday morning meeting. A burst of raucous laughter exploded from the conference room. When one hires college guys, one endures college-guy humor.

"Hey, boss," Josh greeted her.

"Morning. Okay, y'all, boss is here, step away from the coffeepot." She reached for the carafe and held it up, swirling the dregs. "I should randomly fire someone for this."

"Like to see that," Josh said as he took the carafe from her. "I'll start a fresh pot. I told you to invest in one of those Keurig things."

"I should. It's almost cruel and unusual to make me face the lot of you without coffee."

"It's cruel and unusual for you to make us get up at this ungodly hour on a Monday," one of them called from the conference room.

"Whoever said that is the randomly fired guy," she yelled back, and a wave of laughter and hooting rolled from the room. She touched Josh on the arm as he poured grounds into the machine. "I want to talk to you after the meeting."

"Sure thing, boss."

She walked into the conference room where almost every employee was gathered around the large dining table. Others were holding up the walls. A silent scuffle at the end of the table caught her attention. The two went still when they realized she was watching. Malik gave her his best choirboy face. But Eric's redhead complexion was giving him away. She stared at the faces around the table. Everyone had gone still with expressions ranging from innocent to amused. Except Wyatt Anderson. He lounged back casually in his chair, but his eyes were alert and appraising. She got the impression of a cat watching the spot where its prey hid. A little thrill ran through her, and she frowned at her body's reaction. *This had to stop.* She turned Malik and held out a hand.

"Gimme. And it better not be porn again. Y'all drank my coffee, and it's too freaking early for porn."

A folded newspaper made its way down the table to her. She picked it up. The urge to laugh was accompanied by a prickle of irritation. It was an ad campaign by Marcus Canard, her closest competition. Well, she wasn't competing with him. But he definitely was competing with *her*. For the first time, the Cleaning Crew had won the *Charleston City Paper*'s coveted Best of Charleston Award for Best Cleaning Company, beating out Canard's Happy Housekeepers.

The photograph showed a diverse group. Three women, one white, one black and one Hispanic, and two young, handsome men, one white and one black, smiled at the camera. They were dressed in khakis and blue button-down shirts. "We meet *all* your cleaning needs!" the caption proclaimed.

Sadie tossed it on the table. She smiled and shook her head. *Show no weakness.* "They say imitation is the sincerest form of flattery. But, hey, any of you want to go work for Marcus Canard, I'll give you a glowing recommendation."

Josh handed her a cup of coffee, steaming hot

and black. "Forget him," he said as he took his seat. "Dude doesn't get it. Never will."

"Get what?" Wyatt asked, sitting forward and propping his arms on the table. He looked at Sadie. She shrugged and gestured at Josh.

"Simple," Josh said, "you get what you pay for. We work our asses off. We go beyond the basics and go out of our way to make everything right for the client. Why? One, it's what Sadie expects from us. Two, it's what the customers pay more for. Three, it's what she pays us good money to do. Marcus pays his staff minimum wage. He keeps them all part-time so he doesn't have to provide benefits. Sadie offers benefits even to part-time employees, plus extras, like free gym memberships. He doesn't care about his employees, so why should they care about him or his company's reputation?"

Sadie sat down. Her knees were a little weak. Josh's praise meant a lot to her. The guys clearly agreed with him, too, which made tears start in her eyes. She sipped coffee to wash down the lump in her throat. They believed she had it together. None of them knew she was running scared every day. It wasn't about Marcus and the competition. It was about her. She had to succeed. She *had* to. She was supposed to have been a loser living in poverty, probably marrying a similar loser and having a passel of kids.

The Cleaning Crew was a fluke. She'd left her first maid job and was on her own. She'd cleaned private homes from sunup to sundown six days a week. It'd started with a conversation about the Powerball lottery, which was up to some unimaginably huge amount. The client had asked Sadie what she'd do if she won. Sadie replied she'd buy a nice house and hire a team of gorgeous guys to cook and clean for her. The client laughed and said, "Who wouldn't? I'd pay extra for a hot man to clean my house." The purr in the client's voice had amused Sadie. When her client list grew to the point where she didn't have enough hours in the day to do all the work and was thinking of hiring another person to help she remembered that purr. And hired a hot guy. It had grown from there. A joke. But she could point to it and say, "See, I'm not a loser. I'm doing fine, thank you very much. I don't need help. I don't need anything." The fear that at any moment she could do something stupid and ruin it all haunted her. Then everyone would shrug and say, what do you expect from someone like her? She sipped more coffee and forced the doubts from her mind. *Show no weakness. Wrap it up tight, shove it down deep and keep plowing forward.*

"Okay," she said when she thought she could

speak. "Let's get this meeting going. You have jobs to get to."

"I've got a hot blonde in my bed to get back to," Cody quipped.

"I don't want to hear about your sister," Sadie replied tartly, opening her notebook to the list of topics she wanted to cover.

The room erupted with laughter and shouts. Sadie looked up and her eyes met Wyatt's. He was smiling but raised his eyebrows in a question. She shrugged and quirked up a corner of her mouth. Sometimes you had to play the audience.

"All right, come on. First item. We have two new employees, Wyatt Anderson and Aaron Stone. Welcome them." She paused for the guy razzing and grunting that passed for welcoming. "Aaron, you'll be with Sam. And Wyatt, you'll be working with DeShawn. Now for the boring stuff. The state of South Carolina is requiring me to provide proof you know how to properly dilute the new floor-cleaning solution. Molly has the sign off sheets. Go tell her how to do it properly and get signed off. She may give you a lollipop."

She ran through the list quickly. She hated meetings. Hated everyone looking at her, expecting her to be all boss-like and perfect. And she was beginning to hate the way she could feel Wyatt's gaze on her skin. He seemed as though he was going to fit in and do a good job. She was going to have to get her hormones under control. She opened the floor to questions.

"What are you going to do about the ad?" Malik asked.

"Nothing. Marcus Canard advertises. We don't. The work we do is the only advertising we need. Almost all our new clients, about 95 percent, come from referrals. The rest stumble on us by Google search. We have almost zero client loss. The last three clients we lost, it was only because they moved away. No one has canceled the Crew because of our service."

She stood. "I need more coffee, and y'all need to get to work. Anyone who doesn't have a client scheduled in the next hour needs to get Molly to check you off on the cleaner. Wyatt and Aaron, get with your partners. I gave them the packets already. They'll show you what needs to be done. Everyone have a great day. Call me if you need anything. Don't forget first Friday is this week."

She caught Josh's eye and tilted her head, indicating for him to come with her. She ran upstairs to let Jack into the office. He got too excited when so many people were here. While he amused himself by sniffing around the conference room, she poured more coffee and went to her office. Josh sat across from her desk, quiet and watchful as she slurped down the second cup.

"New guy seems interesting," he said.

"Which one?"

Josh grinned and lounged back in the chair, his long lanky legs stretched out before him. He stretched and rested his clasped hands on top of his head. "Come on, Saff, how long have we known each other? You get a little panicky when you know he's watching you."

Was it obvious? "I do not. Do I?"

Josh laughed and her cheeks burned. "Yes, but I think I only noticed because I know you so well. I meant because he's a little older than most of the guys."

"He's not too much older than you. He was a house painter. Economy is still shaky. Got custody of his niece and needed more steady hours and pay."

"Seems like a decent guy. What'd you want to talk to me about?"

Sadie took another sip, appraising Josh over the rim of her mug. He was good-looking, with dark wavy hair and blue eyes. He could probably pass for her brother. He was the hot guy she'd hired for the experiment that became the Cleaning Crew. Barely a man back then. He'd been about to turn nineteen, full of attitude and anger and a desperate need to belong to something. Sadie had understood. She'd taken a gamble with him and it had paid off. Paid off very well. They clicked immediately when he told her he'd aged out of the foster-care system. Eighteen and on the street. Exactly like her. Only he had been lucky and his foster family had let him stay until he finished high school. Sadie hadn't been as lucky. She'd been put on the street the minute she turned eighteen, four months from graduation.

He was one of two people who knew her whole story. And she was the only one who knew his. Her instincts had been right about him. Given a chance, some guidance and sisterly affection, his loyalty had become a fierce thing. And she paid him well for all he did. He'd trained every new guy for years. He set the tone and enforced her expectations in guy speak that carried more weight than her rules and regulations. She trusted him like no other. This was why she hesitated to say what she'd brought him here to say. But she knew her hesitation was nothing but selfishness.

"I've been getting inquiries," she said. "About if we would consider franchising. And Molly's been logging at least five calls a week from the Columbia area asking if we take clients there. So there's a potential market."

"But you're against selling a franchise. Don't want to lose control over the quality."

"Exactly. Here's what I was thinking. Not a franchise, but a second office."

"Uh-huh. Might work. Would keep you in charge."

She sat back, tenting her fingers and pressing them to her lips. "I was thinking about offering it to you, Josh."

He sat up from his sprawl. "Offering what?"

"To head up a new location. To be the manager. Get the whole thing off the ground. Hire the guys, train them, everything. You're the only person I'd trust to do it, Josh."

"Wow." He ran a hand through his hair. "Wow. I'm, um— I don't know what to think."

"I'm floating it out there as an option. As much as I'd hate to lose you, I don't want to waste your talents holding you here."

"How would it work, though? I'd be the manager?"

"We'd have to sit down with Lena and a lawyer and work out the details. I wouldn't be against giving you a franchise so you'd be the owner. I trust you."

"I'll think about it. My gut reaction is to say no because I don't want to leave. But it would be a challenge."

Sadie rose and walked around the desk. Josh stood also and she pulled him into a tight hug. "I wish you were my real brother," she said.

"I am your real brother."

She stepped back and wiped at her eyes. "I

know. I'll miss you if you go to Columbia. But I want it for you. I know you'll do an awesome job."

"I said I'll think about it, Saff."

She swatted at his arm. "Stop it. You'll slip up one day and say it in front of the wrong person."

After Josh left, Sadie took Jack for a walk around the block. An idea began forming in her head. She wasn't the type to engage in a battle. It was far safer to ignore and evade. But this Marcus thing was starting to irritate her. When she got back, she called Lena.

"How much money is in the advertising budget?"

"None. You don't advertise. I don't budget for it. Why? What do you want to do?"

Sadie pulled open the bottom drawer and opened her stash of jelly beans. She needed a sugar high for this. "I was thinking of doing an ad thanking the people of Charleston for voting for us in the *City Paper* thing."

"Uh-huh. I'm liking it."

"A group shot. Of all the guys."

"And you in the center."

"Um. No. I stay out of the limelight."

"Then I won't approve the funds."

"You have to. It's my money."

"Come on, Sadie. This is an awesome idea. Your gorgeous self, surrounded by all that hot beefcake, thanking the people of Charleston? Marcus will choke on his breakfast opening up the paper."

Sadie picked out a cream and a strawberry jelly bean to eat together. While she chewed, she pictured the look on Marcus's face when the ad came out. The image appealed to her after all his nasty comments. "You got names?"

Lena heaved a long, mournful sigh. "This is why I take you to those business association meetings. For you to meet people, build up a network."

"I know. You got names?"

"Hold on."

After scribbling down the name of a woman who ran an advertising agency, Sadie popped another jelly bean in her mouth. "I was thinking about going to see Abuelito this weekend. Would it be okay?"

"Better than okay. We can go together. He'd love to see you."

"Can I wait until then? Should I go sooner?"

"There's time. Not much, but time."

Sadie ended the call and leaned back in her chair, propping her feet up on the desk and holding the jar of jelly beans on her stomach. Jack put his head on her thigh and sighed. She scratched his ears and let out her own sigh. "Oh, Jackie Boy. I don't know if I know how to say goodbye."

A brief rap on the door pulled her attention away from the jelly beans. Molly walked to the desk, holding out an envelope. "Mail for you. Looks personal."

Sadie took the envelope. White business-letter size. Hand written and addressed to S. D. Martin. Her eye and breath caught on the return address: G. Rogers, Florence, SC. "Okay," she said, dismissing Molly with a voice that sounded faint and tremulous inside her head. "Thanks."

After Molly left, Sadie dropped the envelope. Florence. Where her mother lived. Rogers. Her mother's married name. Grant, the baby her mother kept. The one she was pregnant with when she signed away her parental rights to Sadie. *Throw it away. Tear it to shreds and burn it.* She wanted—needed—nothing from those people. Still she remained frozen, her hands curled into fists framing the envelope. But how? Why? Had her mother told her new family about her? And how had he found her? *Open the letter. Find out.* Instead, she swept the letter into the top drawer. Out of sight, out of mind, right? She had a business to run here.

WYATT'S MIND KEPT going back to how Sadie had motioned for Josh to follow her once the meeting had ended. He was beginning to suspect Josh was much more than just another employee. The way he'd joked with Sadie about the dead cat, the way he'd passionately defended her against Marcus Canard and now the way they disappeared to her office together. Maybe Josh needed a little investigating.

He was on a tour of headquarters, following his preceptor, DeShawn, down the hallway, past Sadie's office and the classroom and to the third door.

"This is where you'll start every day. You'll have an assigned group of clients. Each day is scheduled out. I know mine by heart so I don't have to check, but there's a calendar there."

The calendar took up the only wall space not filled with bookshelves. There was a small round table in the center of the room. The bookshelves were filled with white binders. Each binder had a name printed along the spine.

"These are the client books," DeShawn said with a wave of his hand. "We've tried to talk Sadie into going paperless, but she wants to keep these."

"Wow. That'd be a huge job to transfer all this to computer," Wyatt said. He was slightly stunned by the number of books.

DeShawn crossed the room and began to pull binders from the shelf. "We've got a pretty easy day today. It'll be good for your first full day."

They sat together at the small table and De-

Shawn opened a binder. "Every morning, you see who's on the schedule and pull their books. All the information you need is in here. Name, address, contact number. Any special requests will be here." He turned a page and pointed. "See, for example, this is an elderly couple. We moved their cleaning day to coincide with the recycling pickup day because they have trouble getting the full bins out to the curb. We do that for them."

"That's a nice touch," Wyatt said.

"It's more than a touch. Sadie expects this. It's part of what sets us apart. Anytime a client asks for something extra, we do it, every time if needed. If we see something like this we're supposed to offer to take care of it."

"Great."

He had no idea how cleaning services were usually run, but he could imagine this individual attention was rare.

"So we get the books, go over them to remind ourselves of anything extra to do and we take them with us so we can update them. There's a cleaning log here where we log time in, time out and the date. Also, anything unusual goes here. Any new requests or needs are put at the bottom of the special requests list. Got it?"

Wyatt nodded. "Seems straightforward enough."

"Questions?"

Only about a hundred, Wyatt thought. "I'm

still a little concerned about the whole 'guys cleaning your house' aspect of this. I know about the behavioral contracts, but there've been no problems, have there?"

DeShawn shook his head as he stood and gathered the day's books. "It's a thing with some of the newer clients. Most of the people who've been with Sadie for years know it's all about the job we do, not who's doing it. It's an attention-grabbing gimmick, nothing more. Our service is beyond excellent. Now, come on and let me show you how to properly clean a house."

Wyatt, who had been cleaning house since he was twenty and his mother became ill, was a bit offended by that…until they started. He'd known the work would be mostly physical: mopping, sweeping, vacuuming. He wasn't prepared for the military-level precision with which DeShawn went through a house. He could clean a house twice as well in half the time Wyatt could do his own home.

By lunch, Wyatt was beginning to wonder what he could report to Marcus. Every client they'd seen so far had been an elderly couple. Surely they weren't buying drugs or sexual services. Even the idea that Sadie was running the cleaning service as a front to some criminal business was hard to believe. Front operations were usually poorly run. Most attention went to the criminal activity as it was the more lucrative. Fronts were only that—fronts, barely functioning covers. The Cleaning Crew was no front. It was a thriving business.

"So, how're you liking it so far?" DeShawn asked over lunch.

Wyatt smiled at him. "It's good. Pretty much what I expected."

"You're picking it up very quickly. Better than most, trust me."

"Probably the military training. I like order and plans."

DeShawn's eyes lit up. "You were military?"

"National Guard."

"Did you get sent over?"

"Two tours in Afghanistan."

"Can I ask you some questions?"

"Sure." He braced for the usual questions from young men who thought war some exciting real-life version of the video games they'd grown up playing.

"I'm thinking of joining after I graduate next year. I can go in as an officer but I can't decide which branch. The air force appeals to me, but with my engineering degree, some have said the army might be best. What do you think?"

Wyatt dropped the french fry he was holding. Whoa. Okay. This kid was serious. "I'm not an expert on all the different branches. I was in the

Army National Guard. There was a demand for engineers. Mostly for rebuilding. What do you want to do with your degree? Say you enlist, do your twenty years and retire. What experience would you want to have to transfer to a civilian job?"

"Structural engineering."

"So compare what's available in each branch to what jobs are comparable in the civilian market, and go with that."

DeShawn lifted his hand. "Boom! Right to the center of it. Thanks, man."

Wyatt did the fist bump thing and grinned. This made him feel a little better about the whole undercover-and-lying thing. He'd maybe helped this guy. "Let me ask you a question now."

"Shoot."

"Sadie said everyone went out with a partner. But you don't. Neither does Josh. Why's that?"

"There are only a few of us who go solo. The ones who've been here the longest. We have the older client lists. The clients Sadie had back when she worked alone. Before there was a Crew."

Wyatt nodded. That wasn't going to help him much. He needed to get in with the newer clients and newer employees. See what was going on with them. He gathered up the remains of his lunch and followed DeShawn to the trash bin. *This is only day one; give it some time.*

They finished up just after three and headed back to the office. Sadie was in the back room, filling out the next month's calendar when they went in to put the books away. Wyatt felt his heart rate amp up a few notches at the sight of her. The jeans and T-shirt hugged her curves and her hair was down, loose curls spilling to the center of her back. She turned and smiled as they walked in.

"Hey. How'd it go?"

"Good job with this one, boss."

Sadie's gaze moved to him and he felt every inch she looked over. "Oh, yeah?"

"Yeah. Picking it up so fast, he probably doesn't need a full two weeks. In a month, he'll be ready to go solo."

Wyatt grinned at DeShawn. This was good. *Yes, take me off orientation early. Put me on a team with one of the new guys.* "It helps when you've got a great teacher."

DeShawn held out a fist and Wyatt bumped it. "Tomorrow."

"How's Julietta doing?" Sadie asked after DeShawn left. "I've been thinking about her. Is she okay after what happened?"

Wyatt blinked and stared for a moment. People usually avoided talking about Jules. It was messy and painful. "Yeah," he said. "She's okay. I was expecting it to be like a dam breaking but she hasn't said anything more. I called her therapist and told her what happened. She said to let Jules lead the way on when she wants to talk about her mother."

Sadie pressed a hand over her heart. "Good. I was so afraid I said something wrong and made it worse."

"No. The therapist said you did perfect. Didn't make a big deal out of it. So thank you again."

"You're welcome, but it wasn't anything I did. She chose the moment. I haven't forgotten about the curls. I'll grab something from Walmart and show you how to use it sometime this week."

"That'd be great. Anything else I can do for you?"

The faint blush on her cheeks was interesting, but he only caught a glimpse before she turned back to the calendar.

"No. See you tomorrow."

CHAPTER SEVEN

FOUR DAYS INTO the job and Wyatt was starting to feel really horrible about this investigation. Between the morning interactions and midday resupply runs that allowed him interaction with other teams, Wyatt was getting a better idea of how the Cleaning Crew operated. There wasn't anything going on. Better work ethic, better gimmick, better management and leadership. That was it. Marcus was going to have to accept the facts.

He consulted his kitchen cheat sheet. Clean microwave, inside and out. He glanced around to find it. They were in a large, gorgeous home on Albemarle Point overlooking the marsh and the Ashley River. The kitchen was huge. It had two stoves and the biggest refrigerator he'd ever seen in his life. So, this was how the other half lived.

The front door opened and his pulse kicked up a beat or two when Sadie called out. She could really get him going. For all the good it did. *Sure, I know I was lying to you and spying on you, but do you want to catch a movie or something?*

He shook his head. She was the first woman to catch his eye since Victoria had walked out on him. And with the way she'd responded to Jules, a little chunk of his heart was trying to get in on the action.

"Hey, boss. What's up?" DeShawn called from what he'd told Wyatt was the atrium. Looked like a sunroom to him, but fancy houses needed fancy rooms, he supposed.

"Checking in on you. How's it going?" Sadie's voice.

"It's going. No problems."

"Great. Where's the FNG?"

Wyatt snorted out a laugh, one echoed by DeShawn. "Where'd you learn that?" DeShawn asked.

"Josh. He said it meant *former National Guard*."

DeShawn came into the kitchen with Sadie trailing behind him. DeShawn was laughing too hard to say anything. Sadie stopped and put her hands on her hips, her cheeks going from pink to red. Black eyebrows drew together over those denim blue eyes. *Good God, she's gorgeous. And sexy. And completely out of the question.*

"Damn it. I'm going to kill him. What does it really mean?"

"Fucking new guy," Wyatt said, not bothering to contain his own laughter. DeShawn collapsed

against the counter, laughing so hard tears were leaking from his eyes.

"Oh, you guys think you are so funny with your jokes. Maybe I'll add dumping kitty litter and washing litter boxes to the weekly chore list. Who's funny now, huh?"

DeShawn sucked in a loud lungful of air. His hands clamped down on his stomach. "Stop. Stop, you're killing me."

She crossed her arms and tapped a foot. The look on her face would have scared Wyatt straight if he'd been a kid DeShawn's age. Then the corners of her mouth began losing the battle with her own laughter.

"*Former National Guard.* Who even calls anyone that? I cannot believe you fell for it," DeShawn said between gasps for air.

"Oh, Josh is dead meat. Dead. Meat. Go scrub a toilet or something. Let me talk to the fucking new guy."

After DeShawn left the room, still laughing, Sadie turned to Wyatt. Her coloring had returned to the pink, and he was struck again by how pretty she was. And funny. And tough. And smart. And how much she was going to hate him when this was over. All the joy of the little prank left him and his guts turned to lead.

"I'm checking in with you. How's it going with DeShawn?"

He picked up the rag and returned to cleaning the microwave. "It's going well. He's a good teacher. Organized and patient. I can see how good he is, and having a…FNG must slow him down, but he doesn't show it."

Her cheeks pinked again and it made him smile.

"Good. Exactly what I like to hear. How about you? Is the job about what you expected?"

"Mostly. I didn't realize the extent of the planning and record keeping. I can see why you're blowing away the competition."

"We."

"Huh?"

"*We* are blowing away the completion. The Crew isn't me. It's you. You guys do the work. I'm only the ringmaster of this circus."

"Whatever you do, your clowns love you. That's a big part of the success."

Her lips parted and she drew in a breath. Her expression showed a bit of puzzlement, as if she didn't know if she should believe him or not. "Thanks."

"I can see why that guy Marcus is floundering, trying to get an idea of how to compete with you. What you are doing is completely different and not just the guy-cleaning-your-house gimmick. You keep your employees happy. And happy employees do a better job."

"I try."

"I think you're doing better than trying."

Sadie laughed. "I think I'll have you follow me around all day, giving me pep talks."

"Do you need pep talks?"

A brief flicker of uncertainty surfaced in the blue depths of her eyes. His hand twitched, wanting to touch her porcelain skin. Would it be like silk beneath his fingertips? Would he feel the heat of her easy blushes? She held his gaze as if she couldn't quite look away. A wave of desire washed over him. *No.* This was bad. He returned his attention to the spotless microwave and began wiping the inside of it.

"We can all use a pep talk from time to time. Anyway, I was checking in. If you have any questions or need anything, my number is in the information packet." She started to leave but stopped at the door. "How's Julietta?"

He sprayed more cleaner on the rag and glanced over at her. "She's doing well. Told me her mother used to make pancakes on Sunday mornings. We tried it for dinner last night."

"You made her pancakes? How'd that go?"

He paused, looked down, laughed. "She appreciated the effort, I think."

"Are you bringing her to the first Friday feast tomorrow?"

"I meant to ask. What is it exactly?"

"First Friday of every month, Molly and I cook. We have a family dinner."

"Not sure how she'd do in a large crowd of strangers."

"I understand. If she gets overwhelmed, she can play with Jack up in my apartment."

"I'll see what she thinks about it."

"Great. Hope to see you both."

Yeah. That's not going to happen. He had a meeting with Marcus Canard scheduled for later. A meeting during which he was going to end this investigation. He refused to take any more money from Canard. And he was feeling guilty about the money Sadie was spending to train him. Then he'd have to quit the Cleaning Crew. Hopefully without her ever learning what a scumbag he was.

MORE THAN A little angry after Marcus had him wait in the threadbare lobby of his office, Wyatt got straight to the point. "There is nothing illegal going on at the Cleaning Crew."

"You haven't been there long enough. They aren't going to let you in on everything in your first week. I told you this would be a long assignment. You said it wouldn't be a problem and you could clear your entire caseload to take this on. I even asked Henry first before appropriating his favorite private cop."

Wyatt sat back but didn't break eye contact. "That's true. But I have a serious problem continuing an investigation when it isn't warranted. There is no evidence of wrongdoing. You're throwing away your money."

"What I do with my money is my business. And I didn't see anything about your training."

"Now you are talking about corporate espionage. I don't do that. Understand? You hired me to find out if there was illegal activity going on. Not to spy on their business practices."

Marcus lifted his hands. "Fine. You've got principles. I want you in there for at least a week or two more."

Wyatt shook his head. "No. I've concluded this investigation. If you don't like my results, hire someone else to do it."

He stood to go. *To hell with this.*

"Well, that's a real shame, son. If my recollection is correct, when Henry introduced us, he said you did whatever needed to get the job done. A bulldog, he called you. He's going to be mighty disappointed when I tell him you crapped out on me."

"I didn't. You don't like my findings."

Marcus leaned back in his chair and clasped his hands across his gut. He smiled, exposing his teeth, but his eyes stayed cold. "Henry does my insurance. Gosh, if he was so off in his judgment of you, maybe he's off with his judgment of my assets. Maybe I'll have to tell him I'm going to move my business elsewhere."

Wyatt's hands clenched along with his jaw. "That's blackmail," he said.

Walk out, part of him screamed. *Tell him to shove it and walk out.* And six months ago, he would have. He would have banked on his relationship with Henry being strong enough. He couldn't believe Marcus paid more in premiums than he saved for Henry by proving fraud. Surely he was a bigger asset. But now he had Julietta to consider. Keeping her in therapy. And a stable environment.

"I'm not blackmailing you. I'm stating how disappointed I am in a business associate's judgment."

"Fine. One more week. If I don't get a hint of anything by then, then there isn't anything. Agreed?"

"Sure. Thanks. I always appreciate someone who can see the big picture. Because we all depend on each other, don't we?"

Wyatt managed to not slam the door as he left. He wanted to drive straight home and take a shower. Dealing with Marcus always left him feeling dirty. He sat in the car, trying to calm the anger before he went home to Julietta. He needed a plan to get out of this. He was beginning to see that Marcus was a vengeful man. Exhibit A: his fixation on finding anything to ruin Sadie's reputation in return for nothing more than her being a better businessperson. He needed to set up a meeting with Henry and feel him out about his relationship with Marcus. He'd get that done and put in another week.

Then what? Back to his usual life of following insurance cheats around. Back to focusing on Julietta's recovery. Back to sleeping alone every night. He cranked the engine. He didn't miss Victoria, not really. His love for her had been squelched in a single moment.

She had gone with him to Asheville after Maddie's death. He'd found Jules stunned and scared in the care of Maddie's best friend, Kate. She'd put her little arms around his neck and told him her mommy was dead. He remembered sinking to the floor, Jules in his lap as they cried together. After her tears tapered away, she had whispered a question to him. *Who's going to take care of me now?* He'd told her he was. A movement in the doorway caught his eye and he saw Victoria standing there. The words *Victoria and I will* died on his lips at the expression on her face. Horrified. Furious.

That night, they'd argued. She told him to let Kate keep Jules. That she had no intentions of starting their marriage with a half-grown kid.

And he had no business even trying to take on a young girl. He'd listened to her with a dizzying sense of stunned relief. It was as if a mask had slipped and he was seeing into her soul. And it was ugly. When she said if he was going to take custody she might as well leave him, he told her to go home and pack her things. To be out of the house before he and Jules came back.

In the time between burying her mother, settling her affairs and coming home to Charleston, Jules asked if Aunt Victoria was going to live with them. He told her no. He told her he and Victoria had decided they didn't love each other enough to get married. And he prayed Jules would never hear or figure out the truth. Because she'd been disappointed with his answer. Another woman gone from her life. Maybe when they got through this first year, he'd look into that Big Sisters program. Something to get a stable female presence in her life.

He dropped the truck into gear and backed out of the parking space. *This is exactly why you shouldn't be thinking about Sadie Martin. There is no way to make this work.* He shook his head. Damn, he was attracted to her. And he suspected he wasn't the only one feeling the sparks. Guilt squirmed in his gut. He was lying to her. Spying on her. *It's your job. It's what you do.* Somehow, he didn't think she would see it that way.

And even if he quit, he could never do anything about this attraction and not tell her. And she'd never forgive him. *Do the job. Secure your relationship with Henry. Get out. Nothing else to do.*

CHAPTER EIGHT

"WHY ARE YOU so nervous?"

Sadie frowned at Molly. "What? I'm not nervous."

"You are. You're running all over this kitchen like a chicken with its head cut off."

Sadie pointed at the stove with the knife in her hand. "I've got three different spaghetti sauces going. I'm trying to chop up this stuff for salads. I'm not sure if we have enough noodles. And we haven't even started dessert yet."

"Yes? And how is this different from any other Friday Feast? You're about to vibrate out of your skin."

Sadie scowled and returned to slicing tomatoes. "You're imagining things."

Truth was, she *was* nervous. Wyatt had called to let her know Julietta was very excited to come to the dinner and see Jack again. Now she was acting like a geeky high school girl who had the captain of the football team coming to her house. And she hated it. Hated the out-of-control feeling that left her both scared and hopeful. Wyatt was an employee, and her giddy little heart needed to wake up to the fact.

"Are you slicing those tomatoes or slaughtering them?"

The beautiful locally grown beefsteak tomatoes she bought at the farmers' market were now a goopy mess on the cutting board. She put the knife down. "You do it. I'll get the bread ready."

Molly hip checked her away from the counter and began to salvage larger bits of tomato. "Maybe you should go sit down with your jellybean jar for a little bit."

"Ha-ha. So funny." Sadie began opening bags of French bread.

Molly looked up from the tomatoes. "Remember, we need slices, not bread crumbs."

"You're killing me with your razor-sharp wit today, Molls, killing me."

"Come on. Spill it before the guys start showing up. It's Wyatt, isn't it? You two could short out a power grid with the sparks flying off you."

Sadie froze. *No.* It wasn't noticeable. But Josh had noticed. Now Molly. This had to stop. She was setting a horrible example. If she couldn't control herself, what authority did she have to tell the guys to control themselves? Rule number one: no fooling around in word or deed. None. Not even in jest. She took in a deep breath and let it out. Wrapped her jangly nerves up tight and pushed them deep down where she kept her fears and tears. *Don't act the fool.* She stood up straighter.

"He's an employee. One of the guys. There are no sparks."

Molly opened her mouth, but Sadie held up a hand.

"Rules are rules."

"Some rules should be broken."

Josh came in through the conference room. "What rules should we be breaking?"

"No rules should be broken. But I did want to ask you something before everyone gets here. Wyatt's bringing his niece. She's eight and her mother died recently."

Molly let out a little sound and brought her hands to her lips. Sadie hoped she would keep it together when Julietta got here, but then, Molly cried at TV commercials. Josh leaned against a counter, crossing his arms. His eyebrows went up and she scowled at him.

"Eight. Wow. That's tough," he said. But he held her gaze for a long moment. *You were eight, too,* his expression said, *when your mother walked away. Are you going to be okay with this?*

She ignored it. "Should I say something to the guys when they get here? So they don't ask?"

Molly returned to the salad, deftly dicing a

cucumber. "Did Wyatt say anything about it?" she asked.

"No, at first he told me he wasn't sure how she'd do around so many strangers, but then he said she was excited about it."

"Then I'd let him handle it. He knows what's going to be best for her."

Sadie nodded. It sounded reasonable. She had been torn about telling. She didn't want the guys walking on eggshells, but she also didn't want an innocent question to upset the girl. Molly was right, it was Wyatt's responsibility. Not hers. She ached for Julietta. Their situations weren't exactly the same, but she knew the fear in realizing your world wasn't permanent.

Josh gave her shoulder a squeeze. *You okay?* She tilted her head to touch her cheek to his hand. *Yes.* Wasn't she always okay?

The guys began filtering in, and everyone went about setting up the table in the conference room. They ate family-style at these dinners: a table full of food and a room full of laughter. It had started a few years prior when Sadie realized a couple of her college guys either weren't going home or had no real home to go to over the holidays. She had them come to her place for Thanksgiving and Christmas dinners. It had morphed into a monthly affair from there. She loved the ragtag family they'd become.

She was doing a final taste test of the spaghetti sauces, one meatless, one with ground beef and one with super spicy sausage, when the skin at the nape of her neck felt as if it had been brushed by a feather. She turned, and, sure enough, Wyatt Anderson stood in the doorway. Staring at her. He wore jeans and a dark green shirt that brought out his eyes. The sleeves were turned up over those amazing forearms. Her heart skittered in her chest. *You're insane. You can't feel a look.* Her insides turned into a slurry of hot and cold mush. For a long beat, they held a gaze. *Sparks.* Molly's words echoed in her mind.

"Hey, Ms. Sadie! Where's Jack?" Julietta asked.

Grateful for the distraction, she smiled at Julietta. She was so darned cute with her dark hair pulled up in a ponytail bouncing off her shoulders. She wore jeans and a T-shirt with a picture of a princess on the front. Above and below the princess were the words, *I'll save myself, thank you.* It made Sadie laugh out loud.

"Jack's upstairs. I love your shirt."

She looked down at it and smoothed the front with a hand. "My mother had it made for me on the computer."

"It's awesome. I might get one for myself."

She glanced at Wyatt and raised her eyebrows. He showed no reaction to the mention of her mother. He lifted a shoulder in a slow shrug and smiled, making those dimples pop. Sadie turned back to Julietta before she could hyperventilate.

"What can we do to help?" he asked.

"Not sure. I'm waiting for these pots to boil so I can start the pasta. Then we'll toast up the garlic bread. Check with Josh. He's in charge of the drinks."

"Can I go see Jack?"

Wyatt put his hand on her shoulder. "Not right now, Jules. Let Ms. Sadie get dinner finished."

"After dinner," Sadie promised.

DURING THE DINNER, Wyatt couldn't keep his eyes from straying to Sadie. She'd about taken his breath away when he'd walked into the kitchen. She wore a sundress, exposing her arms and legs. And they were mighty fine arms. And the legs, well, he couldn't continue those thoughts while a guest at her table. She had her hair piled up in a haphazard bun at the back of her head. Several of the curls had escaped and one swayed against the nape of her neck, taunting him. He wanted to brush it aside and press his lips to the tender skin below it.

He looked down at his plate and sopped up sauce with a bit of bread. *And you are a lying, deceitful spy who has no right to even think about her.* Pretty soon, he'd "quit" and move on. She'd never know. The idea of hurting her made him feel like an even bigger jerk. Julietta reached up and tugged at his sleeve. He smiled down at her. She was having a good time. The guys, Josh especially, had taken to her and were treating her like a pampered baby sister. Since she'd mentioned Maddie at the park, the mentions of her mother had begun to trickle out. The therapist said this was a very good sign. It was the breakthrough they'd been waiting for. A major step in her healing process.

"What's up, Jules?"

"Can I go play checkers with Josh?"

"Of course you can."

She scampered off as people began to rise from the table and take their plates to the kitchen. He started to get up, also, but DeShawn and two other guys, Cody and Eric, he thought, sat down next to him.

"Hey, guys, what's up?"

"I was telling them about your having been in the National Guard," DeShawn said. "Cody's thinking about enlisting, too, and Eric wants to join the Guard. Can you answer some questions for us?"

"Uh, sure. Let me take this plate…" A hand came over his shoulder and he turned to see Sadie's smiling face.

"I've got it. Convince my guys to not get blown up." She took the plate from him.

"We aren't going to get blown up, *Mom*," De-Shawn said, rolling his eyes.

Wyatt answered their questions. He detailed his two trips to Afghanistan and tried not to glamorize it. While he did, he noticed people were drifting through the rooms, talking, laughing. This was a relaxed, family atmosphere. His admiration for what Sadie had built here grew. When their questions finally came to an end and he'd answered them as thoroughly as he could, he stood. "I'm going to check on Julietta," he said.

She wasn't in the kitchen. Molly pointed to an open door that led to a staircase. "Sadie took her upstairs to see Jack."

He hesitated on the staircase when he realized it led to Sadie's living quarters. The door at the top was open, and when he reached the next to the top stair, he called out. "Hello? Jules? You up here?"

"I've got her," Sadie called out. "Come on up."

The door opened into the living area. She'd done some serious renovating up here. There was a large open living space. Off to his left was a hallway he assumed led to the bedroom. There was little furniture. A couch sat centered on a rug of swirling earth tones. On either end of the beige couch there were end tables, one pine, the other oak, with lamps that also didn't match. A cherrywood coffee table. A small dining room set. She didn't entertain much, he supposed. The garage-sale-collection look of it intrigued him. Why? She was so thorough and organized in her business, why did her home look so temporary?

"Uncle Wyatt, look!"

He approached Julietta. She sat on one end of the couch with Jack beside her. Sadie was holding a bottle of nail polish.

"See what Ms. Sadie did? Pink, purple, pink, purple!" Julietta pointed to each of her freshly painted fingernails.

"Very pretty," he said.

"I hope it was okay. I should have asked, I guess," Sadie said. She dipped the brush back into the bottle and leaned forward to take one of Julietta's hands. She pursed her lips and blew on the wet polish. "Let it dry, honey, or it'll smudge."

"It's fine," he managed to choke out. He couldn't take his eyes off her gorgeous mouth. *Stop it.*

"She's got tons of them, Uncle Wyatt. All kinds of colors."

He managed a smile. "Wouldn't have taken you for the nail-polish type."

She lifted her leg and wiggled her foot, encased in a ballet type slipper, at him. And the urge to take the shoe in hand and pull it off to see what color those toes were sporting roared up out of nowhere. And then, he'd skim his hands up those legs that went on forever and find out what color panties she was wearing. His body reacted to his thoughts and stirred to life. He jerked his eyes away.

"Okay. Uh. Okay. I'll be downstairs."

He fled the room, clomping down the stairs two at a time. He needed a minute. He didn't get it.

"Are you okay? You seem a little flustered," Molly said. She was packing up leftovers in little Tupperware containers and lining them up on the counter.

I bet I do. I wanted to throw my boss down and rip her dress off. I'd say flustered *is about the right word for it.* "Probably from running up and down stairs on a full stomach. That was awesome spaghetti. Are recipes available?"

Molly laughed at him, so he went back to the dining room. Most of the guys had left and the others were getting ready to go. They were young, single guys and it was a Friday night. Of course they wouldn't be hanging around. They descended on Molly and containers were quickly claimed. Sadie came downstairs as they began shouting their goodbyes.

Molly picked up a bag from the counter. "Okay, then. Sadie, the pots are in the dishwasher. You need to finish up the plates and silverware. Everything else is done, so I'll see you Monday. Y'all have a great weekend. Bye."

Sadie put her hands on her hips as Molly scooted out the door. "Well, bye." She turned to Wyatt as he walked into the kitchen. "She could have said she didn't want to wash the dishes. Sheesh!"

She went to the sink, began to fill it with hot water and poured a generous dollop of dish soap over the plates stacked there. "Julietta is reading Jack a book."

"Guess I'm on dish duty with you."

"You don't have to."

"I want to. Owe you for the dinner." He stepped to the double sink. There were two dish racks on the counter. "Wash or rinse?"

"I'll wash. I hate rinsing. It's boring."

They stood side by side, washing and rinsing. He could hear Julietta's voice lilting in a sing-song as she read to Jack. He was overly aware of Sadie's body next to his. The brush of her shoulder against his arm and the accidental bump of her hip sent ripples of heat through him. She handed him a plate and their fingers touched so he held on for a moment. She looked at him, her eyes wide and blue, her lips parted. *God, she felt it, too.*

Her head swiveled back to the sink. "I hope it was okay I painted her nails."

"It's fine. But I may have to hire you for girl-stuff lessons."

She smiled and shook her head, making a tendril at the side of her neck sway. The urge to push it aside and press his lips to the tender spot at the base of her skull went through him. Then he'd work around the column of her neck to that spot where her pulse was fluttering. And then... He tore his gaze away from her neck and shifted against the growing pressure in his groin. *You gotta stop this.*

"I'm probably not your best bet for that kind of stuff."

"No?" He tugged a plate from her fingers and playfully bumped his shoulder against hers. He couldn't help it. He wanted to see her blush. "What are you my best bet for?"

She drew in a sharp breath and peeked up at him. He got his blush and resisted a smile. He leaned in. *One kiss. Just one.* So he could go on with his life with the knowledge of how those lips would feel against his. As his mouth approached hers, she turned to him and tilted her face up to his. He let his hand touch her waist, ready to pull her closer.

"We can't do this," she whispered.

He stopped and let his hand fall away. "I know. I'm sorry."

"Don't be sorry. But we can't."

She couldn't do it because she believed he was an employee. She wouldn't break her own rules. He shouldn't do it because when the truth came out, it would hurt her even more. Jack's nails clacking down the stairs gave them a moment to step apart before Julietta burst into the kitchen.

"Uncle Wyatt? Can we get a dog? I'll walk it and play with it and everything!"

"Getting a dog is a big responsibility. We'll talk about it." He grinned at Sadie. "Thanks a lot."

Her laughter made him feel a little better. He let out a shaky breath. It was going to be a long week.

THIS WAS NICE. Wyatt stretched his legs out in the grass and leaned back in the lawn chair. The sun was almost gone, the mosquitoes were few and the cicadas were loud. Best of all, his friends had brought beer and meat. The bottle of beer felt good in his hand and tasted even better. The scent of charcoal and beef filled the air.

"Been too long," Adam said.

"True. A lot going on."

Adam laughed at the understatement. Adam was his former partner on the police force. Scott leaned over to snag a beer. Scott was a lawyer, a district attorney whom Wyatt had worked with for years before leaving the force. The backyard barbecues and Saturday afternoon basketball games had been a weekly ritual for the three of them until life intervened. Wyatt was beginning to find a new normal with Jules. Adam had a three-month-old at home and Scott was freshly divorced with custody of his two teenagers.

"How's Jules doing?" Scott asked.

Wyatt glanced to the rear of his property, where Jules and Scott's thirteen-year-old daughter where stalking fireflies in the marsh. "Better. Much better."

"How about you, man?"

"I'm good. I'm…"

His words trailed off. What was he? The overwhelming sense of loss had faded to a dull ache. He and Jules had settled into a comfortable routine. But still, he felt a nagging sense of… restlessness. He thought back to last night. Washing dishes with Sadie. That moment when he'd looked into her eyes and saw his own desire reflected back at him. Probably a good thing she'd come to her senses. He wasn't entirely sure he would have been able to stop with a single kiss.

"Missing Victoria?" Adam asked with a smirk. He'd clearly never liked her but had the restraint to have never said so while they were together. Nor had he done the "I told you she was awful" thing once they'd broken up.

"Oh, hell no." He bit back a few other expletives. He had nothing to say about her that he wanted Jules to overhear. He ran a hand through his hair and got up to look at the steaks. "Just keeping busy. This current investigation is taking a lot of time."

"Yeah, you told me you were doing undercover. How's it going?" Scott asked.

"It's a bullshit job," he said as he returned to the lawn chair. "I knew there wasn't anything to find the first day. But the guy who hired me wants me to stay at least two weeks."

"Undercover?" Adam asked, leaning forward. "Doing what?"

Wyatt took a long pull of beer and wiped his mouth with the back of his forearm. "Can't tell you."

"Why? Is it top secret?"

Wyatt grinned. "No. Y'all will make fun of me."

"Male escort?"

"Stripper?"

"You know what? Forget it."

"Now you have to tell us," Scott said. "Or we'll go with stripper."

"I'm not going to be done there for another week, so keep your mouths shut. It's at that cleaning service, the Cleaning Crew. Heard of it?"

"You're undercover as a maid?" Adam's laughter echoed back from the marsh.

"I've heard of it. Um, Sadie? Martin? She's the owner, right?" Scott asked.

He ignored Adam and focused on Scott. "Wait, you know her?"

"Well, well," Adam said in an amused drawl. "Apparently your interest is a little more personal than professional."

Wyatt felt some heat on his face. Yeah, he was interested, all right. Fat lot of good it was going to do him. "Just curious. She seems like an interesting person."

"Go for it, dude," Adam urged.

"Sure. I've been lying and spying on her. Most women frown on that kind of behavior." He turned back to Scott. "So you know her."

"Not really. I've only met her once. She keeps a low public profile, but she's given a ton of money to a couple of the charities I'm involved with."

Wyatt went to flip the steaks. Scott was involved in several local charities and all of them served underprivileged children. This news did not surprise him. The way she'd responded to Jules? She had a soft spot for kids. His guilt felt a little bit heavier.

"She hot?" Adam asked Scott.

"Oh, yeah. Beautiful. But really shy, I think. Like I said, she gives a lot of money, but she rarely comes out for events. What are you investigating her for?"

"Guy who runs Happy Housekeepers thinks she's doing something illegal. But she's not. Like I said, it's a waste of time. But he's holding his relationship with one of my biggest clients over my head. So I'm just going along."

"Marcus Canard?"

Adam's tone was scornful and Wyatt raised his eyebrows. "You know him?"

"I know of him. Came out of a pretty poor family. I'd admire what he's accomplished, but he's as mean as a snake. Totally vindictive."

"I don't doubt it. It's my understanding his cleaning service is going under."

"That would hurt him. He branched out into real estate development. Lost a bundle when the bubble burst. Income from his cleaning company is the only thing keeping him out of bankruptcy, if what I hear is true."

"Huh. Interesting."

More than interesting. It was the entire reason for his investigation. Marcus was calling in favors to try to bring down a rival. Trying to save his only successful business venture. He was desperate. And men in desperate financial situations often did very stupid things. Hiring a PI must be his Hail Mary pass.

He looked up at the shriek coming from the

marsh. It was a happy girl shriek and it made him smile. Jules came sprinting up, jar in hand. He could see the faint glow inside it.

"I caught one! I caught one, Uncle Wyatt!"

She crashed into him and he scooped her up, balancing her on a hip. Barely. Soon she'd be too big for this, and a small part of him was dismayed. He took the jar and held it up. "Good job. Don't forget to let him go in a few minutes."

She wiggled down and took the jar. She brought it close to her face to peer at the glowing beetle within. It was flying around the jar, seeking an escape. "Can't I keep him overnight? For a night-light? I'll let him go in the morning."

He hunkered down and looked into the jar with her. "I don't think he'd like that, Jules. He's probably a little confused right now, wondering how he ended up in there."

Zoe, Scott's daughter, knelt down in the grass beside Jules. "He's probably missing his friends back there, too. We should let him go soon."

Jules's face crumpled and Wyatt's heart squeezed at the compassion in her expression. "You're right. I'm going to let him go now." She ran back to the marsh and her voice drifted back to them. "Bye-bye, firefly. Have fun with your friends."

The men chuckled and Wyatt put an arm

around her shoulders when she came back. "That was very kind of you, Jules."

"Can we go inside and watch a movie?"

"Sure. Dinner will be ready in a few minutes."

"You're a natural at this dad stuff," Scott said after the girls had gone inside.

"I had to learn fast." He glanced at the back door, making sure it was shut, and then looked back to Scott. "I have a question for you."

"Shoot."

"Could I adopt her?"

"Probably. But you don't need to. You're her legal guardian."

"I know. I… I've been thinking about it. Making it a lifetime commitment. I mean, I'm committed. She's my blood, my only family. But I want to make it more. I don't know how she'll feel about it. Just looking at the possibility."

"That's awesome, man," Adam said. "I hear what you're saying. You know, I thought you might have taken on more than you could handle at first. But when Jake was born, I understood. Your family. Your blood. It means everything."

"Where's her father?" Scott asked.

"Don't know. Maddie never said. I went through all her papers and asked all her friends. Didn't find a thing."

"Shouldn't be a problem. You were approved by the court to be her guardian, so an adoption could be as simple as filling out the paperwork and a court date. Let me know when you're ready and I'll give you some names of family practice lawyers."

"Great. Appreciate it."

They all stood and Wyatt took the steaks from the grill. Adam hooked an arm over his shoulders and gave him a shake. "Now about this hot woman you're after…"

"I'm not after her."

"But you want to be."

"But I can't."

"Why not? Just tell her. After it's over. Say, hey, business, you know?"

"I don't know about that."

But now he was thinking about it. Sadie liked straightforward, no-nonsense. Maybe he could go to her, confess all and plead for forgiveness. What was the worst that could happen?

CHAPTER NINE

IT LOOKED LIKE a perfectly ordinary building. Like a library or a school. Sadie tilted her head to peer out the windshield at the sleek brick building. Live oaks and neat beds of azaleas, recently past prime blooming season, embraced it. The wide, inviting porch led to a pretty wood door. Beyond the door people lay dying. Abuelito lay dying.

She put her forehead to the steering wheel and squeezed her eyes against the burn of unshed tears. She clenched the wheel to stop her hands trembling. She couldn't do this. She couldn't walk in there and say goodbye to the first man who'd ever loved her. Loved her like a father should love a child. A tear slid down her cheek as her throat ached. *Leave. Call Lena and tell her you can't do this. She'll understand.* For a brief, blessed moment, the pain and fear went away as the hope of an escape filled her.

She shook her head without lifting it from the steering wheel. No. She'd regret it forever if she didn't say goodbye. She'd walked away from too many people in her life not to have learned that lesson. Avoiding immediate pain always came with lingering regret and doubt, and the shame never went away. She wasn't doing it anymore. If anything, she owed him more than any other. He'd shown her what a family was supposed to be. A weak, wavering smile trembled on her lips. *Una gatita callejero*, he'd called her. Literally a street kitten.

She straightened and brought her hands up to press at her eyes, wiping away the wetness she found there. She took a sip of bottled water. *Suck it up, Sadie girl. Head up, shoulders back. It'd be an insult to the love and time he gave you to run out on him now.* She would go in. As soon as her legs would support her.

Lena waving at her from the sidewalk caught her attention. Sadie waved back. Too late to run now. Lena, as always, was gorgeous and stylish and impeccable. The dark red of the sleeveless linen dress she wore suited her olive complexion. Black strappy three-inch heels still didn't put her up to Sadie's height. How she wore linen without it wrinkling was a mystery. Sadie looked down at her own clothing. Jeans. She'd made a concession to the visit by replacing her Crew T-shirt with a blue top. The top, with its twisted knot of fabric at the scooped neckline, was technically a T-shirt, but it was a *fancy* T-shirt. And she was wearing flats, not running shoes or work boots. Her version of dressing up.

"Are you okay? You're a little pale."

"I'm scared."

"Of Lito?"

"Of goodbye. I don't know what to say."

Lena looped a warm arm around Sadie's waist. "Me, either."

"Well, that doesn't help."

They turned and headed toward the building. "It's so pretty, isn't it?" Lena asked. "Like a school or something."

"I was thinking the same thing."

The realization that Lena was dreading this as much as her crept up on Sadie and gave her courage. She hooked her arm around Lena's shoulders. *"Anda, hermana. Hagamos esto."*

Come on, sister. Let's do this.

Lena dropped her arm from Sadie's waist with a laugh. "Your Spanish still sucks." They began walking toward the door. "After all these years, you still sound like you're reading out of a text book."

"Because the only Spanish you taught me was how to cuss out a man."

Lena let loose a torrent of Spanish, speaking too quickly for Sadie to even follow. She picked up on a few words. *Balls. Dull. Knife.*

"And you wonder why you can't keep a man."

"They play with fire, they know they might get burned."

Sadie pulled open the door and the ribbing stopped as they stepped into the cool, hushed reception room. Gooseflesh rose on Sadie's arms. The room was classic Charleston doctor's-waiting-room decor: lots of burgundy and green. Palm trees on the upholstery and Jim Booth prints on the wall. Oriental rug on the floor. A pretty young woman smiled at them from a desk with nothing on it but a telephone. *Amazing.* Sadie hadn't seen her own desktop in years.

"Hello. How may I help you?"

Lena approached the desk. She answered in a hushed voice that matched the low tones of the receptionist. "We're here to see our grandfather, Luis Acosta."

Gooseflesh stirred back to life and Sadie hugged her arms to her belly. What if someone was dying right now? Her mouth went dry and her heart began a sickeningly fast run of beats. What if Abuelito was? What if he didn't look like himself? What if he was gross and gruesome and… She snapped herself out the thoughts with a physical jerk. *Sadie, you are a grown woman, not a child afraid of the boogeyman.*

A buzzing noise made her jump. So much for not being a child. Sheesh, it was only the door. *The door to the back. Where people are dying.*

She pressed her fingers against Lena's warm palm. Lena squeezed back tight, bolstering Sadie's courage. The clichéd waiting-room decorations ended at the door. They were in a hospital corridor. The hospital smells, faint as they were, washed over her. Antiseptic and stale, cool air. The silence of the waiting room followed them and their footsteps seemed to crash loudly in her ears. A faint beep, the squeak of a nurse's shoe on the polished linoleum floor.

"Room fourteen," Lena murmured. She didn't let go of Sadie's hand.

They stopped outside Lito's room and looked at each other. Lena's lips trembled as she tried to smile. Sadie suddenly felt ashamed of her selfishness. This was Lena's beloved grandfather. She'd grown up with him. He was her blood. Her heart had to be breaking harder than Sadie's. She should be comforting her friend, not the other way around. She lifted a fist to knock on the door.

"Ready?" she whispered. She knocked when Lena nodded.

Lena's aunt Estrella was sitting with Luis. She kissed Lena on both cheeks and did the same to Sadie. She picked up her purse. "I'm going to take a little walk while you visit," she said.

Sadie watched her go as Lena crossed the room to kiss Abuelito. When she turned to face the man in the bed, her forced smile faltered a little. She had not known Luis in his prime, but when she'd met him twelve years ago, he'd been a handsome gray-haired man, his body a little thick with age, his hands gnarled from years of manual labor. Now he lay small and wasted, the white sheets showing how pale his usually swarthy complexion had become. On numb feet, she crossed the room to kiss his cheeks. When had this happened? The last time she'd seen him, he wasn't this pale, tiny little bird of a man.

"Ah, my favorite granddaughters," he said, and at least his voice was the same, rich and thickly accented.

They sat on either side of the bed. Sadie kept her eyes on his hand, clasped in hers. How many times, she wondered, had his hand snuck a ten- or twenty-dollar bill into her purse or pocket? And once he'd learned her secret vice, how many bags of jelly beans had he hidden in similar fashion? A smile curved her lips and she dared to look up into his face. His eyes were the same, too. Two black pools that could have been hard but never were. Always warm, always kind. She wondered how he managed it in a world that had not always been warm or kind to him. Maybe it was because of his trials that he learned to be kind.

He glanced from Lena to Sadie and back again. "It's hard for young people to say goodbye." A small sound escaped from Lena and he turned to her. "No tears, my little Lena. No tears."

"I can't help it. I'm going to miss you so much." Lena bent to press her forehead against his hand.

He squeezed Sadie's hand and turned to her. "Gatita. Can you give me a minute alone with Magdalena?"

"Sure," she said through numb lips. A stab of painful jealousy speared her. Tears started in her eyes. She bent her head to kiss his hand before stepping out.

In the hall, she leaned against the wall and covered her eyes. Of course he'd want to talk to Lena. She was his real granddaughter. Who was she? The stray *gatita* who'd hung around their porch for a few scraps tossed her way. Her throat closed up painfully. She crossed her arms against her chest and lifted her chin. *So what, Sadie? Status quo. You knew you weren't family. You don't have one. The end. Suck it up and deal with it.*

After a few minutes, the door opened and Lena came out, wiping her eyes with a tissue. She handed a clean one to Sadie. "He wants to talk to you now."

The warmth of the request quickly extinguished the flare of guilt. Why did she always assume the worst? Why couldn't she fully believe people cared about her? *You know why.* The whisper came from deep inside the darkest secret of her soul. A secret no one but she knew. She entered the room and he motioned at the chair beside the bed and held out a hand.

"Sit by me, Gatita. I have something to say to you."

She sat and took his hand in hers. "I want to say something first, please. I never thanked you for what you did for me."

His free hand squeezed hers with a strength that surprised her. "Look at me, Sadie."

She met his eyes and the usual warmth there was gone, replaced by a sort of fearful earnestness she'd never seen before.

"Listen to me," he said. His tone was as urgent as the look in his eyes. "You have done nothing wrong. Your mother was a fool not to get you back. I don't know why she couldn't keep you, and I don't care. None of it was your fault. You were a wonderful child. And you've become a wonderful woman. She should be ashamed she didn't try. I would have been proud to call you daughter."

Sadie pressed her cheek to the top of his hand as a ragged sob ripped from her throat. "Lito," she whispered. She wanted to give in to the pain his words stirred and cry the hot, hard tears she'd shed so many of in her life, but not now. She had to say these things. She couldn't let this man die without knowing. "I used to pretend you were my real grandfather and you all were my real family."

He pulled a hand free to cup her cheek. "We are your real family, Gatita. Real family is bound by love as well as blood. We all love you."

It took a while for her to get the tears under control. When she did, she lifted her head and scrubbed at her eyes. "Thank you for showing me what a family is. I know Lena's parents thought I'd be a bad influence on her. I know it was you who made them give me a chance. I was so lost back then. But you showed me how not to be afraid. Thank you."

"If I've done nothing else in this life, then that will be enough for me to enter heaven with a smile. Never be afraid of love, Sadie. You deserve it. You are worthy of it. Don't let her failure be your legacy." He caught her chin in his hand and titled her face up to meet his eyes.

"Lito, there's something else. I need you to tell me what to do. I got a letter from my half brother."

"What did it say?"

"I don't know. I'm afraid to read it."

"Ah, Gatita. He's your blood. Read it. Give him a chance. Promise me."

"I promise."

An easy promise to make to comfort a dying man. But it wasn't that easy. Because he didn't know the entire truth. Her mother not only never tried to get her back, but signed away her parental rights so she could go marry a man and have his children. It wasn't that her mother didn't want children. She hadn't wanted Sadie. And she wanted to hate those children. Not be a part of them.

She begged off dinner with the family, telling Lena she had too much work to catch up on. Now, sitting cross-legged on her couch, glass of wine in hand, contemplating the letter, she regretted the decision. Dinner with Lena's family meant good food and lots of loving strokes to the ego. This letter promised nothing but reopened wounds and pain. A short, bitter laugh burst from her throat. *Right, Sadie, those wounds never healed.*

In one fluid movement, she leaned forward, grabbed the envelope and ripped it open. Trembling fingers found the single sheet of paper inside.

Dear Ms. Martin:
My name is Grant Rogers and I think you may be my sister. I've tried to call you but I can't work up the nerve. My mother is Dawn Martin Rogers.

I graduated from college last December and got a job doing medical research in Raleigh. I was packing up to move when I found an envelope in the attic. It had baby pictures with the name Sapphire Diamond written on the back. There were also papers from the Department of Social Services regarding the placement for adoption of a child by the same name. When I confronted my mother with these, she told me she'd had a baby very young and put it up for adoption. The fact that my real name is Granite and my sisters are named Ruby Jade and Emerald Pearl confirmed my initial suspicion.

I tried searching the adoption reunification sites but found nothing. When I did a Google search of "Sapphire Martin," I got nothing. But a search of "S. Martin, Charleston" led me to an article about your company. There was a picture of you and you look very much like my mother.

I hope I'm not wrong. I hope I haven't upset you. I don't want anything but a chance to meet you. Or just talk. You can call or text me at…

It was signed Grant Rogers. Sadie let the paper fall to her lap and reached for the glass

of wine. Sapphire, Granite, Ruby and Emerald.
Dear sweet jelly beans in a bowl. Even as she
laughed, tears mixed in.

THE PHONE RINGING at 7:00 a.m. would normally
be considered a bad thing. Except when you are
so ready to have work distract you from your life
that you welcome Monday like a long-lost friend.
Sadie had even contemplated the very expensive,
and much-ignored, treadmill tucked away in the
second bedroom. Her wine and jelly-bean binge
after reading Grant's letter warranted some sort
of penance. But alas, someone needed her. Even
a sick call would get her out of exercise and shut
up her brain.

But it wasn't a sick call. Wyatt Anderson's im-
possibly sexy voice, its low baritone sweetened
with a trace of Southern accent, oozed through
the phone. Forgotten in her grieving was the near
kiss after the dinner on Friday. How could she
have forgotten? He had leaned in to kiss her. It
wasn't her idea. A delicious swirl of desire swept
through her as that tidbit sank in. He was attracted
to her, also. She shook her head. Didn't matter.

He was having an emergency. A curl emergency.

"I wouldn't bother you. I'm sorry. But she took
me by surprise. And she looked so dejected when
I told her I hadn't learned how or even bought

whatever it is I need. I didn't know what to do. She keeps saying it's okay, but it isn't."

"Oh, no. This is my fault, too. I meant to pick up a small curling iron last time I was at Wally World and give it to you."

Julietta had bebopped up to Wyatt and asked him to do the curl like Sadie had promised to show him. And she'd never shown him. *You know better than this. Always keep your promises. No matter how small.* Her stomach felt like a bowling ball. "Okay," she said. "Give me an address. I'll swing by the store and grab one and be there as quick as I can."

"Would you? Thank you. I'll owe you. Whatever you want or need. I'll owe you."

She smiled at his relief and a part of her heart went gooey at his devotion to his niece. She plugged the address into her GPS as she clattered down the back stairs with Jack hot on her heels. The address Wyatt had given her wasn't far from the West Ashley Walmart in an older neighborhood of neat brick ranch homes. It took her thirty minutes total.

His front door opened and she climbed from her car. She motioned for Jack to stay.

"He can come in or go in the backyard if he needs—it's fenced."

She turned at the sound of his voice. *Dear*

sweet baby Jesus in the manger. Wyatt stood on the small porch, holding the screen door open. Wearing a pair of sweats dipping low on his hips and nothing else. She'd been right about those six-pack abs. And the amazing pecs. Made more amazing by the light dusting of brown hair across them and the line of hair down the center of those abs. And— She forced her eyes away and her mouth shut. *It should be illegal for him to go shirtless without warning.* Her thoughts were becoming completely inappropriate for this early on a Monday morning.

"Okay," she said. Her voice sounded weak and she cleared her throat. "Come on, Jack."

She used the time it took to get Jack into the backyard to snap out of it. *Employee. We don't drool over the employees, Sadie dear. Sexual harassment suits are not good for business.* But her hormones weren't listening. They were still squealing like fourteen-year-olds. She switched her focus. Julietta. The little girl she'd let down. That doused the flames.

She hesitated on the porch, peering in through the screen door. Wyatt had disappeared. She pulled open the screen and stepped in. Two walls of the room were lined with full bookshelves. A recliner with a side table and a lamp sat on a patterned rug in the corner. On the wall above the chair were several framed photographs. One was of Wyatt and a pretty blonde woman. He looked at least ten years younger. Sadie smiled. He looked better now. That seemed to happen with some men. The little lines and some life experience pushed good-looking to totally sexy.

"That's Maddie," he said from the doorway into the hall.

Sadie continued looking at the picture. Wyatt's hand rested on Maddie's shoulder. She thought of the letter she'd returned to her office desk. What would it have been like to have a brother? Sisters? Squaring her shoulders, she cleared her throat. "She was very pretty." She handed the curling iron to him. "While you break into this packaging and plug it in, I'll talk to Julietta. Where is she?"

"Last door on the left. I'll get some scissors." He turned the package over in his hands. "Or a saw."

She went down the hall. At the end, the door was standing open and she caught a glimpse of a messily made queen-size bed. Wyatt's bed. A thrill shot through her. What would it be like? Tangled in his sheets. Would they smell like him? She looked away and tapped on the closed door to her left.

"Julietta? It's Sadie. May I come in?"

"Sure."

The room was little-girl neat. Purples and blues and greens. Julietta sat on the floor, lacing up a pair of mismatched sneakers. The green shoe had yellow laces and the yellow shoe, green laces. She was dressed in jeans and a white T-shirt with one of the Van Gogh iris paintings on the front. Sadie suppressed a grin. She liked this kid's style.

"Why are you here?" Julietta asked. She didn't seem upset, just curious.

"Your uncle called me. I think I owe you an apology."

Julietta looked up, her eyes serious. "About the curls?"

Sadie sat on the floor across from her. "Yes. I promised you I'd show him how to do it and I forgot. I'm sorry."

Julietta tugged at a yellow shoelace. Her little shoulders shrugged, sending a dart of pain through Sadie. "It's okay."

"No. It isn't okay. I said I'd do something and I didn't. I was wrong. If you'll let me, I'll show him how right now. I brought a curling iron."

Julietta didn't move. Her hands still held the ends of the shoelaces. Sadie held her gaze even though she wanted to gather her up in a hug. She knew she was being evaluated. Kids who'd learned too young how drastically their worlds could change were especially sensitive to broken promises. Earning their trust was difficult. And Sadie, who was still struggling to let herself trust in others, could barely stand the idea that she had let this girl down. No matter how trivial it seemed, she knew it was a big deal to Julietta. Could she be trusted again? After a long moment, Julietta smiled and hopped to her feet. "Okay."

She followed Jules down the hall to the kitchen. Wyatt leaned against the counter, examining the curling iron. To get her eyes off his ass, she glanced around the room. Like the rest of the house, it was simple but homey. What looked like original pine cabinetry and white appliances. The dining room table was messy with books and papers but the rest was spotlessly clean. Test papers and art work made a mosaic on the fridge.

"You have to plug it in first," Julietta said.

Wyatt held up the cord. "I did, little Miss Smarty-Pants. Now what?"

"You turn it on."

Sadie covered her mouth to hide the smile at the exchange. Wyatt glanced at her and the light in his eyes brought a momentary burning of tears to her eyes. He loved this little girl. He loved the teasing.

"Is this right, Ms. Sadie?"

She moved to the counter to check the settings. "You've got it."

"Now it has to get hot," Julietta explained to Wyatt. "It takes a minute."

"Oh. A minute. Well, in that case." He turned to Sadie. "Coffee?"

"I'd love some." Before she could specify black, he handed her a cup he'd already poured. She raised her eyebrows as she took a sip.

"I notice things," he said. A small smile played at the corner of his mouth.

Oh, hell. He noticed things. Her heart kicked up a notch and she sipped more coffee, hoping to diffuse the warmth she felt flooding her cheeks. Julietta saved her.

"The light's on! I think it's ready!"

"Okay, then, let's get this done," Wyatt said. He scooped Julietta up and plopped her on the kitchen counter.

Standing beside him, even with Julietta vibrating with impatience between them, Sadie was uncomfortably aware of him. As a man. His hair was still sleep tousled and she so wanted to comb her fingers through those messy waves and smooth them into place. Why hadn't she let him kiss her, again? *Oh, yeah. You're his boss.*

"Okay, honey. Hold still now."

She hoped he'd just stand there on his side, but no, he leaned close to watch. She could feel his heat and his arm brushing lightly against her shoulder. *Ignore it. You have a burning hot chunk of metal you are putting near a small child's face. Ignore him.*

"How about we do two curls today? I'll do the first one and your uncle can do the second. So we know he's got it."

Julietta nodded. "That sounds like the right thing to do."

She demonstrated how to work the iron. She wasn't very proficient with it. She'd spent more time learning how to tame her curls. But she did it without burning the child or her hair and successfully coached Wyatt through the second curl. She smiled at the sight of his concentration. It looked as though he was defusing a bomb or something. He was determined to get it right. To make Julietta happy.

"Thanks again," he said as he stood on the sidewalk while a squealing Julietta went to get Jack from the backyard. "I owe you."

"No, you don't. I feel horrible for having forgotten a promise. I remember how much it hurt."

His eyes turned to her. Thoughtful, speculative. "Had a lot of promises broken, then?"

"More than I can count," she said. She snapped her mouth shut, mentally berating herself for the slip. Julietta came around the corner with Jack dancing happily in circles around her. "Okay,

Jack, in the car. Julietta, you look incredibly stylish today. Thank you for accepting my apology."

Julietta gave her a quick hug around the waist. "Thank you, Ms. Sadie! Bye, Jack!"

Sadie managed to get away without meeting Wyatt's eyes again. He was right. He noticed things. Too many things.

SHE WAS LATE getting back to the office. *Damn Highway 61 traffic.* Josh and Molly were in the kitchen when she skidded through the back door. "Hi. Start the meeting without me. I'll be right back."

Molly caught her by the back of her shirt. "Whoa. Hold up there, Missy Miss. What are you doing, looking like something Jack dragged in?"

"I had an errand to run. Took a little longer than expected."

"Uh-huh. And what kind of *errand*—" Molly made air quotes around the word "—did you have to run that's making you blush like a schoolgirl?"

"I'm not blushing. And, hey, I'm the boss. Josh, start the meeting. I'll be down in a few." Their laughter followed her up the stairs.

AND THERE WAS Wyatt sitting at the conference table when she went back downstairs. Lounged back with casually contained power and watch-

ing her entrance. *Do not blush. Do not blush.*
Her mind offered up the memory of him shirtless in the morning sun and the blush disobeyed
her command. Her eyes swept the room and she
took her seat. Sipped, okay, gulped down some
coffee. She flipped open her notebook and began
to list names of the guys who weren't there. She'd
have to call them later. Josh finished telling the
group about the *City Paper* award party. She
tipped her chin at him. Keep going.

She forgot about Wyatt and his maddening effect on her as she watched Josh lead the meeting.
Part of her still thought of him as the nineteen-
year-old kid who couldn't keep his hope for better from shining through his sullen affectation.
But he'd grown into a man. Twenty-seven on
his last birthday. He knew the business inside
and out. He was just as responsible for its success as she. No, she couldn't keep holding him
back here. He was too good to be her second-in-
command forever. Time to talk to Lena and the
lawyer about opening a second office. For him.

"Anything else, boss?" Josh asked, drawing
her attention back to the meeting.

"Five o'clock at the photographer's. No excuses. Clean uniform. Clean hair. Clean attitudes.
This is going to be a thank-you to Charleston for
giving you your high-paying jobs. Let's make

anyone who ever voted for Happy Housekeepers weep with sorrow that they were ever so deluded."

That whipped them up. They stood in a cacophony of laughter and insults aimed at Marcus Canard. Wyatt leaned over and touched her hand, sending a flame through her. He'd brushed his hair and the sight of those slight curls so neat disappointed her a little. She liked the way it'd looked before.

"I know you said no excuses, but Jules has an appointment with her counselor at four and I…"

"Oh! Of course. No problem. I meant no excuses like 'we went for pizza and forgot' or 'I was trying to get a girl's digits and forgot.'"

What a shame. She'd planned on putting his gorgeous face and body right up front in the photo. If he didn't stir up a couple new clients, nothing would. She watched him leave the room with DeShawn.

"Oh, I see."

She turned to Molly. "You don't see anything." She stood and stomped to the kitchen for more coffee. "I've got phone calls to make."

THE PHOTO SHOOT was a nightmare. Not really, but Sadie hated be at the center of attention. And she was. The photographer was wonderful. It was like herding cats to get fifteen testosterone-ridden young men to smile at the same time. Then she wanted to do crazy things like have them holding Sadie on their shoulders or have her crowd surfing through them. In the end, Sadie got the shot she wanted: she and Molly in the center of the guys, everyone smiling at the camera. Her guys were hot and she didn't look like a gargoyle. *Perfect.*

The photographer was showing her pictures on the computer when DeShawn came up and touched her arm. His rich sable skin was ashen and his eyes looked lost. She stood. "What's wrong?"

He held up his phone. "My grandmother."

A knot of fear twisted in her gut. DeShawn's grandmother had raised him. Taken him away from his alcohol-abusing parents. No Child Protective Services. She took his free hand. "Is she okay?" *Stupid.* Of course she wasn't. "What's happened, DeShawn?"

"She had a stroke. She's at the hospital. They say it's bad. I've got to go."

Sadie closed her fingers tighter on his. She looked around and caught Josh's attention. He came immediately. DeShawn's grandmother lived in Charlotte, NC, which was a three-hour drive. "Are you going to be okay to drive? Do you need one of us to take you?"

He shook his head. The dazed expression faded and his color began to come back. "I'll be okay. No. I've got to go. I'll be all right. I'm sorry about leaving."

"Don't be sorry. Not one bit. You go, be with your family. Don't think on us for one second."

Several of the guys gathered around DeShawn, offering help. By the time they led him out of the studio, Sadie's concern over him making the drive had faded away. Josh walked up behind her and squeezed her shoulder. He leaned in close to whisper in her ear.

"You'll have to finish orienting the FNG."

Icy horror at the thought of being alone with Wyatt all day for several days filled her. *Nope.* There weren't enough jelly beans in the world. She spun around and grabbed Josh's forearm. He was laughing. Laughing!

He lifted his palms and gave her an innocent look. "I've got those beach rentals out at Kiawah Island to get done tomorrow. It's a major operation and you've never done it before."

Shit. Molly slung an arm around her shoulders.

"You want me to buy some extra jelly beans to bring in tomorrow?"

"You guys are so funny. Ha. Ha. Ha."

She stomped out of the building. What was she going to do? He did things to her. Made her think things. Feel things. Hell, say things. And that almost kiss. Well, he was a guy. If she didn't want to talk about it, maybe he wouldn't, either. *Maybe. Hopefully.*

CHAPTER TEN

WYATT STOPPED SHORT at the door of the conference room. His heart rate kicked up a notch. Instead of DeShawn, Sadie sat at the table with client notebooks stacked up beside her. One lay open and she was skimming through the pages with a serious expression. His breath froze. Had he been found out? Did she know the truth? Regret washed over him as he tried to find some words to soften the betrayal she was going to feel. She looked at him and he braced himself.

"DeShawn's grandmother is in the hospital. He had to go to Charlotte to be with her, so I'm taking over his client list for the week."

Relief flooded him. So much, he almost let out a laugh. Completely inappropriate for the situation. To give himself a moment, he pulled out a chair and sat next to her. His relief was short-lived as he realized what she meant. She would be orienting him. He and Sadie. Alone together all day. Could be tricky. Because not only was he lying to her, he had a strong feeling he wasn't alone in this attraction. Which could not happen. Should not happen.

"Is she going to be okay?"

Sadie shut the client book and shook her head. "I don't think so. I'm hoping we'll hear something today. She's in bad shape."

"Damn. That's too bad. DeShawn's a great kid. Was he close to her?"

"She raised him. Since he was a baby. She's more like a mother than grandmother." She stood and began to stack the client books. "So you're stuck with me for the duration. Are you going to be okay with it?"

He held her gaze. Apparently she could swing from soft and caring to hard as nails in an instant. Her mane of black curls was tightly contained in a bun. Thick black lashes framed the dark blue of her eyes and stood against her fair skin. She wasn't asking if he wanted to orient with her. She was asking if he'd let the almost-kiss thing drop. If he could keep his hands—and lips—to himself.

"You're the boss."

She stood and gathered up the notebooks. "That's what they tell me. Let's get out of here before everyone starts showing up. We've got six clients lined up today, all due for a regular cleaning. They're in the same neighborhood, so it should run smoothly. DeShawn told me you pretty much have the routine down, so show me what you've got and I may cut you loose from orientation."

He took the notebooks from her and tucked them under his arm. Oh, he'd like to show her what he had. *You've got to stop thinking like this, man. Off-limits.* "Let's get it done."

She kept up the prickly exterior through the first two client stops. But she was good. She may have been behind a desk for a while, but she went through the houses with an efficiency that made DeShawn seem slack. No wonder the clients never left her. He found himself pushing to keep up with her. Pushing to earn the little half smile and nod she gave after her sharp eyes swept over his work.

"You should orient everyone," he said as they drove to the third house. "You're fast but thorough."

"I had to be fast if I wanted to eat," she said.

He was learning to read her. After she said it, her lips pressed together. She'd let something slip she hadn't meant to say. *But why?* Why did she hold everything so close? He should let it drop. She didn't want to talk about it.

"What do you mean?"

She glanced over at him with an appraising look that fueled his curiosity. This was ordinary small talk. It wasn't as though he was asking about the deepest secrets of her soul. Of which he was beginning to suspect she had quite a few. She shrugged and hit the turn signal.

"When I was building my client list and working alone. I learned to hustle. Don't get a job done, don't get paid."

"How'd you get started with using guys?"

She pulled into a driveway and put the car in Park. "Why not?" she said and climbed out.

He joined her at the open hatch and began unloading equipment. He waited for her to continue, but she walked away. *Okay. Touchy subject.* Why, he had no clue. *Maybe she doesn't want to chitchat with you, dude. Ever think of that? You're the one who tried to kiss her. She's the one who said no. Remember?* He remembered. He also remembered the way her pupils had dilated, how her breath had hitched and how those gorgeous lips had started to pucker up for him. She'd wanted it, too. Well, Sadie the woman may have, but Sadie the boss did not. He shut the hatch and followed her. This was turning into a big, smelly elephant.

SADIE COULD FEEL his gaze on her back as she let herself into the house. She squared her shoulders. Keep it together for a couple of days. He was doing a great job. She'd figure out who needed a new partner and get him out from under her feet. This week. Because she couldn't take much more of this. It'd started at the first house when she'd walked into the living room and there he'd been, in all his hot glory, reaching up to dust the ceiling fans, biceps bulging and a little flash of flat stomach exposed as his shirt rode up. The wave of lust unleashed by the little tease of skin had shocked her. And annoyed her. She'd worked with guys just as good-looking or even better-looking for years. Why was he setting off her alarms?

Focus. Get these jobs done. She set the client's book down on the kitchen counter and picked up a note. "Don't go into Liam's room," she read out loud. "It's an abomination, and I am ashamed."

"Teenager?"

Sadie shrugged. "Thirteen or fourteen, I think. It'll get us out of here a bit faster. I'll start upstairs."

She sorted through the big carryall for the supplies she'd need to do the rooms upstairs. Wyatt moved to stand beside her.

"Can I ask you something?"

She refrained from heaving a sigh, barely. "That's never the beginning to a question anyone wants to hear."

He ignored her. "Are you angry with me?"

His question took her aback. No, she wasn't mad at him. She was mad at herself for her lack of control. "No. I'm not. I'm worried about De-Shawn. I want to get these houses done. I've still got to go back and do the work I'm not doing now. I'm focused. Sorry if it's coming off wrong."

His eyes held hers. She struggled not to look away. Damn, he could see right through her. He nodded. "Okay. I wanted to make sure. After the other night..."

He wanted to talk about it? She pushed down the irritation. She hated feeling stupid and almost kissing an employee was about as stupid as it got. "The other night was a mistake. One I don't intend to repeat. But it won't impact your job. I promise. And I'm not mad about it. Okay?"

"Okay."

But he didn't sound okay. He continued to pin her in place with those gorgeous hazel eyes. A small smile tilted up a corner of his mouth. *Shit.* He knew what he did to her. She picked up her supplies and headed for the stairs.

She started in the main bathroom, needing the physical release of scrubbing to loosen the knot of conflicting feelings. It had been a mistake. She was right to nip it in the bud. *Does not matter how he makes you feel. Doesn't matter that he seems to feel the attraction also. Does. Not. Matter.*

She sat on the edge of the tub and turned the

faucet on to rinse the cleaner away. Shutting down emotions, shutting out people, came easily to her. Except now.

LATER THAT NIGHT, Sadie made her way to the patio of the Triangle Char and Bar. Two men were flirting with Lena. *Of course.* To her left, the bar was noisy with the after-work crowd of hip, young professionals. Lena had snagged a table at the outer edge of the patio and effortlessly held the two men enthralled with her dark beauty, wicked smile and sharp wit. Her yellow sundress would have made Sadie look as though she was on the transplant list for a new liver. She felt sloppy in her khaki Dockers. She'd pulled off the Crew T-shirt and replaced it with the first top her hand found in the closet, a plain, royal blue blouse.

"There's she is! There's my sister."

Sadie tried to smile as she made her way to the table. Lena loved playing the sister game. The only thing they had in common was the color of their hair. Lena's skin was a flawless golden brown next to Sadie's paleness. Lena wore heels to make up for her five-foot-three-inch height. Sadie wore sneakers or flats because five-foot-nine was tall enough, thank you.

But she wasn't in the mood to play today. The day with Wyatt Anderson had left her cranky.

Self-diagnosis: hadn't-been-laid-in-two-years syndrome. After dealing with him all day, she had gone back to the office to do her work, hampered by intermittent fantasies in which she hadn't stopped his attempted kiss. She wanted a glass of wine. Or two. Or three. And food.

She sat next to one of the men. He made a sweeping motion and elbowed her. And touched her boob in the process. She could smell the alcohol on him. One sip from drunk. Her eyebrows rushed together as her frustration coalesced around a total stranger touching her.

"With a scowl like that, you must be the evil sister."

Sadie glared at the man who'd first touched her and now insulted her: pushing fifty, moderately attractive, desperately holding on to his youth with a stylish haircut, hip new clothes and a spray tan.

"Touch me again and I'll hurt you. Go away now," she said. And meant it. She hadn't survived seventeen years in foster care and group homes without learning *some* skills.

The man stood. "I guess the bitch has spoken." He looked at Lena. "Apparently you got the manners in the family."

"Not really. You weren't stupid enough to touch me. She only *threatened* to hurt you. I would have done it."

After the two men moved away, Lena rolled her eyes. "Why are you such a grump?"

"I had to cover for one of the guys today. *And* do my regular work. Is this my wine? Thanks."

She took a sip without waiting for confirmation. Lena caught the waitress's attention and she came over. "Another round of these."

"So working with Mr. Super Hot New Guy's got you seriously frustrated. I'm going to have to get a look at him."

Sadie almost spit out her wine. "How'd you know that?"

Lena leaned prettily on her elbows, her hands beneath her chin and one black brow lifting in a perfect arch. Sadie wished she could do that. She tried to raise her left eyebrow. Then her right.

"Stop it," Lena said, "You look like you're having a seizure. I called to check how the photo shoot went. Molly told me. So. You and hottie alone all day long."

"I have something important to talk about with my mature, professional accountant."

"Oh, honey, I'm not being professional until I hear the gory details. Does he still make you melty and gooey?"

Sadie glared at her and Lena let out a peal of laughter, drawing every male eye on the patio. Including Mr. Touchy and his pal. Sadie scowled at him and was somewhat mollified when he quickly looked away. Lena rubbed her palms together. Sadie picked up her menu.

"I'm going to take that as a yes. What's happened? Y'all making goo-goo eyes? Playing the innocent touching game? Has he tried to kiss you?"

"I'm getting tired of hummus. Let's try the pimento cheese." She tried for a no-nonsense, we're-not-going-to-talk-about-it tone, but the flare of heat on her cheeks gave her away.

Lena's eyes went wide and she leaned close. "He did! He kissed you!"

"No, he didn't. There was a…a moment."

"*Digame!* I love moments. Was it hot and sexy or sweet and romantic?"

"Nothing. It was nothing."

"Obviously he's attracted to you if y'all are having moments."

Sadie shrugged and smiled with relieved gratitude at the waitress who'd appeared at her side. "We're going to try the pimento cheese for the app. I'll have the chicken tacos. And more wine."

She sipped wine while Lena ordered. She thought back over the day with Wyatt. Her hormones had been singing, but he hadn't done or said anything. Purely professional. He'd brought up the near kiss only to confirm it had been a mistake and wouldn't be held against him. Nor repeated. And it wouldn't be. Still, she felt a little dart of sadness. She covered her face with her hands. When she moved them, Lena's dark eyes were warm and no longer teasing.

"Is there no way to get past the whole working together thing?"

"No. Because we don't work together, Lena. I'm his boss. It's wrong time, wrong place."

"I'm sorry."

"Don't be. Can't miss what you never had."

"Doesn't mean you can't know it when you see it."

Again, Lena cut straight through the murk of Sadie's muddled emotions and shined a light directly on the problem. Because she *could* see it. And it had very little to do with his gorgeous face or that body she wanted to turn into her own personal playground. It was in the way he'd taken Julietta in, his obvious love for and commitment to her. For a woman who'd been thrown away by her own mother, that struck deep to her core. It was in the way he'd gotten every stinking last one of her *Napoleon Dynamite* jokes. It was in the quiet competence he showed on the job. It was in the way he got along with the guys. She'd been worried about him being older, but he'd found a role among them already: the cool young uncle.

She shook her head. *Didn't matter.* She tried to wrap it up and stuff it down deep where she kept all her other broken dreams, but it kept floating up. She swallowed it back down with a slug of wine.

"I want to talk to you about something big. I need to know if we can do this."

Lena smiled up at the waitress as she set the appetizer between them. "Thank you." She turned her attention back to Sadie. "Is this where I have to be accountant-y?"

"Yes."

Sadie scooped up cheese with a cracker and popped in her mouth, taking her time. The moment she said this out loud, it would put things into motion.

"I want to investigate opening a second location in Columbia."

"Not selling a franchise?"

"No. We've been averaging four unique calls a week from the Columbia area asking if we take clients there. I think it's time to start looking at expanding."

Lena clapped her hands together. "Finally! This is awesome. What changed your mind?"

"Josh. He's too good at what he does. He's built this business with me. It's not fair—or smart—to waste his talents being my second-in-command for the rest of his life."

"So you want to put him in charge of the Columbia branch?"

"Yes."

"Say it again like you mean it, Ms. Martin."

"I know. Josh is like my brother. I depend on him for so much. But it's time for both of us to grow up a little. Do I have the money to do this?"

"Girl! Do you have the money? You don't spend a penny you don't put back into the business. And I look after that for you. You've got plenty of money. Making people rich is my job." She took a sip of her drink, one pinky raised from the glass. "And I'm very good at my job."

"So there is enough?"

"What do you do with the statements I send you?"

"Molly files them somewhere. You know numbers make my brain shut down and I start to drool. That's why I keep you around."

"I feel so appreciated. Yes. Expand away."

"How?"

That was the problem. She didn't have a clue. The Crew had grown organically from her own client list. Little by little so the steps had seemed like a natural progression. To start from scratch in a city where she didn't know a soul? It was like staring up Mount Everest.

"How do I know? I'm a financial manager, not a business planner."

"Is there such a thing? Can I afford to hire one?"

Lena laughed. But Sadie wasn't joking. She'd

never finished high school. She had always meant to go back and get her diploma in night school or something, but working for poverty wages required putting in eighty or more hours a week to survive. And then she hadn't needed it.

"Have you talked to Josh yet?"

"A little bit. He isn't sure he wants to, but I think he will. He'd want the challenge."

"Then start with him. I'll bet he's got some ideas."

"I'M NOT TAKING him off your hands."

Sadie scowled at Josh as he slid into a chair beside her in the conference room the next day. She seemed to be scowling a lot lately. "That's not why I wanted to talk to you. But feel free to shove it."

"I reserve little-brother rights to tease, harass and generally annoy you as much as I please."

"Then I reserve big-sister rights to punch you in the throat."

She took a sip of coffee, now in a much better mood. Josh had that effect on her. She could completely be herself with him. He knew all her secrets. And she knew his. He was more open about his past than she was, but only she knew of his search for the little sister he'd been separated from on the night his parents died. How many late nights had they spent telling foster-care horror stories that somehow ended up in hysterical laughter? How many websites had they scoured looking for any clue to find his sister? They'd worked the poison of anger and resentment out of their souls together.

He got up to get coffee and when he returned, they drank together in a comfortable silence.

"I talked to Lena last night," Sadie began when she'd finished her cup. "The Columbia expansion is a go if we want it."

Josh's blue eyes met hers. "Do we?"

"If you want it is the real question." She leaned back in the chair, trying for casual even though her heart was beating faster and the coffee was sloshing in her suddenly quivering stomach. She was being selfish, but it was scary to think of not having him here with her every day. The one person she could confess her fears to. The one who understood her completely.

He played with his coffee mug, spinning it with the tips of his fingers. "I've been thinking about it."

"Tell me what you think we should do. To get it going."

"We should start small. I'll go back through the requests. See who's interested and what services they want. Put together a team. Columbia's close enough we don't need to start out renting office space and spending a ton of money on it.

Get some clients, take a team up, do the cleanings, come home or overnight at a hotel if we need. If it catches on, I can move up there. Rent an apartment and run it from there until we get big enough to need a separate location."

"In other words, sort of how we built it here."

"No. Exactly how we built it here. It worked. We didn't get in debt. We didn't have to cut corners to pay bills. There's no rush on this."

Sadie nodded. It made perfect sense. Get some clients on board and let it grow by word of mouth. She knew Josh would see it without the anxiety clouding her thinking. She smiled at him. "Sounds like you've been doing a lot more than thinking. You've come up with a solid plan."

"So it's a go?"

"It's your baby, Josh. It's a go if you want it."

He nodded. "I'll start getting it together."

They both stood and Sadie pulled him into an embrace. "You're going to do awesome."

"You going to be okay if this takes off and I move away?"

She hugged him tighter. That was the million-dollar question. "Yes. I will."

He kissed her forehead. "Thank you for lying."

She rested her head on his shoulder and he put an arm around her. "I'm not lying. I mean it. You are going to do an awesome job."

"Still not taking him off your hands."

She pushed him away. "Brat."

He picked up his coffee cup. "If that's all, boss, I've got to get to Kiawah and finish up the rentals."

"Yeah, yeah. That's all. Get out of my face. I've got real work to do."

Real work. Like keeping her hands off Wyatt Anderson. Like stopping her mind from imagining all sorts of ways he could end her two-year drought. She pulled the client books for the day and poured another cup of coffee. She loved this time of the morning before Molly got in and the guys started to arrive. She and Josh had created this. It was more than a business. It was a family. She frowned as she thought about it. She could only think of two of her guys who came from solid, intact, middle-class families. Most were children of divorce, not uncommon these days, but many were from bad situations. Drug-addicted or alcoholic parents. One was gay and had been forbidden to return home on his eighteenth birthday. She hadn't hired the guys because of their circumstances. Not purposefully. Maybe subconsciously. Like Wendy, she was collecting Lost Boys.

Her thoughts drifted to the letter from her half brother. She needed to decide what to do about that. She wanted to ignore it but Lito had made her promise. To give Grant a chance. If it were only him, she might. But to open a door to her mother? No way.

"Is that frown for me?"

She startled, sloshing a bit of coffee on the table. Wyatt. She hadn't heard him come in. He leaned in the doorway, his arms crossed, displaying those biceps and forearms. He smiled. *Those dimples.* She looked away, flustered. *No more hiring guys with dimples. There. Problem solved.*

"Sorry. Thinking deep thoughts. You aren't the first person to point out I look angry when I concentrate."

He sat next to her. "Eight o'clock in the morning seems an odd time for deep thoughts."

She looked into his eyes. She loved his eyes. Loved the sparkle of humor and the flare of desire she saw in them. "And what time is most appropriate?"

He leaned back, hooking one arm over the back of the chair. "I'm staring at the ceiling at two in the morning."

"I've got some of those, too," she said. *Liar.* Those weren't deep thoughts keeping her awake. They were simple thoughts. *I want you. I want your body.* Her cheeks began to warm.

He lifted his arms and stretched, tempting her to peek at the display of pure male muscle. Damn, he was hot. *Okay, see, right there. That is not helping with the "sleeping through the night" problem.* And neither was the way his biceps flexed as he rested his hands on top of his head.

"Anything you want to talk about? These deep thoughts of yours this morning?"

"No, just boring business stuff. What about you? Anything I can help with?"

WYATT SMILED AT her sincerity. Her entire manner changed. Her face softened from its worried frown, her eyes and voice warmed. She did care about her employees. Deeply. *What must it be like to have her care about you, as a man?* An aching pull returned to his chest. That was what had been keeping him up at night. The hope there might be some way to get out of this without her hating him. The idea there might be a way to see if this attraction could be given a chance. He'd like that. But he couldn't see how. And it ate at him. He sat forward and brought his arms down.

"Nah. The usual. Worrying over Jules."

Her fingers, warm and soft and tender, touched his arm. His breath stopped in his lungs for a moment as the heat raced up his arm.

"Is she having trouble?"

"No. The opposite. She's taking giant steps. Has a friend, even. They walked to school together this morning. I worry about how we lost Maddie and now I'm it. I'm all she has in this world."

"That'd keep anyone up at night, I'd think."

He shrugged. He hadn't meant to reveal that. He preferred to keep his fears to himself, but she invited confession. The sense of truly caring about her employees. He focused his attention on her fingers still lingering on his arm. Which was much more pleasant than the fears haunting him in the night. He leaned back again, trying to nonchalantly pull his arm away.

"Don't forget you're still grieving, too, Wyatt," she said quietly.

The words rocked him to his core. Yes, he was still grieving. Maddie was his baby sister. Their father had died before Maddie was old enough to remember him. She was nineteen when their mother lost her battle with cervical cancer. It had been the two of them for so long. He'd helped her with college. Helped her with Julietta. They'd been close. And he'd pushed his own grieving aside to help Jules. Confined his pain and tears to the privacy of his bed. He took Sadie's hand in his.

"I know," he said, his eyes on hers. "I'm doing okay. It's difficult. To be strong for Jules. To not let her see me falling apart."

"Maybe she should."

"What? See me fall apart?"

"No, not that. But maybe she should see you be sad. See you miss her. So she knows it's okay."

He squeezed her hand. Then regretted it when she noticed and drew back.

"How'd you get so smart?"

She stacked the books and stood. "Oh, I'm not smart. That's for sure. I just know..."

"People?"

HIS WORD CHOICE surprised her. *Pain*, she was going to say. She didn't know squat about people. Hadn't she proven that time and time again? She got drawn into those eyes and their gazes locked and held. The air between them filled with all the things she wanted to say. If only she could say them. If only she wasn't his boss. The front door banged open and Molly called out a cheerful greeting.

"There's coffee in the kitchen if you want a to-go cup. I'm going to bring Jack down. We've got a busy day today."

She went upstairs and took a moment to get her emotions under control. *What was that? One of those bonding moments you hear about on* Oprah *or* Dr. Phil? He'd held her hand. And it hadn't been sexual. It'd felt—she groped for a word—*nice. Comforting. Right.* She wanted to shake off the rules and sit and talk with him. Tell him how amazing she thought he was. The way he was committed to Jules. Only a truly good man would rearrange his entire life to help a child. And be glad to do it. She shook her head and headed back down with Jack leading the way.

"Jack. Go sit with Molly," she said, pointing.

Jack ran in circles around the conference room, greeting each of the guys who'd arrived. Wyatt leaned against the counter, at the sink where he'd almost kissed her. His eyes were dark, serious, contemplating. Had she upset him with her comment about grieving? *Open mouth, insert foot. Again.* She sighed and picked up the books. Wasn't the first time she'd said the wrong thing at the wrong time.

"Ready?"

He pushed off the counter and took the books from her, tucking them under his arm. "Let's do it."

Okay. He's going to have to stop saying things like that.

They powered through the morning. They knocked out two residential deep cleans before ten and headed downtown to the *Saga* magazine office. All eyes swiveled to her when she pushed open the door. DeShawn's arrival seemed to be a much anticipated event.

"Where's DeShawn?" one of the women asked, clearly disappointed with Sadie until Wyatt walked in behind her. "Oh. Hello."

"DeShawn who?" a second woman asked, pure lust dripping from every syllable.

"Hi, ladies, good to see you, too," Sadie called. "DeShawn's out with a family emergency. This is Wyatt. He's a new guy. I've warned him about you people. Remember the rules."

Hands hit the air amid laughter. "Lookie, don't touchie," the women called out in singsong.

Wyatt glanced at her. A slow grin crossed his face. Expect catcalls, she'd told him. Good-natured ribbing. Mostly harmless. His gaze swept the small crowd of women with that grin and those dimples on full power. The estrogen level in the room rose about a million points judging by the sighs and face fanning. Her own lust was like a low-grade fever.

"Hi, ladies," he drawled out in a bedroom voice. "Hope you don't mind, but we might take a little longer than usual today. I'm still learning, and I like to go slow."

"Stay as long as you like."

"We can show him everything, Sadie, if you want to take a break, pick him up later."

Sadie set the supply cart down. "I'm not leaving him alone with you degenerates."

SADIE HAD INSISTED on treating him to lunch at Hominy Grill after finishing at the *Saga* office since they were only blocks away. They had the best shrimp and grits in a town where every restaurant had it on the menu. While he would happily pay nineteen dollars for that dish, he was eating the turkey club instead because Sadie was buying. She was working her way through the curried chicken salad sandwich with a gusto he liked to see in a woman. He hated salad pickers and calorie worriers.

Sadie pointed a French fry at him. "You handled that very well. Played them perfectly."

He grinned and shook his head. It had been a performance. The women pretended to gush over him. He'd played the role of the polite good old boy by enhancing his accent a bit and tossing out lots of "yes, ma'ams" and "no, ma'ams." Before they left, the women thanked him for being a good sport and he even got a round of applause.

"How do the younger guys handle responses like that? The sexual innuendo? I'm old enough to know it was a game, but it could be misconstrued by someone barely out of high school."

"That's what the preemployment testing is for. Extroverts with high emotional IQ and strong social skills do the best. Josh and DeShawn are the only ones who go solo. Everyone else is partnered up. Speaking of which, I think we can cut you loose from orientation and put you with a partner starting next week."

This announcement startled him. He'd hoped

to turn in his resignation and walk away from Sadie Martin as soon as he figured out how to get clear of Marcus without repercussions. But a few days with an employee not in the top echelon of the company would give him the opportunity to show Marcus he'd exhausted every opportunity to find some wrongdoing.

"You sure?"

"Positive. Unless you feel you need more time?"

He shook his head. "Not if I'll have a partner to keep me on track."

She took a sip of iced tea. "Good. Noah needs to be partnered up. His partner is taking an internship ahead of graduating next December. I think he's ready for more of a leadership role."

Wyatt nodded and tried to keep his face neutral. Noah. He was the kid Aaron said got the extra tips. The one he'd wanted to ask what he did to earn them. Now it seemed he was going to get the chance to find out. Perfect. He'd do a few more days. He concentrated on his sandwich for a minute. "So what's the story with that Canard guy?"

A flicker of annoyance crossed her face before her expression settled back into a careful neutral. He was beginning to know that expression. It meant he'd hit a nerve.

"There's no story."

"But he seemed to be trying to mimic the Crew with that ad. He's a rival, isn't he?"

She bit into a French fry and shook her head. "I don't consider him one. We serve different clienteles. His business is losing customers—I know that. Some of them are coming to us, but not that many. We're too expensive. I think he's just mad about that stupid *City Paper* award."

"Ever met him?"

Her dark blue eyes went hard. She glanced at the traffic passing on Rutledge Avenue and sighed. "I used to work for him."

He managed to put an appropriately interested expression on his face. There it was. Now he'd found the reason for Marcus's grudge. "Really?"

"My first job. I lasted less than a year. He was a terrible boss. A bully."

"And he carries a grudge, I guess."

She wilted back in her chair. "Yeah. I don't like to talk about it. But he's fairly vindictive."

"What do you mean?"

"A couple of his clients wanted me to keep working for them when I quit. He tried to sue me, said I had signed a non-compete agreement with my employment. Said I used what he'd taught me to steal his clients. When he couldn't provide the documentation, because there never was any, he withdrew the complaint."

"Did you?"

"Did I what?"

"Use what he taught you to steal clients?"

"The only thing I learned from Marcus Canard was how not to treat employees. Everything I learned about cleaning houses came from the women who worked for him. Please don't repeat any of this to the guys. I don't want it spread around. I prefer to ignore Marcus."

"I won't. Was just curious."

So this was revenge. Marcus was going broke and he was blaming Sadie. After all this time. He'd have to be careful extricating himself from this situation.

CHAPTER ELEVEN

WHY COULDN'T JULES'S first new friend's mother have been a happily married woman? Or a dude? A simple my-two-dads situation would have been great. Anything but this. Shiloh's mother had been divorced too long. He knew because she'd told him. Several times. Wyatt declined her invitation to come inside, opting to remain on the porch. The small ranch house was a street away from his place. Not a plus right now.

Charlotte—*call me Charlie*—stood in the doorway holding open the screen. He hoped she always looked like this and hadn't gone to such trouble on his account. More makeup than he'd seen on the last four women he dated. Combined. A miasma of desperation clinging to her words and laugh. He was sure it was hard to be a divorced fortysomething mother, but he had no intention of helping her back into the dating pool.

But he'd seen her daughter make Jules giggle like an eight-year-old girl should, so he would deal.

"So she did okay?" he asked. This was the first time he'd left her anywhere other than school.

"Perfect. She's a doll. A real doll."

Charlie stepped out on the porch and pulled the door almost closed behind her. The flirtatiousness disappeared. "She did mention her mother like you said she might. Said they used to watch a movie together after school on days she didn't have to work late. I said it sounded like a lot of fun. She said it was, and they went to color."

Shame stung him for his unkind thoughts. Charlie was a good person. She'd been appropriately concerned when Wyatt had talked to her about Jules's situation. It hadn't scared her away. He'd run across that a few times. Mothers who didn't want their children to know parents could sometimes die. She'd simply asked him the best way to respond.

"Thanks," he said. He started to say more, but the door pulled open behind Charlie and the two girls peeked out. Jules's dark hair and eyes contrasted with Shiloh's blond hair and blue eyes. "Hey there, Jujube. Ready to go?"

Her eyes rolled so hard in her head he worried she'd hurt herself. "Uncle Wyatt. Don't. Call. Me. That."

"Can she stay for dinner, Mr. Wyatt? Can she? We'll do our homework and everything. Please?"

"It's okay with me," Charlie said. "In fact, both

of you can stay. For dinner. Dessert. I've got a nice bottle of wine."

Wyatt responded carefully. "Sorry, Jules. We've got to go see a friend of mine. I was thinking we could go out to dinner tonight."

She came along without any further protests. It'd been a lot for her to spend a few hours in a new situation. Maybe she was tired. And he realized he didn't want to go home and eat alone. He smiled at how quickly he'd become used to her company. She was a funny, bright little girl. Much like her mother had been. The comparison tugged at his heart. It was becoming less painful, the stabs now mellowing to these unexpected tugs.

"Who are we going to see?" she asked when they got in his truck and he made sure she was buckled up.

"A man I used to work with. I know it won't be very exciting for you, but it won't take long. Then we can go out to a real restaurant and have dinner."

"I haven't done my homework yet."

"You can start it while I have my meeting. We won't be out late. You can get it done before bed."

She nodded and it brought another tug. Maddie had been the same way. Always had her homework finished. Always had clothes for the next day picked out before bedtime. He reached across the seat and took her little hand. "Did you have fun with Shiloh?"

"Yes. We colored and her mom let us put glitter on our pictures. Mine is still drying so Shiloh is going to bring it to me at school."

He smiled. One woman had come close to settling him down, but it was this little girl who captured his heart and had him rushing home. "Where to you want to eat?"

"Can we go to McDonald's?" she asked.

"Yuck, no."

"Wendy's?"

"How about Ladles Soups? You can get soup and a sandwich."

HENRY MOODY'S OFFICE was on the fifth floor of a newish building off I-526 on the North Charleston side of the Westmoreland Bridge. His secretary greeted Wyatt with an amused smile. "Now this is a sight. May I take a picture?"

Wyatt supposed it was a different look for him to be toting an eight-year-old girl. He grinned at Susie, who was a neat, efficient woman in her midforties. She had pictures of her family—four kids, two dogs and a husband—on the wall beside her desk. She was determined to get everyone she knew married off and having kids as soon as possible. Wyatt's single status at thirty-one was a horror she couldn't imagine.

"Hey, Susie. This is my niece, Julietta. Can you keep an eye on her while I talk to Mr. Moody?"

"Of course. Honey, you can help me, if you want."

Jules held up her backpack. "I have to do homework."

"Of course you do. What a good girl."

She came over and helped Wyatt clear off the coffee table in the waiting area. She touched Wyatt on the shoulder. "Mr. Moody is ready for you. Go on in. I'll get Miss Julietta set up."

Henry Moody came from a long line of insurance men in Charleston. He was approaching seventy with no signs of retiring anytime soon. He had such an easy Southern grace and charm that a competitor might miss the sharp business acumen that had transformed a sleepy family company into a large corporation.

"Good to see you, Wyatt. Tell me you are done with this other business and are ready to come back to work. I'm losing money without you."

He said it with a smile and waved Wyatt to a chair, bolstering his confidence in what he had to say. The good-old-boy system was alive and well, but it was never spoken of directly. He was going to break an unspoken rule. Best to do it and get it over with.

"I wish I could say I was. One more week at

the most. Think your bottom line can hold out that long?"

"We'll try. So, if you aren't here for to give me good news, what is it?"

"I want to talk to you about Marcus Canard."

Moody's lips twitched, as if something bitter had touched his mouth. It was gone quickly and if Wyatt hadn't been looking for a reaction, he would have missed it.

"How is Marcus?"

Wyatt shifted in his seat, feeling his pulse rise and a touch of sweat at his hairline. "I have some concerns."

"Oh?"

"Yes. This investigation he hired me to do? I'm not sure it was legitimate."

"Meaning?"

The word was spoken mildly enough, but Henry had leaned forward slightly and his gaze was direct. Wyatt shifted forward in his chair and clasped his hands together. He'd better be right, or he was going to blow everything.

"He wanted me to find some sort of illegal activity at a rival cleaning company. His suspicion was that it was a front for a male prostitute ring. I went in undercover and took a job there. It was fairly obvious from the beginning that nothing illegal was going on. He didn't like my results."

"I'm not surprised. Marcus can be...difficult."

"That's the thing. I started wondering where his interest in this lay. There is very little overlap between the two businesses. Some, but the Crew's clientele tend to be upper middle class to wealthy. They weren't Marcus's clients to begin with. And why was he so adamant that I do this investigation?"

Henry smiled. "Because I told him you were the best."

"Besides that. I've checked him out. He took a huge loss in the real-estate market when the bubble broke. The cleaning company is the only thing keeping him afloat, and it's going under. He's not just hoping to find something dirty to boost his business. He wants me doing corporate espionage. He isn't happy that I've refused."

"If you've found nothing, why are you continuing? I need you back here."

"There's one more angle I want to look at. After that, I can honestly say I did everything I could for Marcus. That I gave him my best effort. But he's not going to like it."

There was a long, painful silence while Wyatt willed Henry to pick up on the implication of his last sentence.

"And you worry he may want some revenge on you for not reporting on their operations?"

"Yes, sir."

"How? He'll pull all his dealings with me? Since I recommended you?"

"He's threatened me with that."

Henry stared at him for a long moment. Then a quick smile crossed his lips. "Promise?"

Wyatt let out the breath he didn't know he was holding and sank back in the chair. He should have come to Henry much sooner.

Henry leaned forward. "Son, do you know how much money you have saved my company?"

"Exactly? No."

"Last year alone, it was close to three hundred thousand dollars. I trust you. I trust your instincts."

The number surprised him. He whistled. "Maybe I should raise my rates."

"Maybe you should. Maybe I should put you on the payroll."

"Are you offering me a job?"

"Would you want one?"

Wyatt thought. Would he? Running his own business was a pain at times but it gave him flexibility with his schedule. He needed that now with Jules. On the other hand, a steady job, a steady paycheck with benefits would help him ensure the stability he needed for her.

"I might."

"How about I put together an offer?"

Moody glanced at his watch and stood. Wyatt did also. "Can I think about it? Let you know?"

"Of course. And if you can get Marcus out of my company, I might give you a sign-on bonus."

Wyatt shook his hand and left, feeling better than he had in days. Now he could move forward. Put in his resignation and disappear from Sadie Martin's life. The light feeling of relief left him, replaced by something suspiciously like sorrow.

LADLES SOUPS HAD begun in the West Ashley location. Wyatt was pretty certain he had eaten there enough to have funded at least one of their expansions. He loved the simplicity. Soups, salads, sandwiches. Perfect. He and Jules sat at one of the high tables along the windows because she wanted to. He pretended it was the sun in his eyes that had him rubbing them, not the sight of Jules swinging her dangling legs back and forth in the air beneath her chair.

She was cracking him up with her food. One bite of grilled cheese, one slurp of chicken noodle soup. Back and forth. Just like her mother. He turned his attention to his loaded potato soup and BLT before the lump in his throat grew any larger. *Nice. Big tough former cop, two-war-zone-tour vet and private investigator almost re-*

duced to tears by an eight-year-girl acting like an eight-year-old. You're getting soft, man.

"Can we go see Ms. Sadie and Jack?"

Whoa. Where did that come from? Jules didn't know this was temporary. He set his spoon down and leaned forward so he was eye to eye with her.

"I think we should wait for an invitation."

"Can you ask her to invite us?"

He smiled; he couldn't help it. "I'm only working at Ms. Sadie's place for a few more days. It's a temporary job. Do you understand?"

The touch of sadness in her eyes tore at his heart. That there was nothing he could do about it hurt worse. "Then you'll be catching cheaters again?"

"Yes."

She sighed and seemed to deflate in her seat. She picked up the crust of her sandwich and bit into it. She chewed then her face lit up with a smile. "We might see them at the park again!"

Problem solved. In her mind. The sting of guilt and remorse faded. "That's always a possibility."

He pushed away the remnants of his meal, his appetite gone. The past six months of adjusting to Jules being in his life, he'd put almost everything else on hold. Including women. Victoria had walked out and he'd had no desire to start dating. Until he met Sadie. Now he realized even the simplest of dates would have an impact on

Jules. He'd have to be very careful who he let into his—no, *their*—life. He couldn't have her bonding with women who came and went, echoing the loss of her mother over and over.

"You about done there? Let's get home, and I'll help you finish your homework."

She held her arms out. "Piggyback!"

He swept her onto his back and carried her out of the restaurant. In the parking lot, he spun them around and around in circles as they made their way to the truck. Her squealing laughter was making his ears ring, but it was the sweetest sound he'd ever heard. *Face it, man. She's going to be your number one girl for quite a while.*

CHAPTER TWELVE

She knew she should stop crying and let go. The guys were going to start showing up soon. But she needed this right now. The early-morning light flowing soft through the kitchen windows and Josh's arms around her were exactly what she needed. The peacefulness of both. The tears she never let others see came freely in his arms. He didn't say a word. Just held her.

A 5:00 a.m. phone call from Lena had awakened her. If she wanted to say goodbye, come now. She'd sat paralyzed with fear on the edge of her bed for a full fifteen minutes before she was able to force herself to move.

She'd come home to find Josh making coffee. He'd taken one look at her and asked what was wrong. And the tears had come. What was wrong? Everything was wrong. Her heart was a bruise in her chest and every beat hurt. It was real. He was going to die. Soon. Today. She'd been calm and dry-eyed once she reached his bedside. Had been able to whisper "I love you" and kiss his pale cheek. Josh didn't need to say anything because he knew. He knew Abuelito was the first person Sadie had loved. She pushed back and he let her but didn't take his arms from around her.

"Sorry," she said, swiping at her face with both hands. "Your shirt is ruined."

He reached to rip a paper towel from the holder and handed it to her. "It'll be okay. Snot is pretty washable."

She snorted out a half laugh. "Let go. I'm going to be unladylike."

He let go. She turned away while she took care of her drippy nose. She hated crying. Hated it with a passion. But this morning she recognized the catharsis in tears. She did feel better, as if she'd worked out a nasty splinter. It still hurt, but in a cleaner, more focused way. She'd faced her fears. She hadn't run away from pain. She hadn't left things unsaid. Losing Abuelito was terrible, but she didn't have the underlying emotions of guilt and shame to make it even worse.

Josh handed her a cup of coffee and touched her cheek. "You going to be okay? I can shift things around and take over if you need the day off."

She shook her head and slurped down half the cup of coffee. She was going to need to main-line it to get the boost she needed this morning.

"No. I'm okay. If I sit around all day waiting, I'll lose my mind. Lena's going to call me when…"

She stopped because the tears were there again. She polished off the coffee instead. She moved to pour a second cup, but Josh caught her and pulled her into his arms again. She pressed her cheek against his shoulder.

"Call me if you have to, Saff. Don't play tough girl," he said. His hand rubbed along her spine, warm and comforting.

"Okay."

"Promise?"

She hugged him tight. "Promise."

Letting go, she stepped back to get to the coffeepot. Wyatt Anderson stood in the doorway. *Damn.* She'd never heard the door open. Her eyes met his. Her cheeks burned at the intense speculation in his eyes.

"Coffee's fresh," she said. She turned to pour a cup, breaking the eye contact.

"Something going on?" Wyatt asked.

His tone was casual, but his eyes were on her face where she was sure the ravages of her little crying jag were still visible. Some women could cry pretty. She was not one of them. Her eyes probably looked as if she'd been toking weed all night. Her red nose was surely highlighted by the blotches on her face. She turned away.

"No, everything's cool. I'm going to let Jack out."

She gave Josh a look as she headed to the stairs. *Keep your big fat mouth shut.* She didn't want her business bandied around. Didn't want people's sympathy. Didn't know how to handle it. She had enough to handle right now, thank you very much.

Upstairs, she ducked into the bathroom to check her face while Jack whined and walked in circles around her legs. She leaned close to the mirror. Yep. Bloodshot eyes and red nose. The rest wasn't too bad. She splashed cold water on her face. *You need to pull it together. It's going to be a long day. You've done all you can do for now. Get through this day. Focus on getting Wyatt checked off on his orientation.*

Wyatt was sitting at the conference table with the day's books in front of him when she came back downstairs. Jack whined at the back door. Grateful for the distraction, she went to let him out. She stood on the back porch watching as Jack made his perimeter inspection before selecting which plants to water. The sun, now fully up, was bright and warm on her face. The air was still cool and the birds sleepy in their nests. She reached into her jeans pocket and pulled out a ponytail holder.

"Ready when you are, boss," Wyatt said from behind her.

She remained with her back to him and finished securing her hair. She didn't want to look at him. She knew he would see the sorrow in her eyes. He saw everything. Then he'd ask questions and she didn't want to answer them. Because she didn't know what the answers were. She clapped her hands. "Come on, Jack. Daylight's wasting."

Jack scurried past her and she had to turn and face Wyatt. He stood at the conference room doorway, one shoulder propping up the jamb, arms crossed, biceps popped. The smile and dimples were missing in action and she had a sudden longing to see them. To see the little glint in his eyes that made her think of fallen angels. His gaze held concern and a hint of a question. *Yeah, that look.* Exactly what she was trying to avoid.

She turned away and headed for the conference room table, careful not to touch him when she passed through the door. She dived into her most comfortable role: all-business. Focused on the issue at hand. She sifted through the books. They had five cleanings scheduled for the day. Two deep cleans and three regular. Big houses. The day was going to need serious organizational skills. *Well, let's see what he can do with it.*

"You went through the books. What are you thinking for the day?"

"It's going to be tight. There's a lot of square footage here. There won't be time for a resupply run. I'd say double the usual to make sure we've got everything we need. Looks like DeShawn had them on an alternating schedule. Regular, deep, regular. If we hustle on the regulars, we'll have enough time to do proper deep cleanings."

She flipped through the books as he spoke. He had it. The most important detail was the supplies. It was normal to break the day in half and resupply for the afternoon appointments. She liked the critical thinking and planning he'd shown. He was going to do well. *Perhaps too well.* Not for the first time she wondered why he was here. He had a college degree. Even if he hadn't wanted to be a cop anymore, he could have found something other than a manual-labor-type job. *But maybe that's what he wants. Not everyone wants to sit at a desk all day.*

"Perfect," she said, closing the books and tucking them under her arm. "Let's go check the inventory and see what we need."

She made it through the first cleaning. It was a big house, but the owners were a retired couple who traveled frequently. She'd bet they hadn't even been home since the last cleaning. Wyatt had the routine down. He still carried a little cheat sheet tucked into his back pocket, but he was quick and thorough. She did a walk-through inspection.

Once she was satisfied, she gave Wyatt the

go-ahead to start packing up. She pulled out her phone. Nothing from Lena yet. She sighed and tucked it back in her pocket.

"Are you okay?"

She jumped. *Seriously!* He was too quiet on his feet. She picked up a container of cleaning supplies and pushed past him.

"Yes. Fine. We need to hustle, like you said. This next one is going to be a doozy."

He followed her out with the rest of the supplies. "You've checked your phone every five minutes, and it looked like you were crying this morning."

She put the container in the hatch and moved aside for him to do the same before closing it. "What? You want to talk about my feelings or something?"

She gave him the scowl designed to strike fear into the souls of the crew. Didn't seem to faze him. "Thought maybe I could help."

He moved away to wait at the car door. Feeling like a complete jerk, she hit the unlock button. She wasn't a people person. She wasn't a feelings person. Trying to deal with the loss was sapping every resource she had. She wanted to run and hide. She wanted to lash out. She wanted to be with the family as they waited, but didn't feel worthy. She wanted to cry, but couldn't. She wanted to stop hurting. Most of all, she wanted this scared-little-girl feeling to go away. The part whispering to her that Abuelito was the only one in the family who loved her and once he was gone, she wouldn't be welcome. She knew it wasn't true. But she'd thought she'd had a real family once before and that had all been a lie. All those familiar feelings of rejection and abandonment were floating to the surface. She had more experience with abandonment than love, so it was winning out at the moment.

She wrenched open the door with a sigh and slid into the driver's seat. She sat with her hands on the steering wheel for a moment. She could feel the stiffness in the way he sat and it kicked off a little puff of regret. *Had she insulted him? Hurt his feelings?* She wanted to bang her head on the steering wheel.

"I'm sorry." In her peripheral vision, she saw his head turn toward her. Felt the brush of his gaze along the side of her face. She swallowed down the tears threatening to surface. She realized she'd never talked about what was going on with Abuelito with anyone but Lena and Josh. "Someone very dear to me is going to die. Today. He's in hospice. I've been to see him for the last time this morning. And now I'm…"

What? Hiding. Because she was still a coward. Still afraid to love fully. Her first reaction when someone was leaving was to protect her heart.

Push away. Run away. She hadn't gone that far. She would never be able to look at herself in the mirror if she had. But she'd kept her pain between her and the old man. She'd run from the family gathered to wait and mourn. Oh, she'd been there when they were showering her with love and acceptance and food. She didn't have a problem letting them in then. It was now, when it was hard and when it hurt, she'd made a token effort and run.

"Trying to cope?" Wyatt asked.

His words were spoken so quietly it took a moment for her to comprehend them. She turned to him. *God, his face.* Now he did look like an angel. Not a sweet, pure angel, but one who'd walked around among humans for a while and had seen suffering. Her cheeks burned. Of course he'd seen suffering. His sister had died in a horrible accident. His niece was suffering before his very eyes while he tried to comfort her. She turned the key and cranked the engine to life.

"Yes, trying to cope."

He reached out and warm, strong fingers closed gently around her hand. Sadie froze. The lightning fast shock of his touch didn't zing along her nerves this time. This was pure tenderness. He squeezed her hand in his and her fingers flexed, returning the gesture. Comforting. The muscles in her shoulders relaxed. She looked from their hands to his face. The understanding and compassion she saw there drew her in, mesmerizing her.

No. Oh, no. Don't do this. Don't get sucked into this, Sadie girl. She pulled her hand free and dropped the car into Reverse. A sudden new fear rose within her. This wasn't her hormones talking, this was her heart. And that was simply not going to happen.

Wyatt seemed to understand she wanted to keep busy and keep moving. He was all business as they tackled the deep cleaning at the next address. It was the smallest of the scheduled houses and the time advantage they'd gained with the easy first cleaning helped them keep ahead of schedule. She was more than happy with her inspection of Wyatt's work. First-rate. Proving her point he was too smart for this job. Or trying to impress the boss. She pulled out her phone, pushed it back in her pocket. Only to pull it out a minute later to make sure that the volume was turned up. It was. She knew it was.

Every nerve in her body seemed poised at the breaking point. Maybe she should call. Maybe he was already gone and Lena forgot to call. She shook her head. Lena wouldn't forget. *Would she?* She pulled the phone back out. *What are you going to say? Oh, hi, it's me, is he dead yet?* She tucked the phone away and covered her face with her hands. *Maybe you should go. Go be with the family.* No, she'd flat-out lose her mind sitting there waiting. Watching him slip away inch by inch. She gulped in a shuddering breath. Then a purposeful breath, deep and slow. *Pull it together.*

"Hey," Wyatt said from behind her.

"Seriously, dude!" When her feet touched back down, she put a hand on her galloping heart and spun to face him. "I'm going to bell you like a cat."

His startled expression melted into laughter. "Sorry. I'll try to stomp. Everything's packed up and ready. We're way ahead of schedule. Can we call the next appointment and see if we can come early? Seems a shame to waste an hour's advantage."

She rapidly shifted gears from her heartache to being startled to being warmed to the core by his laughter. It left her a bit dizzy. The businesswoman was too pleased with his suggestion to let the rest bother her. It was just what she'd been thinking of doing. Critical thinking skills turned a good employee into a great employee, and he had them.

"Great idea. Get the number from the book and give them a call."

SHE WAS WALKING up the stairs, carrying the vacuum cleaner, when her phone rang. She froze.

The vacuum cleaner slipped from her numb fingers to land with a thud on the step. For a brief, irrational moment her brain screamed at her to ignore it. *Don't answer.* She managed to get the phone out of her jeans pocket without dropping it.

Lena sounded calm and in control. The words washed over Sadie. About ten minutes ago. Everyone going home. Her parents were going to the funeral home. Arrangements. Come to the house for dinner tonight. Sadie tried to say something but her throat seemed to have closed and the pressure building in her chest was making it hard to breathe. She forcefully pulled in a long breath. She said some things. What exactly, she didn't know. Ended the call.

Ten minutes ago. Shouldn't she have sensed it? She covered her face with her hands. Never again would she hear him call her his *gatita callejero.* A homeless street kitten. She felt as if a hole had been ripped open in her soul and she was slipping away through it. A strange sound slowly seeped into her consciousness and it wasn't until Wyatt came at a run from the kitchen, skidding to a stop at the foot of the stairs that she realized the sound was coming from her. Weeping.

She suddenly found herself with his arms around her, and the tears broke loose. For a long time she was aware only of the waves of pain and loss coursing through her. Expecting his death had taken none of the sting away from the reality of it and her heart broke with this new emotion, this grief she'd never experienced.

She became aware of the feel of Wyatt's chest against her cheek, of his hand in her hair. His voice was low and soothing in her ear. She pressed closer into his warmth, sliding her hands around his neck and nestling closer. The tears faded away. His shirt was soaked with them. She started to pull away but he held her tight.

His hand drifted from her hair to cup her cheek and turn her face up to his. The rough strength of his hand contrasted with the tender concern in his eyes. The pain and fear left her as a wave of warmth filled her. Without a thought, she leaned forward and pressed her lips to his. *Yes. Oblivion.* She tightened her arms around his neck. He hesitated. His lips left hers for a moment and crashed back as he gave in to the kiss.

He held her even tighter and she could feel his heart matching the mad rush of her own beat for beat. She skimmed her fingers across the faint stubble of his cheeks. At his low moan, she hooked her fingers behind his neck and deepened the kiss. He tasted sweet, so sweet, as an angel should. And smelled like sunshine on saltwater. One of his hands was buried in her hair and the other was rubbing a line of fire down her back and…

Shit! She pushed back so hard she slipped to the stair below. She clapped her hands over her mouth and stared up at him. *What on earth are you doing? Abuelito is dead and you're tongue kissing an employee in a client's home? Have you lost your ever-loving mind?*

Wyatt held out a hand. "Sadie."

She scrambled to her feet, heat and horror and shame filling her. "I'm sorry. I'm sorry. I don't know what I was doing."

He remained sitting. "It's okay. Sit down."

She grabbed the vacuum cleaner. "No, it isn't. It's terrible. I'm a horrible person. I mean, I'm sorry, that will never happen again."

You suck. That's all there is to it. She sank back down on the stair and buried her face in her knees. Wyatt's hand pressed lightly on her back and the gesture set loose a fresh torrent of tears.

"Give me your phone."

When she didn't respond, he pulled it from her pocket. This was about as bad as kissing him. Sobbing like a child. On the job. *You are working, Sadie. You aren't allowed to fall apart.* She sat up and savagely wiped the tears from her face. She started to stand but Wyatt closed his hand around her wrist and shook his head. He pointed to the stair and she sat.

"Hey, Josh, it's Wyatt. We're going to need some help out here."

"We don't need help. Give me a minute."

Sadie reached for the phone but Wyatt twisted away. "Yes," he said into the phone. His eyes were warm as he looked at her and he took her hand in his. His palm was hot against her icy fingers. He ended the call. "Josh is on the way."

"Okay. We can get this finished up before he gets here."

"We can sit here until he gets here."

She couldn't. She couldn't sit there with him. Not after she'd shoved her tongue down his throat. Her cheeks burned. Her legs twitched with the desire to jump and run away. She covered her face with her hands. There was something seriously wrong with her. "I'm sorry."

"Don't be."

"I don't know what to do," she whispered.

"You go home when Josh gets here. You go be with your family. You cry. You remember the good things. You cry some more. You put one foot in front of the other."

He dropped an arm around her shoulders and gave her a friendly squeeze. The knot of confusion loosened and she leaned into his warmth.

"I'm such a dork."

"No. You're a pretty awesome person, Sadie Martin. And a damn good kisser."

She buried her burning face in her knees but a brief smile played at the corners of her lips.

SADIE DROVE SOUTH along Savannah Highway with one hand on the wheel, the other wandering absently to her lips from time to time as she made her way south. Her mind was a pleasant blank as familiar landmarks came and went. The Coburg Cow, that landmark of the West Ashley area of Charleston, caught her eye. Since the 1960s, it had been an early morning rite of teenage passage to climb the tower to the rotating sign and ride on the back of the cow. Sadie had not participated in this ritual.

So many things she never did because she never knew when or where she'd be moved. No sports. No clubs. No close friends. She spent the entirety of her teen years keeping her head down and trying to stay out of trouble.

She rubbed at her throat, trying to soothe away the ache there. Abuelito was gone. It hardly seemed real. When she finished this drive, when the homes and business parks that crowded this section of Savannah Highway thinned out, when she passed through Red Top and Ravenel, when she turned off onto the farm road, she'd be at Lena's family home. And he wouldn't.

Fear whispered in her ear, telling her to turn around, to go back home. Told her she couldn't handle this. She shook her head. *No. Not this time.* Her fingers drifted back to her lips. The memory of Wyatt's lips pressed against them rose in her mind, but what lingered were his words. *You go be with your family. You cry. You remember the good things. You cry some more. You put one foot in front of the other.* There was no right way to do this.

Sadie sighed as she pulled to a stop on the side of the road. The driveway was overflowing with cars. She climbed out and, as she always did, stood for a moment staring at the house. Deep down an oak-lined country road, it stood in a small meadow surrounded by oak, pine and maple forest. It was a simple home really, for all its size. Two stories, redbrick with steeply slanted black rooftops, it had a deep covered front porch with rows of glistening white rocking chairs. The window frames and eaves were also painted white, providing a bright contrast to the dark red brick. The front yard was small and neatly landscaped. The land went on seemingly forever in the back. Lena had built this for her family. Mobile home or grand mansion, they were the same loving people who had taken her into their home and lives.

The front door opened as she walked up the front steps. "Sadie!"

She smiled as Lena's cousin Sam stepped out.

Five years ago, he'd had a horrible crush on Sadie and had once asked her to marry him. He'd been fifteen at the time. He'd grown into a tall, darkly handsome man, and after the Marine Corps had given him the body of a god, she'd almost had reason to regret her decision to turn down his proposal. She held out her arms and he lifted her to her toes with his embrace.

"Who all is here?" she asked after he let her go.

"Who isn't here? Everyone." They stepped through the door and Sam called out, "Hey. Look what I found!"

The buzz of conversation quieted then rose again as Sadie was pulled into the house and was passed from arm to arm. She let it wash over her, the love, the tears, the laughter, the memories. She made her way to the kitchen, the heart of the house, where she knew she'd find Ana.

"Mamacita," she said as she put her arms around Lena's mother. Tears stung at her eyes at the strength of the arms that circled around her, squeezing her tight. *"Lo siento."*

Ana stepped back and wiped at her eyes. Abuelito had been her father. "I'm so glad you came, Sadie. I was worried about you this morning."

Sadie kissed her cheek. "I'm okay. I've just never…" The words died on her tongue and she moved aside as Ana turned back to the counter and resumed mixing up a bowl of what looked like corn dough.

"Lost a loved one?" Ana asked.

"Yeah."

Sadie leaned against the counter and smiled at the other women who were seated at the kitchen table, sifting through a large box of photographs. Lena's aunts. She knew Estrella and Paula but not the other two.

"Come here," Estrella said. She held out a photograph.

"What's all this?" Sadie asked as she crossed to take the picture. "Oh!" She sank into a chair, holding the picture in both hands. It was of Abuelito and her. He was sitting in his place at the head of the family table and Sadie had leaned down from behind, her cheek pressed to his. He had one hand pressed against hers.

"We're sorting through them. The funeral home will load them into a computer and they will show on a monitor at the viewing. Isn't that nice?" Estrella said. She tapped at the top of the picture in Sadie's hand. "But you keep that one."

"May I?"

"Of course you can."

Sadie looked down at the picture. She tried to remember exactly when it was taken, but there were no real clues. Before he got sick, that was for sure. Two, three years ago? Ana had taken it. She was the only person Sadie knew who still used film. A warm, liquid feeling washed over her. It was like a family snapshot. She didn't have many of those. Few of the foster parents had thought to send pictures with her when she moved on to a new home. She had some school pictures, a couple Santa pictures, but that was about all. She tucked this one away in her purse.

"Where's Lena?"

"Upstairs. On the phone. Making money for someone," Paula said.

Sadie frowned slightly at the disapproving tone. This was new. Lena was the family's golden child. Could do no wrong. Yes, her grandfather had passed away, but surely they understood Lena would have to wrap up some business before the end of the day. She looked to Ana, who said nothing. Sadie decided to follow her example.

"What can I help with?"

Ana tilted her head toward the pile of fruit on the counter beside her. "You can start cutting this up for the sangria."

As she cut the fruit and dropped it into the line of pitchers Ana had set out, Sadie listened as people came and went at the kitchen table. Everyone had a story to tell. Usually about some kindness or help that Lito had given to them. Sometimes funny. Lito's youngest sister was there, telling stories of their village in Mexico and how the whole family had moved across the border into Texas when she was only three. She told them how hard Lito worked and studied because the only thing he wanted was to become an American citizen. A goal he accomplished on his twenty-fifth birthday.

Her eyes kept straying to the kitchen window. From there she could see the edge of the forest. Her eyes must have been playing tricks on her because she could swear she saw a cat there in the shadows but there were no more feral cats. Lito had caught them all years ago to be neutered or spayed and released. The colony had died out slowly.

"Do they forgive you?"

"Some. It's the same with people, you know. Some know you are trying to help and forgive what might seem cruel. Others refuse to see beyond their hurt feelings."

The memory rose in her mind and she cleared her throat against the lump that was trying to form there. One of the many memories she had of sitting with Lito while he taught her what family was. What love was. She put the knife down and wiped her eyes with her sleeve.

"I'm going out back for a minute," she said. Her voice wavered and wobbled, but Ana only nodded.

She stood for a long moment on the back

porch. Her heart squeezed painfully when she saw the blanket draped over the back of a chair. The patchwork quilt blanket was frayed at the edges but its colors were still bright. She caressed the fabric. Her fingers closed around the edge. This was stupid. People were going to think she'd lost her mind. A few steps through the yard and she lifted the blanket, flinging it out, spreading it across the patch of grass where they'd always sat. She sat with her knees pulled up to her chest, and wrapped her arms around them and watched the forest.

Her thoughts drifted back to the letter and her promise. Could she take that first step in trusting her brother? She tilted her head back, eyes closed, and felt the warm sunshine on her face. Sifting through her conflicting feelings, she felt she could open a line of communication with Grant. But her mother? That was another story. She wanted nothing to do with that woman.

She shook her head, trying to shake away the wave of bitter anger that washed over her at the thought. Instead, she thought back to the first time Lito had asked her to sit with him. It wasn't here, but at the trailer park the family used to live in in North Charleston. The yard had been much smaller and there wasn't a forest. Just a strip of trees separating the trailers from the speeding cars along Rivers Avenue, but the cats had been the same. Wary. Hungry. She hadn't wanted to sit with him then. She was still too raw, too angry and too fearful of letting anyone close.

How many times had she sat with him and said nothing? Just listened to him? Listened as he told her everything he knew about the feral cats and how to win their trust. When had his voice begun to calm and soothe her? When did she first feel relaxed and comfortable sitting next to him? She didn't know. It'd happened so slowly that she hadn't noticed. She did know that by the time Lena had this house built and Lito had found another colony to tame, she loved him. Loved him and counted on him. It was no longer a one-sided conversation. She could ask him the questions she was too embarrassed to ask others. *What is love? How does it feel? How do you handle the fear? The anger?*

She pressed her face against her knees and wiped away the tears that were streaming down her face. *Oh, Lito. Thank you. I wouldn't have anything if not for you. You taught me how to care about others.*

"Sadie?"

She jumped at the softly spoken word and finished wiping away the tears as Ana gracefully sank to the ground next to her. "I didn't mean to interrupt."

"It's okay. I was just remembering."

Ana reached out and took Sadie's hand. "Me, too." She pulled a photograph from the pocket of her apron. "I found this. I want you to have it."

Sadie felt her lips curve into a weak smile as she looked at the picture. Another one she hadn't seen. Taken from the back porch, it showed her and Lito sitting on the blanket, shoulders touching as Sadie leaned toward him. Beyond them, a ginger tom stood at the edge of the forest. *El Roja.* He was the last of the feral cats to trust them. "Thank you."

Ana squeezed her hand. "I have to say something. I need to apologize to you."

Sadie felt her mouth drop open. "For what?"

"All those years ago, I told Lena she couldn't be friends with you. It was Papa who told me to allow it. He saw the good in you. I saw only what the world had done to you. I was afraid for my Lena."

"You were probably right, Ana. I was a mess. I had no right to have a friend as good as Lena."

Ana closed her other hand around Sadie's and looked into her eyes. Her eyes, so like Lito's, were usually kind and warm. Today they were full of pain and regret. "No, I wasn't right. I was fearful and selfish." She reached up and wiped tears from her eyes.

"I wanted to adopt. But we were poor. And Lena's father wasn't a citizen yet. I was afraid. Afraid to have the government poking around in my home and my life. What if they thought I wasn't taking care of Lena properly? We were poor and didn't have much."

"That's understandable. You did a wonderful job with Lena. And all your nieces and nephews adore you."

"But I hadn't been brave enough to try to save a child from that life. Why did I think it was okay to shun you because of it?"

"Oh, Ana. Don't. Please don't ever think that. You and your family did save me. All these years, you've included me, made me welcome."

"I want you to know that in my heart, I have two daughters. I know you were closest to Papa, but I want to tell you that we all love you. You are family. And I don't want that to change now that he's gone. Promise me you won't pull away from us."

Sadie felt the tears rising from some deep spot in her soul. Tears not of sorrow, but relief. She reached out and pulled Ana into an embrace. "I promise," she whispered.

Ana pushed Sadie back and her hands came up

to brush the curls from Sadie's face. Her hands were warm and tender. "I love you."

Sadie choked on a sob. "I love you, too."

CHAPTER THIRTEEN

"Jack!"

Sadie looked up at the jubilant sound. Jack yipped joyfully as he raced to Julietta, who was ditching her bike. If her heart hadn't been plummeting to her shoes, she might have found some humor in the way the two ran to reach other like long lost lovers.

"It's Jack, Uncle Wyatt!"

Sadie lifted her eyes from Jack and Julietta, and her heart tried to burrow into the dirt beneath her shoes. Her cheeks burned in shame. She had come today, Sunday, hoping to avoid this. Wyatt leaned down to pet Jack before turning his gaze in her direction. Her lips spasmed in what tried to be a smile, but failed miserably. He wore running shorts and a loose tank, showing off muscled legs, arms and that yummy chest. Julietta spotted her and ran to her, Jack hot on her heels.

"Hi, Ms. Sadie! Can I play catch with Jack?"

"Of course you can. He likes to play with you."

Wyatt approached them and Sadie kept her

attention on handing the tube of tennis balls to Julietta for as long as possible. She didn't want to see his eyes. Shame burned through the exhaustion of grief. She couldn't believe the utter loss of control she'd displayed. He squatted in front of her and she was forced to look in his general direction. He had a nice forehead. Tan and smooth. Not too high. Nice eyebrows. She could stare at the spot between them and...

"How're you holding up?"

She had to look at his eyes. And once she'd done it, she couldn't stop. Why did he have to be a nice guy? Why did he ask as if he really wanted to know? Why had his kiss been the most amazing kiss she'd ever had in spite of the circumstances?

"Tired."

That was an understatement. After spending Friday night and all Saturday with Lena's family, she was exhausted. Too many people, too many words, too many tears and even too much laughter. She'd been over already once today for brunch. There must have been fifty people gathered together to mourn the loss and celebrate the life of Luis Acosta. A large, loud crowd in which no emotion was forbidden. Laughter, tears, anger, love. It flowed in a messy, loud river of sound. She'd escaped the brunch, promising to return in time to ride with the family to the viewing later.

He moved to sit beside her. Good because now she didn't have to look directly at him. Bad because she could feel the warmth of his body, could smell his tantalizing scent. She focused her attention on Julietta and Jack romping around in the grass. Julietta's happy laughter floated back to them.

"Last time they played here, you were hoping she'd laugh."

"I remember. I think I said I'd kiss you if she did."

Sadie cut her eyes in his direction and found him grinning at her. "Well, you got that."

"I certainly did."

"I'm sorry. I don't know what to do about it except promise it will never happen again."

"It's fine. But I'm not sure what you are apologizing—repeatedly—for."

She turned to stare openmouthed at him. "I'm your boss! We were on a job! It was completely unprofessional."

"You weren't my boss at that moment. You were a human being who'd received very bad news and needed comfort."

She turned away from him at those words. She focused on Jack as he jumped to catch the balls Julietta was lobbing in the air. She plucked a clover from the grass and spun it between her fingers. "Didn't give me the right to attack you."

"You didn't attack me. And it was a perfectly normal reaction."

"No, it wasn't. Disrespectful to you and Abuelito both."

"You know what I did when I got the phone call about Maddie?"

She leaned forward, running her fingers through the clover, searching for a four-leafed one. Maybe her luck would change and she wouldn't have to talk about feelings and how normal people acted.

"I told my fiancée, and when she hugged me, I kissed her and we ended up in bed. It's a form of denial. The shock of death is so strong, the mind retreats from it initially."

Sadie's cheeks went hot. There was way too much in that sentence. He was engaged? She did not need to hear about his sex life. Not when imagining new chapters in his sex life was the number one reason she hadn't been getting a full night's sleep recently. *Great, Sadie.*

"You're engaged?"

"I was."

He stretched his legs out and leaned back on his hands. Julietta ran back to them. Jack was hot on her heels. Sadie poured water from her bottle into the little bowl she brought for him.

"Ms. Sadie? Can I put Jack's leash on and take him for a walk?"

"That's up to your uncle. He may not want you wandering off."

Wyatt pointed. "If you don't go any farther than the sign right there."

Julietta made a face. "That's not very far."

"That's as far as you're going to get."

"Okay. Can I, Ms. Sadie?"

She snapped the leash on Jack's halter. "He can be strong when he wants to go somewhere. If you can't keep hold of him, call out for us."

"Oh, he'll be good for me, won't you, Jack?"

Jack wagged his tail. Sadie watched closely as Julietta led Jack to the paved trail and began to march him back and forth along the short distance. Jack was heeling perfectly. Something he refused to do for her.

"She left me," Wyatt said.

"Your fiancée?"

"Yes. Maddie had appointed me as Jules's guardian but her best friend was also mentioned. I considered it. For about a minute. Kate is married and has two kids already. She was willing to take her, but I couldn't let her go. She's my only blood family left."

Sadie turned to him. He was watching Julietta. Her throat ached at the love in his eyes. She took a swig of water.

"Victoria told me I was being selfish. Told me Jules would be better off with an established family. With brothers and sisters close to her age. My parents were only children of only children. We never had aunts or uncles or cousins. Kate has a large family. So Jules would be getting the real deal."

He shifted to sit cross-legged and now his hands sifted through the clover. She wanted to take his hand in hers. He'd done what her own mother refused to do for her. "You couldn't let her go," she whispered, unable to get any more volume.

"No. She's mine."

Tears stung her eyes. The ferocity in his words made her heart ache worse. He'd disrupted his entire life to take on the task of raising a grieving little girl. Abuelito had taken on the task of showing her, a stranger, what a family's love was. She pulled her knees up and wrapped her arms around them, needing something to hold on to.

"So she gave me an ultimatum. She wasn't going to start marriage with a ready-made child. She wanted her own children."

"And you chose Jules."

"It wasn't even a choice for me."

Sadie rested her forehead against her knees. She was trying her damnedest not to sniffle when Wyatt's hand, warm and gentle settled between her shoulder blades. She managed not to arch into the caress like a purring house cat who was no longer a wild kitten.

"What about you? How's your family doing? Was it your grandfather who passed?"

She turned her head with a sigh. "Sort of. My best friend, Lena, he was her grandfather. He'd sort of adopted me."

His hand remained, tracing small circles that sent ripples to her core. She locked her fingers together to keep from repeating the disaster of the other day. Because she wanted to crawl into his arms and draw from his strength. This was a whole new feeling. This feeling of comfort and warmth that was a separate thing from the sexual attraction she felt. She didn't know what to do with it. She sat up to stop his hand before she lost control again. Forget what, she didn't know. She did know throwing herself at him again wasn't going to end her confusion.

"I'm gathering letting people close isn't easy for you," he said, his words lightly tinged with humor.

A small snort of laughter escaped. "Yeah. You noticed?"

"Families of choice. Those bonds must be stronger than blood," he said.

"Really?"

"Don't you think?"

"I never had any family to bond with," she said. *Hell.* She hadn't meant to say that. Her cheeks burned. Now he'd want an explanation. And she hated explaining. The shame of it was too much. She didn't want him to know this. Didn't want to see the look in his eyes. She climbed to her feet and waved at Julietta. Cupping her hands around her mouth, she called out, "I need to get Jack home now, honey."

She waited for Julietta to walk Jack back to them. Wyatt rose to stand beside her. He touched her elbow and she reluctantly looked at him. Instead of the pity she expected, she saw regret.

"I'm sorry. I didn't mean to upset you further."

"You didn't."

His hand lingered on her arm and he shot a quick glance at Julietta, who had stopped while Jack watered a bush. "I wish…"

Whatever he wished for was lost in a piercing scream from Julietta that had him sprinting to her. Sadie followed on his heels.

"A spider," Wyatt told her. "Only a spider."

Sadie took the leash from Julietta's hand. "We should be going. I've got the viewing tonight."

She knew he was watching her as she walked away and concentrated on Jack. He was tugging at the leash and trying to smell all the smells before going home. What did Wyatt wish? She knew what she was wishing for.

MONDAY MORNINGS USUALLY started with a staff meeting led by Sadie with her giant cup of coffee and snarky wit. Not this morning, though. Josh presided at the head of the table. Wyatt lounged back as he watched the young man. He'd seen Sadie in this man's arms. He was someone she trusted, and he was beginning to understand the list of people Sadie trusted was short. She had claimed Josh was like a brother to her, and he could have been. They shared the same dark hair and dark blue eyes. Josh, however, had the complexion of the Black Irish, so unlike Sadie's fair skin.

He'd spent a good deal of time wondering what she'd meant when she said she had no family to bond with. Clearly she hadn't wanted to let that slip and had all but run away. But why? She was such a contradiction. She threw up walls and came off tough as nails, but he'd seen her immediately respond to others when they were in need. He'd been on the receiving end of her caring, and it was real. She wasn't faking her compassion. But God help you if you tried to show her any compassion.

"Where's our fearless leader?" one of the guys asked Josh as they settled down around the table.

Josh flipped open Sadie's notebook. "She's had a death in the family. Funeral is today so she's taking a personal day. Means you have to deal with me."

"Who died?"

"I didn't know she had any family."

"Is she okay?"

The questions flew at Josh. He waited until there was silence. "Her friend Lena's grandfather. She was very close to him."

"Was he the old dude who used to take her to lunch every month?"

"Yeah."

"Is it too late to take up a collection and send flowers or something?"

"We totally should do it. When my grandmother died, Sadie sent flowers and a note to my mother."

"When my aunt died, she helped me with the airfare to get back home."

Josh held up a hand. "Molly arranged flowers for the funeral already."

"We should still get some for Sadie," Noah said. He dug his wallet out of his back pocket and threw a five in the center of the table. "Come on, guys, ante up."

Wyatt tossed a five into the growing pile as the guys argued over what kind of flowers they should get. Noah scooped the pile toward him and began to count it. "Pink roses," he said, and the entire table fell silent.

Wyatt looked at Josh, but his face was as closed off as Sadie's could be.

Noah glanced around the table. "Don't you think?"

Josh nodded. "It'll make her cry, but in a good way, I think." He reached down and pulled a small poster from a satchel at his feet. "We got the mockup of the thank-you ad."

He handed it to Wyatt who was sitting at his left. It was a mounted eleven-by-fourteen photograph. Molly was perched on a stool, and Sadie stood behind her. Her hair was down, and the smile on her face took Wyatt's breath away. The two women were surrounded by the guys, who were facing into the camera with varying expressions from gee-shucks grins to smoldering smiles. The bold print along the top simply read "Thank You." Below, it read "Thank you, Charleston, for voting the Cleaning Crew the Best Cleaning Service." He slid it to Noah, sitting on his left.

"The ad is going run in the next *City Paper*, and will be in all the local media soon. I'm expecting we will get a boost in our client list. For the next week, we'll probably be doing more first contacts, so be ready."

"Marcus is going to have a stroke," Noah said.

Josh grinned but said nothing as he took out another mockup and handed it to Wyatt. It was essentially the same positioning, but instead of the smiles, the guys were posing with crossed arms, looking cocky. The copy at the top read "Coming Soon" and below, "The Cleaning Crew. Coming soon to the greater Columbia area." There was a phone number listed.

"We're beginning to offer service in Columbia. This ad is going to run a few times in late May to introduce our name to a new market. We'll go back to word of mouth recommendations once we have a client list started. We want to time this with summer break. The plan is to see how strong the interest is, then take on limited numbers of customers. We'll run the cleanings from here at first. If it takes off, I'll move up there and start hiring a new team."

This news was greeted with a wave of questions. Josh answered them patiently. "That's it, and daylight's wasting. Noah, Sadie told me she talked to you Friday. You and Wyatt are teaming up for the time being. If you need anything, call me, not Sadie. I'll be representing us at the funeral so I might not call back right away. Noah, before you leave, get with Molly. You never got checked off on the new floor stuff. Do it. This morning or I'll kick your ass."

"Gee, where'd you learn that management technique?" Noah said as he rose from the table.

"Sadie Martin's School of Not Taking Lame Excuses," Josh replied. The room erupted in laughter.

Noah nudged one of the guys. Brad, Wyatt thought his name was. "Remember the time Sadie sat and listened to you go on about the test you had to ace and how you were up all night studying and that's why you overslept?"

Brad laughed. "She sat there and let me ramble on for about five minutes then said, 'it sounds plausible, except for the drunk pictures you put on your Facebook page at three this morning.' You can't get anything past her. Nothing."

"Hey, man," Noah said to Wyatt. "Let me get with Molly and get this done. Our first appointment isn't until ten, so we've got some time."

After the guys cleared out, Wyatt sat in the waiting room while Noah did the paperwork. A clack of toenails caught his attention and he smiled as Jack came bounding into the room. "Hey, Jackie Boy," he said, holding out a hand. The dog came to him and accepted ear scratches before abandoning him for Molly.

"You big goofball," Molly said. She reached into her desk drawer for a doggy treat. "Sit. Good boy. Do you need to go pee?"

Jack yipped. Wyatt stood. "I can take him out."

"Would you? That'd be great. I can finish up

with Noah and you two can get going. He can be off leash in the backyard."

He took Jack out and watched as he ran the perimeter of the fence, stopping to lift his leg all the way around. There must be some border collie in him. He made his way back to Wyatt and sat, panting up at him with his tongue hanging out the side of his mouth. Wyatt squatted down to take the shaggy head between his palms.

"You're a good dog, aren't you?"

"Depends on whether he knows if you have treats or not."

Wyatt stood and turned at the sound of Sadie's voice. *Wow.* His mouth fell open and his eyes may have bugged out of his head a little. She had her hair down, black curls cascading in a river of silk, and her hands were slipping an earring into a lobe. The picture he'd seen did not do justice to how incredibly beautiful she was. She was wearing a black dress that made her skin glow. It was a perfectly modest dress with sleeves to the elbow, the hem below her knees and a not-too-deep V at the neck, but it clung to every curve on her body. He forced his eyes off her body and up to her eyes. He was having trouble breathing. And thinking. Perhaps because most of his blood had shifted farther south.

"Jack. Inside."

The dog slipped past her with a whine, but

his tail whacked against her leg on his way. She frowned and bent to brush off the dog fur, and he was given a wonderful view down the front of the dress. Now he couldn't breathe at all. Spots danced before his eyes. She straightened and a frown crossed her face.

"What's the matter?"

He shook his head. "Huh? Nothing. Waiting on Noah."

"You looked weird there for a minute."

You're beautiful, he wished he could say, *and I'd like to kiss you and peel that dress off and do things to you.* "No. I'm fine." He cleared his throat and forced himself to remember why she was dressed up. "You holding up okay there, boss?"

Her eyes held a bit of sadness when she looked into his but a small smile played at one corner of her mouth. "Yeah. Tired but holding up." Her hands came together, fingers rubbing against themselves. "A little nervous," she continued in a whisper.

"Why?" He stepped closer and put his hand over her entwined fingers. Their restless motion ceased and she didn't pull away.

"I've never been to a funeral before."

He looked up from where his hand rested against hers to her face. And there it was: the quick little quirk of the lips before she pressed them together. Another tidbit she hadn't meant to let slip. *Wonder if those slips are just for me. Or does she do it with everyone?* He suppressed the question of how one could get to be Sadie's age and never have attended a funeral. He ignored his urge to pull her into his arms and tell her it'd be okay. "They're all pretty standard. Hymns, prayers, preaching."

Her gaze dropped to their hands, and he squeezed hers a little more firmly. He thought she'd pull away now, but she still didn't. When she looked back at him, she gave him a lopsided smile. "This is going to be a full mass, communion and everything. Catholic funeral."

"Ah. Jumping in the deep end, I see. You'll be okay. I was at one once. The priest knew there were non-Catholics in attendance and he let us know what to do when." He saw the tension leave her shoulders and gave her hand one last squeeze before letting go.

"Thanks," she said.

"You're welcome." He wanted to hug her. Put an arm around her shoulders. Something. A movement in the kitchen caught his eye. Josh. Staring at him. Like a brother daring him to put one finger on his sister. "You'll be fine," he repeated.

He followed her through the kitchen to the waiting room. She picked up her purse and told

Molly she wouldn't be back until late. Wyatt couldn't keep his eyes off her as she walked out the door. Noah peeked out of the conference room.

"One minute, dude. I'm about done."

"Okay," he said, crossing the room to collapse in a chair. *Dear God.* He had to get out of here. He had to get off this job. Molly was staring at him. A sympathetic smile crossed her lips.

"She keeps her heart locked up pretty tight. But I'll bet you could find your way to it."

Wyatt started to protest but she gave another one of those smiles and turned her back on him, keys on her keyboard clacking in time to his racing heart.

WORKING WITH NOAH had none of the awkwardness that his first days with DeShawn had. Noah was an outgoing guy. Talked almost nonstop. This was a good thing. Talkers loved to answer questions. He watched the younger man as they drove to their first stop. Noah was outlining their day. He was as detail oriented as DeShawn and had his routine down to a fine science.

"How do you do this full-time and go to school?" Wyatt asked.

"I'm part-time at school. Usually do evening or night classes. Some of the guys are in school full-time. They'll work one or two days a week, put their classes on the other days. Sadie's very flexible with school schedules. She wants us to finish school."

"What else is she flexible about?"

Noah laughed. "Not much. She's got her rules. You're just off orientation, so you know what I'm talking about."

Wyatt appraised the young man sitting beside him. He'd taken no offense to the "flexible" question. Straight up would work with him. "No kidding. But I heard there were ways to pick up extra tips."

Noah shot him a hand-caught-in-the-cookie-jar look. *Huh.* Was he wrong? Was there something going on behind Sadie's back?

"There are. But you gotta keep it quiet."

Wyatt waited him out. They pulled into the driveway of a house perched at the edge of the Wando River. It was an ordinary brick ranch, but Wyatt knew the location put it in the million-dollar range. Sadie had some wealthy clients. Noah shifted in the seat so he was facing Wyatt.

"It's nothing. Like, this lady." He motioned with a thumb at the house. "Sometimes she'll call and ask me to pick up her dry cleaning. Leaves me a ten-dollar tip. There's one who likes to put new flowers by her porch every couple of months. She'll leave them out with a twenty and I pop 'em in the ground. Got a hundred once for hauling junk to the dump. But you can't let Sadie know. She worries about us getting to the next job on time. Doesn't want us cutting corners because we're running late."

Wyatt almost laughed at Noah's conspiratorial tone. Marcus was hoping they were running a male prostitute ring, and they were picking up dry cleaning.

"My lips are sealed," he said and climbed from the car.

He stood for a moment, looking out at the water. The sunshine held a hint of the summer heat to come but the breeze off the water was still cool. He took in a deep breath. He was out of this mess. He had Henry Moody's assurances and a pending job offer. He was satisfied he'd gone above and beyond for Marcus Canard. He'd turn in his report. Canard could go to hell if he didn't like it. He could turn in his resignation. The good feeling drained from his chest. *Then what? Never see her again?*

He turned away from the water and began hauling equipment into the house. That's the best solution: never see her again. If he wanted to, he'd have to tell her the truth, and she'd never forgive him. He'd rather be able to imagine she thought kindly of him at least. *It's a bad time anyway. You don't need to be starting anything up with any woman. Jules doesn't need any more abandonment in her life. She's already too attached to Jack. Walk away, man, walk away.*

He had to turn in a resignation to Sadie soon. He felt bad about the expense of training a new employee and he didn't want to compound the guilt by leaving her in the lurch with no partner for Noah. He decided to give it a few days and chose not to explore his growing sense of loss.

"SO WHAT'S THE story with the pink roses?"

He and Noah had met up with a couple other teams at Jack's Cosmic Dogs in Mount Pleasant for lunch. They were gathered around two tables pushed together. Josh's comment about it making Sadie cry had made him curious. He had no reason to dig into Sadie's life. Except he couldn't help himself. The table went quiet, and the guys looked to Noah. He washed down a giant bite of hot dog with a swig of iced tea.

"The guy who died? He wasn't her real grandfather, but he came every year at Sadie's birthday. Brought her pink roses and took her out to lunch. He was a cool old dude."

"Wait," one of the guys asked. "He wasn't her real grandfather?"

Noah shook his head. "No. I heard her talking to Josh about it once. Josh was the first guy she ever hired. He had just been kicked out of his foster home because he was eighteen. I think the same thing happened to Sadie. That's why they're so close. But I don't think it's something that either of them want spread around, so keep your mouths shut."

From the flabbergasted faces around the table, Wyatt surmised this was news to many of them. It explained a lot. Her tough-as-nails exterior. Her difficulty letting people get close. Her bond with Josh. His admiration rose even higher. Cut loose at eighteen with no family and she'd built this successful business that at its core owed its success to the feeling of family she'd created. Not an easy feat.

Noah elbowed him lightly. "Ready, dude? I want to try to finish up early so we can stop somewhere and get those flowers."

CHAPTER FOURTEEN

SADIE DROVE SOUTH on Savannah Highway thinking about Wyatt Anderson instead of what lay ahead. She hadn't missed the flare of heat in his expression. That wasn't what had stayed with her, though. It was the touch of his hand against hers and the gentle, quiet warmth with which he tried to comfort her. She'd seen the same thing over the long weekend with the Acosta family. Women turning to their men. Mothers holding their children. And she'd stood alone.

What would it be like? To have someone like Wyatt at her side? Attending this funeral with her? To stand beside each other through all the ups and downs of life? She shook her head. *Wish in one hand, spit in the other. See which fills up first.* That kind of life wasn't for her. She was too messed up. Didn't even know what to do at a funeral. How was she supposed to build a life with another person?

You're lonely, Sadie.

She shook her head against the thought. Her throat tightened and her fingers clenched on the steering wheel. *No. Don't go there. Not now.* She drew in a deep breath. *Besides, you aren't lonely. You have Lena and her family. And Josh. Molly. The guys. You have tons of people in your life.* She blinked back the tears. *Stop it. Stop feeling sorry for yourself.* She dialed up the volume, drowning out her thoughts with Freddie Mercury.

The long drive to the church gave her time to get her emotions under control. The church was a small white clapboard building hugged by live oaks dripping with Spanish moss on the banks of the Edisto River. Sadie parked next to Lena's BMW. Other cars parked nearby let her know that she was probably the last to arrive. *No, second last.* A nearly silent Prius pulled into the space beside her and she looked over. Sam smiled at her from the passenger seat. She smiled back as he climbed out, handsome and sexy in his Marine dress blues. All sorts of ribbons decorated the front. She didn't know what they meant, but knew that he'd worked hard to earn them.

"Remind me again why I turned down your marriage proposal," she said as she stepped out of her car.

He took her hand and closed the car door for her. "Remind me why I didn't try harder."

She smiled as he kissed her cheek. He settled an arm around her waist. "Do you remember Carl? He's our cousin."

Carl was dressed in the formal blue of the army. Sadie shook his hand. "I don't remember meeting you before, but I know who you are. Lito was so proud of you both."

"Really? All I ever heard about was Lena and Sadie. That old man thought the world revolved around you two."

His teasing brought tears to her eyes. Sam hooked an arm around her shoulders. "Buck up, woman. No crying in the parking lot. You've got to pace yourself."

Carl offered his arm and Sadie took it. She drew in a deep breath and nodded. "I'm bucked up. Let's go."

The front door of the church opened and Lena looked out. "There you are," she called while waving in a frantic "come here" gesture. "Aunt Estrella is about to have a fit." She took Sadie's hand as she drew near and pulled her into the church.

Sadie had a brief impression of wood and stained glass and hushed coolness as Lena pulled her down a short hall. The Acosta family was gathered in a small room. "Here she is," Lena announced.

"S-sorry," Sadie stammered to the gathered crowd. "I didn't know you were waiting on me."

Ana stood and took Sadie's hands in hers. Sadie leaned down and kissed her cheek. "Of course we were waiting on you. I have something important to ask of you."

A little wave of motion spread through the room as people shifted. Estrella looked a bit stormy around the eyes and a vague sense of caution rose in Sadie. Lena's carefully composed face gave her no clue. She looked back to Ana. "Anything, Mamacita."

"I would like for you, along with Magdalena, to present the Eucharist."

The whisper of caution drowned in a wave of rising panic. Present? The what? "I—I…" she stuttered.

Lena put an arm around her. "It's okay, Sades. The wine and wafers for communion. We'll bring them up and give them to the priest."

Sadie's arm snaked around Lena's waist. "Uh. Sure. I don't know what to do, though."

Ana took Sadie's hand and squeezed. "Lena will show you."

"Okay." She felt faint with the sudden worry and fear. She turned to Lena when Ana walked away to greet Sam and Carl. "Is this a problem? Estrella looks like she wants to stab me."

"It's me she wants to stab," Lena whispered.

"Why?" Sadie was truly shocked. Lena was the family's standard to which all the cousins were held. The princess, the perfect one.

Lena led Sadie to a love seat along the far wall

of the room. She sat close to Sadie and leaned close to whisper. "I can't take communion. And neither can you. Estrella is upset because neither of us is in a state of grace but Mama wants us to present the Eucharist."

Sadie felt the panic begin to rise again. She didn't have a clue what Lena meant. She'd never been a church kind of person. She'd been dragged along with a few foster families but it had always seemed like their church, not hers. Most of what she knew of communion and church was from television and movies. "Should I have said no?"

"No. It's perfectly fine. You don't have to even be Catholic to participate. It's a funeral. People are tired and grieving. She'll get over it."

"Okay. So what do we have to do?"

"Basically, get up, walk to the back, get the wine and wafers, walk to the front and give them to the priest. Easy."

"Unless I freak out and drop something. What would be worse? Dropping the wine or the wafers?"

Lena raised her eyes to the ceiling and shook her head. "I'll carry the wine."

Sadie leaned back against the sofa cushion. She closed her eyes, listening to the low buzz of voices around her. Her initial panic at being asked to do something in public was fading. They wanted to include her. Like they always did. Holidays, birthdays, she was there. Why did she still feel like an outsider? Why couldn't she break through the fear and the walls and believe she was wanted? Her thoughts were interrupted by Lena's elbow being rammed into her ribs.

Lena was rising to her feet. "Father Greg," she whispered. "We're about to start."

Sadie stood also, her throat squeezing tight. She pressed her lips together against the tremble she felt there. About to start Lito's funeral. She took Lena's hand as they walked from the room. She felt Lena freeze the same moment she herself had to slow her steps: at the sight of Lito's coffin waiting in the foyer. The church doors were propped open and the sunlight was warm and golden on the rich wood of the bare coffin.

She thought she'd cried all the tears she had the night before at the viewing. When she'd finally worked up the courage to see him and touch his hand for the last time. Her heart broke for wanting to see the warm glow of his eyes just once more.

A gentle push from behind got her feet moving again. She put her arm around Lena's waist and pulled her along. They followed the casket as it was moved to the front. People filled the pews of the small church. Most of the faces were a blur, but Sadie saw Josh sitting alone and looking handsome in a dark suit. He tapped over his heart with his fist and she felt a small smile tremble at the corners of her mouth. She hesitated at the pew, watching as people knelt and crossed themselves before sitting. Should she? Was it only Catholics? She pinched at the waist of Lena's dress. Lena turned and nodded. She felt stupid and awkward doing it, but when she sat beside Lena, she also felt a strange sort of calm.

The service began. Sam and Carl rose to drape a white cloth over the casket. The priest sprinkled holy water. Sadie couldn't keep her eyes off the casket. She had never really thought about what Lito had done for her when he overrode Ana's command that Lena not be friends with her. Where would she be without any of the Acostas?

At least she'd let him know how grateful she was for his intervention and love. At least she had that. She had no unfinished business with Lito.

Words and music and reciting responses flowed over her and she found it comforting. Maybe that was part of the healing. This coming together of those who loved Luis Acosta. To remember him. To honor him. Maybe that's what would fill those holes. Memories. She had a lot of them.

A gentle nudge from Lena brought her back from her memories. "Get up," Lena whispered. Something similar to terror flooded through her. She'd almost forgotten. She hesitated, unsure if she was supposed to kneel and cross while exiting the pew. Lena's firm hand pushing on her butt answered that question. She stood in the aisle feeling her cheeks go hot. Lena took her by the arm and they walked to the back of the church.

She didn't drop the wafers. So that was good. As the people rose, pew by pew, to take communion, she leaned in to whisper to Lena. "Why aren't you doing it?"

A shrug rolled through Lena's upper body. "Not in a state of grace. Haven't gone to confession."

"Oh." Sadie didn't know what that meant. She searched her small knowledge base of religious terms. She knew about confession and taking communion. She just didn't know what the two had to do with each other. Her gaze returned to the white-draped coffin.

After the communion was done, after more prayers were chanted, Lito's sister rose to speak. Sadie half listened as Elena spoke of Luis. Her throat tightened. He'd saved her. Saved her from a life of misery and loneliness. She'd never have had a best friend like Lena. She'd never have had Josh and Molly and the guys. She'd not have her business if it weren't for Lito's support and nurturing. She'd not have anything if not for Lito reaching out to her. A sob tore at her throat and she leaned forward, hiding her face in her hands. Lena's hand came down, soft and warm, on her back.

Her sobs were clearly audible in the small church, but for once, she did not care. She didn't care that people were looking at her. *Thank you, God or Jesus or whoever is in charge up there for letting me have him for a little while.*

A warm presence pressed in from her left and a familiar strong arm came down across her shoulders and pulled her close. Josh. She pressed her face against his shoulder.

"Careful there, Saff," he whispered. "This jacket is a lot less washable than the T-shirt you snotted up."

She laughed through the tears and wiped at her face and nose with the tissue he offered. A few hiccuping sobs twisted the deep breath she tried to take, but the storm seemed to have passed. She put her head on his shoulder. "Thanks."

"You okay?"

"Yeah."

And she was. Not completely, but she realized that the tears weren't for losing Lito. They were the tears of gratitude that she'd been allowed to have him in her life, however briefly. This knowledge somehow made it a bit easier to say goodbye.

CHAPTER FIFTEEN

"JACK, YOU ARE not helping. I know you think you are, but really you aren't."

Jack didn't care. He continued snuffling his nose through the little bags of screws and nuts and bolts. Sadie pushed him back and gathered the bags for their own protection. She stretched her legs out over the pile of parts destined to become a new bookshelf. The project was just complicated enough to keep her mind off Lito. Nothing had been the same since he died. The funeral the day before had been more draining than she expected. She'd taken today off to recuperate. But she needed something normal to do. Leaning back to retrieve the wineglass from the end table, she popped a few jelly beans in her mouth. *Fine dining at its finest.* She tried to read the instructions. Part A with bolt B to part C with nut D. *Sheesh.* The pictures didn't help. She put the wineglass back. This project definitely had a "one glass of wine" limit.

She sighed and climbed to her feet and began sorting the boards. Once done, she rewarded herself with more jelly beans. She stood, tossing the candy down her gullet and trying to cheerlead herself into getting this done. Tonight. The box had been shoved under her bed for three weeks now. The joy her ringing phone brought did not bode well for the completion of the project. She snatched it up. Unknown number. Usually meant business.

"Sadie Martin."

"Hey, Sadie, it's Wyatt. I was hoping I could talk to you."

She sat down, pretending it was to reach the wineglass, not because the sound of his voice, rough man edges smoothed with a honeyed accent, was making her knees wobble a bit. No, not at all. "Talk away."

"In person?"

"Now?"

"I'm in the parking lot."

She moved to the window. Sure enough, there he was leaning against the side of his truck, looking like every woman's dream come true. He wore a dark green polo shirt that clung to his shoulders and chest. His jeans were faded, well-worn and taut across the thighs. As if sensing her gaze, his dark blond head tipped up and he grinned. Oh, dear God, that lopsided grin was going to kill her.

"Come on around to the back door."

She ended the call. *Oh, no.* Her hands flew to her hair. It was caught up in a messy bun to keep it out of her face while working on the bookshelf. No makeup. Probably jelly-bean bits caught in her teeth. She cupped her hands in front of her mouth to check her breath. *Cinnamon and wine. Could be worse. Jeez. Stop it. He's an employee, not a date.* She ran down the back stairs, realizing meeting an employee while dressed in yoga pants and a tank top was probably not too professional. Neither were her bare feet and bright purple toe nails. Well, he was the one who'd showed up unannounced.

"Hey, what's up?" she asked as she opened the back door to let him in. His gaze swept over her and came back to hers. Her body responded to the pure male appreciation in his eyes and her heart began a double-time beat. She bent to grab Jack's collar to keep him from escaping, grateful for the reason to break eye contact.

"I need to talk to you."

"Is Jules okay?"

He smiled and his shoulders relaxed. The dimples appeared and nothing on Sadie relaxed. "Yes, she's fine. Can we talk?"

"Sure, come on up."

Perhaps it was a mistake, asking him upstairs. But she wasn't going to go sit in the conference room braless and barefoot.

"Did I interrupt something?" he asked, looking around at the piles of parts strewn around the living room. He stood with his hands stuffed in his back pockets, one booted foot nudging at the wood. He had to stop that, it made his chest look a mile wide and made her remember the bare view she'd seen of it. Her fingers twitched at the memory of the dusting of dark hair across those amazing pecs. *And don't forget that line leading down...*

"Interrupted some serious procrastination. Thanks, by the way—I was running out of excuses."

She waved at the couch and sat nervously at the very end. He sank down on the opposite end, turned to face her.

"How are you doing? With everything?"

She resisted the urge to chug more wine. "Okay. The funeral helped, believe it or not. I guess having a formal ceremony and remembrance sort of turns grief to a new chapter."

"Good."

He looked around the room. Rubbed a palm against his jeans. Turned back to her. Petted Jack. Nervous. She leaned forward. "What's on your mind, Wyatt?"

He ran a hand across his lips and jaw. "This is harder than I thought it'd be."

"I'm a big fan of putting it all on the table."

"I bet you are. Okay. I've had a job offer. It's a good one. Pay-wise, benefits for Jules. I can't pass it up."

Her heart sank. Sank hard. He was shaping up to be one of her best employees. "Take it. You have to do what's right for you and Jules. Family is always first."

"I feel bad. I'll finish out the week so you can find a partner for Noah."

"That'll be great. But only if it's not going to cause a problem with getting the new job."

She felt a smile on her numb lips and heard the right words coming out of her mouth even as bitter disappointment struck her. No, she wanted to say. *Don't quit. Not allowed. I'll miss you.* Miss the way his eyes would meet hers during staff meetings whenever one of the guys was being a kid. Miss the way his smile would quirk up on one side at her jokes.

"You're a good person, you know that?"

His tone was low and earnest. He leaned forward and her body wanted to move toward him. She leaned back instead. "I don't know about that."

He picked up the instructions that had come with the bookshelf. "The least I can do after quitting with such short notice is help you put this together. This doesn't seem to be a one-person job."

"What about Jules?"

He touched the breast pocket of his shirt where she could see the outline of his phone. "Having her first sleepover. So I may be called away at any minute. I'm not convinced she's ready to be away from home overnight. She swears she is."

Say thanks, but no. Tell him you don't need the help. Trouble was she did need help. She'd never be able to wrangle the pieces together alone. It had five sections. The tallest was almost seven feet and the shortest was five feet. It was perfect for the long wall of nothing in the large open area of the apartment. And it meant she could get the rest of her books out of the boxes in the second bedroom and stop living as though she'd just moved in. Maybe start gathering matching furniture. Like a real grown-up.

"If you have the time."

He stood and looked around the room. "It's going there against the wall, I guess?"

"Yep. Any advice? My problem's been figuring out the logistics."

He picked up the instructions and studied the picture. "I think we need to clear a spot and lay it out. It shows how it should be laid out here. This way, when it's done, all we have to do is lift it into place."

She leaned in to look at the diagram. Mistake. Too close. Twisting her fingers together against the urge to run them through his hair, she took a few deep breaths. That did nothing but fill her with his scent. Her heart double-timed a few beats. "Sounds like a plan."

What wasn't in the plan was the way she could barely concentrate after a half hour of crawling around on the floor, watching the flex of his biceps, catching glimpses of his amazingly ripped abdomen as he reached and stretched. If there was a hell this was it: all that male muscle only inches away and not being able to touch. And she wanted to touch. And taste. She wanted to feel his hands on her skin. She wanted him.

"Earth to Sadie."

"Huh?" She dropped her gaze and pretended to fuss with the parts. He'd caught her staring at his ass. But it was impossible not to. She would have to be dead to not notice that denim-clad perfection.

"We're ready to start assembling. I'm going to need six B bolts with the D washers."

She sorted through the bags on the coffee table. She moved to sit by him and hand over the parts while he fastened them and tried not to sigh each time his fingers brushed her palm. After a while, though, the deliberately slow sweep of his fingers triggered the desire to feel those fingers move up her wrist and beyond.

The tiny tastes she'd had of him taunted her. She wanted to have her hands on him. His on her. She wanted to touch him, taste him, to feel him against her. She couldn't ignore it. "You're doing all the work," she said. Trying to distract herself from her growing hunger.

"You're doing the organization. Teamwork."

His gaze met hers. The man made her absolutely stupid. He finished the frame of the tallest section and sat back against the wall with the instruction sheet.

"What's next, boss?" she asked.

He looked at her over the top of the paper, and the screws she was sorting slipped through her fingers. She grabbed at them before they could skitter off the edge of the table.

"There seems to be a rather serious gap in the instructions."

"There always is."

"Sometimes you have to go off book and improvise."

She stopped pairing washers and bolts and looked at him. His back against the wall, legs pulled up, his forearms propped on his knees. He held the instructions. *Oh, go off book?* What if she plucked the paper from his fingers and tossed it aside? Pulled that shirt up over his head and put her hands on him? *Improvise, uh-huh.*

"…don't you think?"

"What?"

Great. You're brilliant. Dork.

They muddled through it. Where Sadie would have been cursing in frustration, Wyatt calmly went through the remaining parts and pieces and came up with how they were meant to go together. An hour later, they lifted the finished product against the wall.

"Looks good," Wyatt said.

"It's perfect." She did a little happy dance and clapped her hands. "I can't wait to get my books in it."

He hooked an arm around her shoulders. "We make a good team."

She froze for an instant. Her initial response was to jerk away. She did not like people touching her unexpectedly. She'd fought off the first person who thought foster kids were easy pickings at age seven when the brother of a foster mother came to visit. It hadn't gotten much better from there. Even the hugs and caresses of foster parents had seemed slightly sinister after that. She'd learned young that touch was fraught with peril. She'd gotten better with being touched over the years and had even been able to see that most of her foster mothers had been sincerely trying to reach her, but she had been unable to open up to them. Josh, Lena, Molly and Abuelito had become her family and she relished the warm hugs and touches from them.

But Wyatt's arm, hot against her nearly bare

shoulders wasn't uncomfortable. Wasn't unwelcome. It was a temptation she could barely resist.

"Do I make you nervous?"

She slipped away from the warm, strong arm. *Nervous? No. Unbelievably turned on? Yes.* "No."

She turned away and his fingers closed gently around her upper arm. "Then why are you running from me?"

She stopped and forced herself to meet his eyes. "I'm not running."

But she was. Running, not from his touch, but from the feelings he stirred. Warmth. Comfort. Need. She didn't know if she could control her reaction. She wanted him. Wanted to get lost in the pleasure of a man's body. *No, the pleasure of his body. Be honest. It's him you want.*

"You are."

She couldn't look away. Couldn't speak. Couldn't even breathe.

"Is it because of what happened?"

"No." *Yes.*

"Then what?"

His hands moved to her shoulders as he turned her to face him. *One step. Take one step forward, put your hands on his chest. Do it, Sadie.* She couldn't. Because he didn't make her nervous, he made her scared. Scared because it wasn't only her body, her heart wanted him, too. She had to look away from the heat in his eyes.

"Because I want it to happen again," she whispered.

The momentary tightening of his fingers on her shoulders signaled his response. His body went tense. His hand left her shoulder to skim her jaw. It settled under her chin and with gentle pressure, forced her to look back into his eyes. The heat there made her knees go more than a little wobbly. She gripped his forearms to keep steady.

"What do you want to happen again?"

He uttered the question in a husky whisper. Her gaze dipped briefly from those captivating hazel eyes to his full lips. Heat flowed through her veins. Her breath quickened as her lungs tried to keep up with the pace of her runaway heartbeat. He stepped closer and the hand under her chin slipped around to the back of her head, tangling in her curls. She could feel the heat of him inches away. Less than one tiny step and she'd be in his arms.

"Tell me, Sadie."

Why are you hesitating? He quit. He's leaving. There was no reason to say no. Do it, Sadie. Do it. End your two-year drought. Scratch this itch and move on. She had no problem moving on. She didn't need love and promises and flowers to have sex with a man. She pressed her hands lightly around his waist. His breath was coming as quickly as hers. His chest hitched with his low gasp at her touch. He wanted her as much as she wanted him. *Do it.* She slid her hands under his shirt. Up over his washboard abs and through the dusting of hair over his chest. She pressed her palm over his heart. Its frantic beat matched hers and she barely suppressed a moan. She stepped an inch closer.

"You know."

His head lowered and his lips hovered a millimeter from hers. "Say it."

"Kiss me."

He slipped a hand around her waist and pulled her against him. His lips touched hers. For one perfect, long moment, he held the tender kiss. He pulled back and his breath tickled across her lips. She moved her hands to his hair and pulled his mouth back to hers. It was perfect. Perfect. Their bodies fit together so well. Her lips parted and her tongue met his in a slow, deliberate dance. Her hands left his hair to scrape along the stubble of his jaw, to slide along the edges of his shoulders. Better. Much better than her desperate flight into oblivion with their first kiss. His hand on her back dipped beneath her shirt and skimmed white-hot up the skin of her back. Desire boiled over and she moaned against his lips, pressing her belly against his and the hardness there.

He broke the kiss, turning his head and pressing his cheek against hers.

"Sadie."

She let her fingers wander back down his chest and hooked them over the waistband of his jeans. His response vibrated through his body.

"Yes?"

"Maybe we should…"

She was done with maybe. Her hand slipped down the front of his jeans and found him. He groaned as her fingers closed around him and his mouth came back to hers.

"Protection?" she asked against his lips.

"Yes."

"Good."

WYATT TIGHTENED HIS arms around Sadie as she tried to slip from the bed. He buried his face in the curls at the nape of her neck, inhaling the scent of her shampoo, something spicy and exotic, and her skin. His heart had not slowed from its frantic pace. She'd been everything he imagined and more. He never wanted to let go. Never leave this bed.

"I'm not finished with you yet," he whispered against her neck and his body stirred at her shiver. His lips curled into a smile as he remembered the shuddering waves of her orgasms. He'd like to cause a few more of those.

Her hands closed over his. "You only had the one condom."

"A mistake of epic proportions."

She turned in his arms to face him, her hand tracing lazily up and down his chest, driving him mad. He caught the roaming hand and brought it to his lips. "Do you have any idea how beautiful you are?"

He liked the pretty pink of her cheeks. Of course she knew that. So the blush, he surmised, was because she didn't like it pointed out. Which only made the guilt dig a little bit more. He hadn't meant to end up in her bed. One kiss was all he'd hoped to take with him when he walked out of her life. But then she'd touched him and had he'd lost all reason. Now he was going to leave a large chunk of his heart here with her.

"We have to get up at some point."

"True. But now isn't that point."

It was getting late, and the sun was almost gone. Dusky shadows filled the room and obscured the dark blue of her eyes as he wished he could say what he was thinking. How much he wanted to stay with her. He wanted to make this into something. Wanted to see if they could make this last. If only it weren't for the big lie sitting there between them. If only he hadn't just made it much worse. He pulled her against him and kissed the top of her head.

"I'm going to miss you. Miss your stupid jokes in the morning meetings," he said.

"My jokes aren't stupid." Her chest rose and fell with a sigh. "I'm going to miss you, too."

He waited. There was no more. No asking or hinting if there was going to be more than this. Of course, some women wouldn't say it out loud. No, they'd stay silent, waiting on the man to make the promises in the dark. He didn't think Sadie was one of them.

"Tell me about this fabulous new job you got."

That startled him. His mind scrambled. Truth is simpler than a lie, he decided. "Fraud investigation at an insurance company. I did similar work with the police department."

She pushed back and propped up on an elbow. "Can I ask you something? It's been bothering me."

"What's that?" He kept his tone light, but guilt nestled at the base of his stomach. *This was bad. This was wrong.* He was digging a deeper hole. He should have controlled himself. Should have walked away with his conscience clear. His heart ached. He didn't want to walk away at all.

"Why didn't you go back to the police department after your service?"

His body tensed and he closed his eyes as he concentrated on relaxing his muscles. He kept his eyes closed as her fingers found his hand and laced through his.

"I'm sorry," she said. "If it's something upsetting, I didn't mean to…"

"No. It's all right."

He shifted around so he was propped up facing her, their fingers still laced. He could tell the story, and it wouldn't be a lie. He'd spent six months with Maddie and Jules, paid for counseling on his own with the back pay he'd saved and healed his guilt. The scar still ached from time to time, but the wound was healed.

"I killed a man," he said, testing out the words. "My unit provided base security. I was on duty and a car pulled up and a man jumped out. He ran up to the gate, screaming in Arabic, and I shot him. They found explosives taped to his body."

Her fingers squeezed against his. "So you also saved lives."

"That's what they said. But you want to know something?"

Her hand slipped from his. She reached up and smoothed his hair back from his forehead. "Tell me," she whispered.

"It didn't matter. I was glad no one else died. But it didn't help. I'd killed a person. And once I knew how horrible it was, I couldn't go back to a job where I might have to do it again. I'd be a danger to my fellow officers if I hesitated when I needed to take action."

"I'm sorry that happened to you."

He closed his hand over hers as his throat closed up. No one had ever said that. Everyone who knew tried to convince him it did matter. Gave him the hero line. He didn't feel like a hero. He felt as if he'd taken a life. Was it justified? Yes. Had it been for a greater good? Yes. But it didn't change how it felt. She was the first to simply let him have his own feelings about what had happened. *No. Don't fall for her, man. Don't.*

"Now you have to tell me something about yourself. A secret."

She laughed. And in the dark, it was the most beautiful sound he'd ever heard. *It was too late.* His heart had gone ahead and tumbled without his brain's permission.

"Nothing to tell. I'm a pretty boring person."

"Why does Josh call you Saff?"

And, wham! Up went the walls. He felt her entire body stiffen. She pushed away and he stopped her by pulling her into his arms.

"Running away again."

"I'm not running away. Let go of me."

He let go, giving her space. Instead of bolting off the bed, she wilted back against the pillow and stared into the darkness. "Where did you hear that?"

"That morning you were crying in the kitchen. Josh called you that."

"Damn Josh. I told him to stop."

Wyatt waited. And waited. The words were on his lips to tell her never mind when she let out a sigh. "You can tell no one."

"No one," he echoed.

She rolled up on an elbow and poked him in the chest. "I swear. No one."

"It must be good, then."

"Promise?"

He traced an X on his chest. "Cross my heart."

"I was hoping for something more like, 'may my dick fall off if I tell.'"

"Wow. You're a hard-core secret keeper."

"It's supremely embarrassing. Okay. So you have to know up front my mother had me young. Got pregnant at fifteen and had me a little after her sixteenth birthday, so she was immature and I guess profoundly stupid. My real name isn't Sadie. I sort of adopted it over the years."

"What is it?"

"If you laugh, I'll hurt you."

Wyatt pulled the pillow from behind his head and put it over his groin. "I'm ready."

Sadie laughed and traced her fingers down the center of his chest to the edge of the pillow. "Nah, you're safe there."

"You're trying to distract me. Nice technique, but unsuccessful. Tell me."

"Sapphire Diamond."

He struggled not to grin at least. "It sounds like…"

"A stripper name."

There was something in her tone. She was making fun of the name, but buried deep was an echo of pain. He remembered Noah telling them she'd grown up in foster care. Taken away from her teenage mother? He pulled her into his arms.

"I'm sorry that happened to you," he said.

She snorted out a half laugh. "Me, too."

He let his hands drift down her back to that amazingly gorgeous ass of hers. He slipped his thigh between hers and rolled her to her back. He began kissing his way along her throat.

"No condom," she whispered.

"There are other ways."

His lips found hers and he kissed her deeply, feeling himself growing hard at her touch. Yes, there were several ways he wanted to watch her lose control again. Then his cell phone rang from whatever dark spot he'd thrown his shirt. Jules. He sat up and scanned the floor. There. A glow from near the door. He rolled off the bed and scooped up the phone.

"Hey, Jules. Having fun?"

"Can I come home, Uncle Wyatt? I think I'm scared."

He looked at Sadie who was sitting up and holding a sheet against her chest. *Damn.* "I'll be there in a few minutes, baby girl."

"She's scared?" Sadie asked.

"Sorry. Yeah. She wants to come home."

"Go."

Sadie climbed from the bed, winding the sheet around her as he found and pulled on his scattered clothes. He kissed her at the door.

"I'm sorry."

She went up on tiptoe to kiss his cheek. Her fingers traced down his neck, shoulder and arm and closed around his fingers for a quick squeeze. "I'm not."

He wondered what she'd meant as he sped to pick up Jules. She wasn't sorry they'd slept together or not sorry he was leaving so suddenly? What did he think he was doing? Starting a relationship here? As much as he wanted her, he couldn't forget he'd been lying to her since the day they met. *This is what happens when you think with your dick, dude.*

Trouble was it wasn't his dick thinking. It was his heart. She'd slipped right into it. Sapphire Diamond. Maybe her mother hadn't been stupid in naming her child after two precious jewels. Because Sadie was a jewel, this he'd come to know.

The outer shell of beauty only seemed cold and hard until you looked into its depths and saw the light buried deep inside.

He was falling in love with her and he had to walk away and hope she never learned the truth about him.

CHAPTER SIXTEEN

SADIE AWOKE THE next morning and rolled to her side, staring at the pillows where Wyatt had rested his head. With the memories came flashes of heat running along her limbs and deeper. Dear God, she'd had slept with him. *Why?* Her body offered up an echo of the sensations he'd stirred as a reminder. She pulled the pillow over her face. She, who might usually eke out one climax, had gone off like a bottle rocket by the time his hand had slipped between her thighs. She recalled his husky chuckle and her cheeks burned. *"Now we have to start all over again."* And start over again they had. Two. Two solid, screaming, lose-complete-control orgasms. It had been good. Better than good. Slow and easy and perfect. They'd moved together as if made for each other. No rushing, no fumbling.

With a frustrated groan, she threw the pillow off her face. She'd cuddled! Canoodled. Spooned. And told secrets in the dark. As though he was her lover. Even worse, she'd liked it. Hadn't even known she was doing it. It just happened. She smiled as she remembered the warm feeling within his arms. A clatter of nails and heavy breathing that sent doggy breath washing over her pulled her thoughts away from the very talented Wyatt Anderson. She rolled out of bed. Jack ran happy circles around her, tripping her up at least twice on the way to the bathroom.

Twenty minutes later, she was showered, dressed and awaiting caffeination while Jack performed his duty in the backyard. The front door opened and her heart slammed up into her throat. *Shit.* Wyatt was going to be showing up soon. With the others. She didn't want to see him. Didn't want the guys to see her blushing or melting into a pile of mush. Didn't know if she could look into his eyes again without blabbing out completely embarrassing pleas for more. Her stomach clenched in an agony of embarrassment. Not for the sex, but for what had come after.

Molly strolled into the kitchen. "Morning."

Sadie whistled at Jack from the doorway and he actually obeyed immediately. "Hey. Good, you're here. I've got a ton of paperwork to do and phone calls to make. When Josh gets here, have him supervise the morning rush."

"You okay?"

"I'll be in my office, and I don't want to be disturbed. Between covering for DeShawn and being out for Abuelito's funeral, I am so behind it isn't even funny."

"You hiding from someone?"

"No."

"Why are you blushing?"

"I'm not. And I'm your boss. Stop with the fifty questions."

"I bought those jelly beans you like so much. They're in the pantry behind the beet chips so the guys won't find them. In case you need extra today."

Slamming her door was probably childish, but it helped ease her annoyance at the teasing. Jack whined and scratched at the closed door. She opened it enough for him to slip out and go play with the guys. She hadn't been lying. There were stacks of paperwork piled deep on her desk. Inventory forms. The financial papers Lena sent over and now required Sadie to at least initial as proof she knew what was happening with her accounts. And government forms. *Holy paper pushers, Batman—the government forms.* Federal, state, county and city.

She got comfortable and began with the easiest. Lena's monthly financial statements. Despite her aversion to numbers, Sadie had no problem understanding the columns of figures, the credits and debits. She looked at the bottom line. In the black. That was all she needed to know. After working through those, she rewarded herself with a little break and finished her coffee before it cooled. Remembering the kiss that had started it all last night destroyed her concentration, and her stomach fluttered. Parts farther south joined in on the flutters. She pushed back against the memories with a growing sense of unease.

She pulled the worst of the piles, the dreaded federal forms, closer and took the first off the stack. Nothing like a little governmentese to kill the sexy. But the nibble of malaise wouldn't leave her alone. She gave up halfway through the stack. She wanted to go get another cup of coffee but could hear some of the guys milling around out there. She'd rather go without coffee than run into Wyatt right now. She settled for a raid on her jelly-bean jar. She propped her feet on the opened bottom drawer and leaned back in the chair. A loud rumble of male laughter drifted through her partially open door and her heart raced as she recognized Wyatt's laugh in the mix. Warmth seeped through her, and she became a bit short of breath.

She got up and quietly shut the door. Jack, who had returned, lifted his head from his bed. "Oh, hell, Jack." She covered her face with her hands. *You're acting like a lovesick idiot.* She leaned back against the door as her feeling of anxiety became a full-fledged beast, devouring her. *You're falling in love with him.* She crossed her arms against her chest and held herself tight but it was too late. Her heart was free-falling into disaster. She did not do love. She did not do the happily-ever-after, two-point-five kids, two-car-garage thing. She didn't know how.

She straightened and strode purposefully to her desk and picked up her pen. The residue of fear still tinged her nerves and it made her angry. *Good. Anger was good.* She knew exactly how to harness its energy. Right now she was going to use it to plow through this paperwork. Use it to burn the thoughts of Wyatt Anderson out of her mind. She wiped at her stinging eyes and focused on the paper before her. *Jeez, what? What is this? IRS? OSHA? EPA? WTF?*

The distraction worked. Well enough she was startled when Jack yipped and scratched at the closed office door. A quick glance at the clock showed almost two hours had passed. *Who knew this bureaucratic stuff was the cure for...for what? Falling in love?*

"You need a potty break, Jackie Boy? I need a coffee break."

Jack pushed through the door the moment she opened it, ruining her effort to discreetly check if any of the teams were back for resupply runs. The office was silent except for the sounds of Molly clacking on her keyboard.

"I'm heading out to lunch in a minute," Molly called out as Sadie went into the kitchen. "Want me to bring you something?"

"No. I'm good. Letting Jack out."

She poured a stale cup of coffee, took a sip and dumped it in the sink. Jack was whining at the back door. "Okay, all right."

He made a beeline for the bushes and Sadie sat on the back step, enjoying the sunshine on her face. Once out of the paperwork fog, her mind went immediately back to Wyatt. She shook her head. There was nothing to be done for that. He had Jules to look after. He didn't need her messing up his life. Because that was what she did— messed up every romantic relationship she ever had. She would push and test and push until the man finally had enough.

Jack came back and she ruffled her hands through his fur. "Why, Jack? Why do I do this?"

Jack didn't answer, but she didn't need him to. She knew why. Trust issues. Abandonment issues. Blah, blah, blah. She could list everything every counselor, shrink or social worker had ever said to her. The real question was not why, but how. How to stop doing these things.

Immediately, the letter hidden in her desk drawer came to mind. She covered her face with her hands. Lito's voice echoed. *Promise me.* And she had. She'd promised him she would give her brother a chance. Give her blood family a chance. As usual, he was right. If she wanted a future with Wyatt, she was going to have to face her past.

Before she lost her nerve and talked herself out of it, she herded Jack back to the office and locked the door behind them. Her heart was pounding, and she felt slightly dizzy as she spread the letter out on the desktop. Now was the time. No one was in the office to disturb her. *Now, before you chicken out!*

He had a nice voice. Young and upbeat. Hers, on the other hand, was tremulous. "Is this Grant Rogers?"

"Yes, it is."

"This is Sadie Martin." A long moment spun out in silence. "I got your letter."

"Oh! Uh…okay…hi."

"Hi."

Another silent moment played out.

"Well," Grant said. "This is only slightly more awkward than I imagined."

Sadie laughed. "Yeah. I didn't really plan what to say after 'I got your letter.'"

"And I never thought of what I'd say if you called."

"Wh…why do you think I'm your sister?"

"Like I said in the letter, I don't want anything

from you. I just need to know. I've wondered about this most of my life."

"Wondered about what?"

"You. Or the possibility of you. It started when my mother was pregnant with my youngest sister. I was ten. I remember going with Mom to a doctor's appointment. I can't remember it all, but a nurse was, like, confirming the history or something. And she said 'so you've had three full-term babies.' And my mom said yes and it confused me because there was only me and Emmie at the time. When I asked her about it, she said I didn't hear right. But I knew I had."

"She wasn't talking about the baby your mother was pregnant with?"

"No. She told me a few months ago. She told me the truth. I was moving out. I graduated from Wofford in December. I got that job in Raleigh and I was home packing when I found stuff in the attic. The baby pictures. *Sapphire Diamond* written on the back. And an envelope with papers from the Department of Social Services. I showed them to her."

"What did she say?" Sadie asked through numb lips.

"She told me she'd gotten pregnant when she was very young. And she'd given the baby up for adoption."

Her head bobbed in a nod. "Yeah."

Wow. Even now, her mother was lying. The story skimmed over the ugly details and compressed the timeline to make her appear noble but it was essentially the truth. But she remembered almost everything. She'd been too young to remember being taken away, but there had been an entire childhood of being dressed up and taken to the social services office where there was a small room with a little table and chairs. Books and games. There she would sit with her mother and listen to her say how as soon as she got a place to stay, as soon as she got a job, as soon as she got everything together, Sadie would come home to live with her. She'd have a pretty pink room and a bike and a kitten.

Every month. Until she was five. Then it was maybe every other month. By age six, it was her birthday and Christmas. By age seven, she'd stopped coming. By age eight, Sadie had known it was all a lie. When Sadie had turned eighteen, her social worker told her some things. Her mother had never been able to stay sober long enough to get her back. She had been turned away on visiting days for showing up reeling drunk or high. She finally signed the papers terminating her parental rights when Sadie was eight. She could then be adopted. Except no one wanted her. No kid over four had a chance of a real home. Later, Sadie learned that two months after the papers were signed, her mother had gotten married. Five months later, Grant was born.

She simultaneously hated him and envied him. He'd had it all. House, parents, school, sisters, Little League. *Bet* he *had a stupid bike.* If only she could stop trembling. If only she could calm her arms and legs. She felt untethered from reality. Floating over her body. A warm weight touched her thigh. Jack had put his head there. Tears stung at her eyes. Jack loved her. Her dog cared about her. Unlike her mother.

"Was she a good mother? Did you have a good childhood?"

"I guess. They both, mom and dad, had had problems with drugs and alcohol in the past. Hell, they met in rehab. Dad had one short relapse when I was a baby, but that's it. They've been good parents."

Her throat hurt. Ached. She rubbed at her burning eyes. It was too much. Baby at sixteen. Overcoming addiction. Making a new start in life. All very difficult things to do. Sadness washed over her, pressing down on her, forcing a little of the anger away. She drew in a slow, wavering breath.

"Yes, I'm your sister."

He huffed out a sound of relief. "Okay. Whew. I was scared to death I'd made a mistake. Mom's been talking about you since I found out. Wondering about you. I think she'd like to see you."

"No. And I'm not mad at you, but I don't want our mother to know you've found me or talked to me. I have no interest in having any type of relationship with her."

"I understand. I was just throwing it out there. But we can talk?"

"Yeah, sure. I mean, it's a lot for me right now, talking to you. I'd like to meet in person. But I'm not ready to even think about meeting her."

"Why weren't you adopted?"

Because she waited too long. She held on and told me lies and made promises she never kept until it was too late and I was too old and no one wanted me. She swallowed it down. Whatever her mother had done to her, she'd obviously tried to make up for it by being a good mother to him and his sisters. Hurting Grant wouldn't ease her pain any.

"I don't know."

They made plans to talk again over the weekend and said goodbye. Sadie crossed her arms on the desktop and lowered her head to them. She was still shaking, but there was also a strange brew of relief and giddiness coursing through her. The door opened at the same time there was a sharp rap.

"Hey, Sadie," Josh said. He paused. "You okay?"

She sat up. "I don't know."

"What's wrong?"

"Nothing, I think." She took a deep breath as she stood and walked to him. "I talked to Grant."

He stared at her. "Your half brother?"

"Yeah. He found me. Sent me a letter. I just talked to him."

Josh's eyes went cold and his entire body stiffened. "He found you?"

Sadie lifted a hand to her mouth. "Josh, I'm sorry. I didn't think…" She reached out for him, but he took a half step back.

"He wrote you? When?"

She shook her head, "A week or so ago. I don't remember."

"And you didn't tell me about it?"

Josh, whose decade-long search for his baby sister was still no further now than on day one, took another step back. She could see the pain in his eyes as he turned and left the office. She followed.

"Josh!"

"Not now, Sadie."

THERE WAS SOMETHING going on. Wyatt noticed the tension in the air the instant he and Noah walked through the back door at the end of the day. Josh sat at the conference room table. Doing nothing. Wyatt couldn't read the expression on his face. Either he wanted to kill someone or someone had killed his dog.

"Dude," Noah said. "We're done. Nothing to report."

"All right." Josh went back to staring a hole in the tabletop.

Wyatt looked at Noah. Noah shrugged. "Hey," Noah said to Wyatt. "I'm out of here. See you tomorrow."

Wyatt bumped Noah's offered fist. "What's up?" he asked Josh.

"Nothing."

Wyatt stared for a moment. *Whatever.* He was out of here in two days. He went to his truck and got the formal resignation letter he'd written up for Sadie. She hadn't asked for it, but he was going to do this as if he'd really been an employee. He turned the envelope around his fingers. For what seemed the millionth time, he tried to find a solution to this mess. He was falling in love with her. He dared to think she might care for him also. Last night had about blown his mind. Her body. Her response. He grew firm at the memory. *And that's all it's ever going to be, man—a memory. You made it even worse. If you hadn't slept with her, you might have had a chance to come clean and explain. But you slept with her under false pretenses; no matter how real your feelings were, it's unforgivable.*

He slapped the envelope against his palm. *Get it over with. Walk away. Live with the regret.*

"I thought you guys were done for the day," Molly said as he went back in through the front door to avoid Josh.

Even she looked stressed out. Her fingers played at the pendant hanging from the chain around her neck. He realized Jack hadn't come out to greet them as he did whenever someone came in. There was a tense, gloomy mood hanging over the entire office. He held up the envelope.

"I have something for Sadie."

Molly frowned and her hand clenched at the pendant. "Ah. I can take that for you."

So whatever was going on involved Sadie. He hoped it wasn't about last night. She'd seemed fine when he left. But then, she hadn't been anywhere in sight this morning. A knot grew in his stomach. "I need to give this to her in person. She's expecting it." Not quite the truth, but not quite a lie.

Molly appraised him before drawing in a long deep breath and letting it out in a rush. "Fine. Enter at your own risk."

He wondered what she'd meant until his light tap on Sadie's door was answered with an extremely surly "What?"

He cracked the door open and peeked in. "Got a minute?"

She threw the pen in her hand down and rubbed at her face. "Sorry. Come on in."

"Are you okay?"

Slumped back in the chair, she looked exhausted. "Crazy day."

He perched on the side of the desk. He wanted to pull her into his arms and hold her for a while. "Anything I can do?"

"No."

He lifted his eyebrows.

"But thanks."

"It must have been industrial-strength crazy."

"I'm sorry. It was. What can I do for you?"

Tell me why you are completely ignoring the fact we had some of the world's most amazing sex last night? He'd like to start there. She was either very good at compartmentalizing or whatever had happened today had made her amnesic.

"It's not anything to do with last night, is it?"

Her eyes met his and there was a flare of heat before the walls went back up. "No, not at all."

He set the envelope down on the desk. "Letter of resignation. To keep it formal."

She seemed to sag even lower in the chair. One hand came up to touch the edge of the envelope. "Oh."

"I'm sorry about the short notice."

"It's okay."

He covered her hand with his. "Can we talk about last night?"

Her guarded expression should have warned him to shut up. But he had to say something. He practically ran out on her last night.

"I'm sorry I had to leave like I did. I wish we could have spent more time."

She pulled her hand out from beneath his. "It's fine. It was great. Thanks. But it was sex. Thanks for the nice-guy effort, but I'm fine. I don't have any expectations. We both knew that last night."

Words that would make almost any guy happy. Would even have made him happy on a number of occasions in his life. Now they stung. Because he cared about her. A lot. And unless he told her everything, there was nothing more he could say. She was upset. Something bad had happened. Now was not the time to tell her about his lies.

"I'm not playing at something here. I wanted you to know that I feel bad about leaving so abruptly."

"Don't."

"Don't what?"

"Don't feel bad. Don't worry about me. Don't do anything. I'm not who you think I am. I'm a messed-up-in-the-head loser..."

She broke off and looked away. Rock-hard lines of anger made her body stiff, but her throat worked as if swallowing down tears.

"You aren't a loser. What happened today?"

She jumped to her feet and crossed the room to open the door. "Thanks for the formal letter. Good luck with your new job."

He followed and stopped at the door. Torn. He hated seeing her like this. Hated hearing the pain in her voice. Hated knowing that if she found out the truth, it would only add to her pain.

"Sadie."

She wouldn't meet his eyes. "Just go."

"Can't we talk? Maybe I can help."

"You can't."

"You don't know that. You never let anyone try. Let me try, Sadie."

Her jaw clenched and she shook her head. He could see tears forming in her eyes and reached for her hand. "Talk to me."

She jerked her hand away. "Stop it. Go. Please."

He wanted to pull her into his arms and hold her until the walls she put up crumbled. But he didn't have a clue what to say now. What to do. So he left. The door shut loudly behind him. Not quite a slam. When he reached the front door, Molly called his name. He stopped but didn't turn around.

"The closer you get to her heart, the harder

she's going to push you away. If you want it, don't quit now."

"I don't deserve her heart."

HE SAT IN his truck wondering what had happened. He should feel better. She'd all but pushed him out the door. It solved his dilemma about how to move forward with a relationship. She didn't want one. The end. Still, it left a hollow feeling in his gut. He pulled out his phone.

"Hey, Charlie. It's Wyatt. Can I talk to Jules?" He smiled at the little-girl giggling he heard as Jules came to the phone. "How're you doing there?"

"We're bowling. Can we get a Wii?"

"Honey, I don't know what a Wii is."

"It's something I need. For my education."

"Uh-huh. Good try. I've got one errand to run. I'll pick you up when I'm done. What do you want for dinner?"

"Spaghetti and meatballs."

"Got it. See you in about an hour. Love you, kiddo."

She didn't say she loved him back. She hadn't yet. Instead, he was given smacking kissy noises.

One last meeting with Marcus Canard, two more days keeping up appearances at the Crew, and it would be over. He pulled open the door and strode straight to Canard's office, bypassing the receptionist. He was expected. Canard was on the phone. Wyatt sat and stared. When Canard hung up, he put the file on desk. "I gave you more than the extra time I promised. There is nothing illegal going on at the Cleaning Crew."

He stood to leave.

"Well, son, I sure appreciate that."

He turned to see Marcus leafing through the report. His piggy little eyes met Wyatt's. "Sit down. I have some questions."

Wyatt remained standing. "I have no answers."

"There's nothing in here about operations, training, services."

"I told you before I don't do industrial espionage. You hired me to find evidence of illegal activity. I found none. The end."

"I need something for the money I've spent on this."

"Your money. Your problem."

Walking out was so satisfying, he wished he'd done it a week earlier. As he drove home, he left a message with Henry Moody.

"It's Wyatt Anderson. If the job offer still stands, I'd be open to hearing the details. Give me a call."

He drove home feeling lighter and freer than he had in weeks. Until he thought of Sadie. *No way to fix that. Let it go.*

"S-l-e-e-p."

"Very good."

Wyatt stirred the spaghetti sauce and checked the spelling list. "Dream."

"D-r-e-a-m."

"Blanket."

"B-l-a-n-k-e-t."

"Perfect, Jules. You're going to ace the test tomorrow. Now finish your math while I get the pasta going."

He watched her dark head bend over the paper as she worked through the problems. Amazing how much his life had changed. Six months ago, he was a single man who had no idea what to do with a child. Engaged. Now his fiancée had jumped ship and he was playing single father. And loving it. He had a family. Teeny tiny as it was, he and Jules were family.

"Uncle Wyatt?"

"You done?"

"Yes. Will we go to the dinner at Ms. Sadie's house again? It was fun."

He sat down next to her and covered her hand with his. "No. I'm only going to be there for a few more days, then I'll start a new job. The dinners are only for people who work there."

Her little head tilted down and about broke his heart. He'd done this. He'd let her get attached. He'd do better in the future. He brushed his palm against her dark hair. "Let's see that homework." He skimmed through it. "Perfect. You're a genius. A pure genius."

"If we see Ms. Sadie and Jack in the park, can I still play with him?"

"Of course you can."

He got up to stir the pasta. He was going to have to be much more careful.

THE PHONE WOKE him from the doze he hadn't known he'd slipped into. The book he'd been reading had fallen to his chest and slipped to the floor as he reached for the phone. He scrubbed a hand across his face.

"This is Wyatt."

"Hey. It's not too late to call, is it?"

Sadie. He swung his legs over the edge of the couch and sat up. Her voice was soft, hesitant and made him long to pull her into his arms. "No. Are you okay?"

She breathed into the phone for a moment. "Yes. I called to apologize about today."

"Accepted. Obviously something happened to upset you. Is it anything I can help with?"

"Not really."

She sounded as exhausted as she'd looked that afternoon. He leaned back and put his feet up on the coffee table. The silence stretched out.

"Last night was fantastic," she said low and whispery.

"That's a fact."

"I wish we'd met under different circumstances. I'm…I'm struggling with some stuff here. I don't think I'm in a good place."

He let his head fall back against the couch back and rubbed at his chest. He wished they'd met under different circumstances also. Like ones where his entire presence in her life wasn't based on a lie. He closed his eyes. Which was a mistake because with her breath whispering in his ear, his mind offered up the memory of her in his arms.

"I understand. I wish that, too."

"So, we're good? Apology accepted?"

"Apology accepted, but we're not good. I have a few things I want to say to you."

"Oh?"

"Yes. Number one. You are not a loser. I know I don't know everything, but I've heard enough. You had a crappy childhood. Raised in foster care, out on the street at eighteen. Maybe statistically you should have ended up a loser, but you didn't. You built a successful business."

"That's different."

"How's it different? Tell me."

"I wasn't talking about my business when I said I was a loser."

"Then what?"

"Me. *Me.* I'm a loser. I don't know how to care for people."

He couldn't stop the burst of incredulous laughter. "You? All you do is care for people. Josh. You took him in off the street, right? Gave him a job. Gave him a life. Your guys love you because you care about them. I've heard them talking. You paid for one of them to fly home for his aunt's funeral. You care for them."

"That's still different."

"What are you talking about then? Who don't you know how to care for?"

She didn't answer and he heard a muffled sniffle.

"What happened today?"

"My past came back to haunt me. I'm sorry. I didn't call to cry on your shoulder. I'll let you go now."

"Wait. I have one more thing to say to you. About the way you came through for Jules and the curler thing. You went out of your way to keep a small promise. It says a lot about how much you care for others."

"After I forgot about it."

"I forgot, too."

She didn't respond. He thought he'd made her mad. Which he didn't really mind. He liked a sassy Sadie better. "She asked if she could still play with Jack if we saw you in the park."

"Is that what you want? To be friends?"

"I think you and Jules can be friends."

"But we can't?"

"I don't think I can be just friends with you."

"Friends with benefits?"

There was a definite increase in the snark level. It made him smile. "No, I think I'd want more."

He waited. Molly had warned him. The closer he got to her heart, the more she'd push away. He needed her to push away. He was playing a dangerous game here. His logic knew he should walk away before she knew he'd lied to her. His heart didn't want to let her go.

"I don't know if I have it in me."

He pressed his lips together to stop himself from continuing to try drawing her out. *Walk away while you're ahead.* "Wrong place, wrong time."

"Tell Jules I hope I'll see her at the park."

Wyatt held the phone to his ear long after she'd ended the call. A crazy idea was circling his mind. *Tell her. Sit down and tell her everything. Beg for forgiveness.* She liked direct. She respected honest. He put the phone down and got up. He made his rounds. Checked the locks. Checked the lights. Stopped to watch Jules sleeping in her bed. Then he went to stare at his ceiling.

CHAPTER SEVENTEEN

SHE HADN'T BEEN avoiding him. Not really. Maybe a little. She'd been around the morning after her phone call, seeing the guys off and making sure the day started smoothly. Wyatt had been there briefly. The heat in his gaze knocked her a bit off-kilter. He'd broken the eye contact, but as he left he'd given her shoulder a little squeeze.

This morning, she was pretending she wasn't hiding in her office, letting Josh handle the morning rush. It was Wyatt's last day. She couldn't face him. She was having crazy thoughts. Like why does it have to end? Why can't they try? Truthfully, why couldn't she try? And therein lay the problem. It was her. She knew herself well enough to recognize the urge to run from anything that made her feel vulnerable. Talking to Grant had amped her flight response to critical levels. Since she couldn't lash out at him, she'd taken it out on the closest target. Wyatt.

She sighed and rubbed at her face. *Concentrate.* Wyatt's quitting left a hole in her teams. Aaron needed an experienced partner but she couldn't put him with Noah. Those two were too close. Fraternity brothers. That was asking for trouble. She sighed again and shifted through the papers. DeShawn was coming back on Monday. She could put Aaron with him for a while. But maybe he'd need a break from having a new guy. And it still left Noah without a partner....

She pushed the papers away and reached down to grab the jelly-bean jar. She swung her feet up on the desk and sifted through them. *Cinnamon and vanilla cream. Yuck. Strawberry and vanilla cream. Better.* Why couldn't she concentrate? A memory of Wyatt's face above her filled her vision. Her hands on his jaw, stubble rough beneath her fingertips. Watching the lines of pleasure etched on his features. She sighed. Those thoughts were not helping.

She swung her legs down and paced around the room, Jack alert to her every move. In case she started dropping doggy treats or something. *You're in love.* She stopped in her tracks.

No.

Yes, you are.

No. Her heart pounded against her ribs and she wiped her suddenly clammy palms against her hips. She didn't do the love thing. But that's what it was. She didn't want to let him go. Didn't want to let him walk away.

She returned to the desk and the papers stacked there. *Tell him. Oh, that's not gonna happen.*

Why not? She set the papers in order. Put the jelly beans away. Wiped up the slosh from her cup of coffee. Lined up her pens. *Doesn't matter. He's leaving.* She straightened from her slump.

He's not an employee anymore. Tell him. Tell him you want to…to what? What do you want to do? Her hormones sent out a surge. *Besides that! Date?*

Didn't matter. She'd never be able to do it. The very idea made her nauseous with the stress of it. What if he said no? What if he said she was crazy? She'd certainly given him enough evidence of that over the past few days. Unbalanced. Unfit to be around Jules.

"Why are you torturing yourself with this?"

Jack lifted his head and gave her the one-ear-up head tilt that never failed to make her smile. Even today.

"Your owner is crazy, Jack. Do you know that?"

He put his muzzle on his front paws and did the doggie eyebrow thing. Goofball. She put her forehead down on the desk. *Damn. You are in love with him. Only question left now is what are you going to do about it? Two options. Tell him, or let him walk away.* She pulled the pile of paper closer. She had an exit interview scheduled with him for whenever he and Noah finished up for the day. She and Molly would go over paperwork, make sure everything was in order. Her stomach jiggled around in her gut at the thought, but a goofy grin kept appearing on her lips while she made her way through the never-ending forms on the desk. Maybe she'd work up the nerve to say something by then.

She managed to get her seesaw emotions under control and finish off most of the paperwork mountain. Until Molly tapped on her door. "We're set up and ready in the conference room."

Her heart rate immediately jumped a few notches but this morning's giddy swirl of emotions was replaced by a towering fear. No way. There was no way she could do this. No way she could confess her feelings. She followed Molly down the hall to where Wyatt was waiting at the table. She hesitated at the door. He was staring down at his hands with a troubled look on his face.

"Wyatt?"

He looked up and smiled but the smile quickly fell away. Sadie and Molly sat across from him. He smiled again but there was something in his eyes. Some emotion Sadie couldn't quite identify.

"What's wrong?"

"Nothing," he said.

"Jules?"

"She's fine."

Sadie sat back and studied him as Molly went through the paperwork. He was nervous, she finally realized. She'd never seen him like this before. His eyes kept meeting hers and sliding away. He nodded and signed where Molly pointed without comment. A dim bit of hope began to grow. Maybe he wanted to say the same things to her that she wanted to say to him. Maybe he didn't want this to be over, either.

"That's all." Molly announced as she gathered the papers. "We're sorry to see you leaving so soon but hope the best for you in your new job."

"Thank you," Wyatt replied, his eyes on Sadie.

Molly glanced back and forth between the two of them. "Well, then. I'll leave you two to…talk."

When the door shut, Sadie leaned forward on the table. "Want to tell me what's really wrong now?"

He sat back and scrubbed a hand across his jaw. "No. But I will."

That didn't sound as if he was about to ask her out for dinner and movie. The trickle of fear came back.

He reached out and covered her hands with his, his eyes intense on hers. "Know this, Sadie. I didn't plan for any of this. I feel terrible about it. About sleeping with you. I do care about you. But I have to tell you the whole truth."

Fear became foreboding at the urgency of his words. He pulled a business card from his shirt pocket and held it between his fingers. "I was just going to walk away. Hope you never found out, but I can't. I don't want to walk away, but I can't ask to be a part of your life if you don't know everything."

Every part of her was numb. Except her heart. It was kicking in her chest like a rabbit seeking escape from a trap. His words made no sense. She shook her head. "What are you talking about?"

He put the card down and slid it to her. "I'm a private investigator. Marcus Canard hired me to find out if you were doing anything illegal here."

She looked down at the card. Thomas W. Anderson, Private Investigator. Specializing in insurance fraud. She stared at it for a long time, unable to move. Maybe she could stay here floating in this bubble of shock for a while. It was nice in here. It didn't hurt yet.

She'd always thought something wasn't right. She'd wondered often why someone like him was doing a job like this. There was her answer. He was a fake. A liar. He'd lied to her about everything. Spying on her. On her crew!

"Sadie?"

A bubble of rage began to float up through her gut. She could see his lips moving but she could hear nothing but the pounding of her heart. Felt only the urge to hurt him like she'd been hurt. She pushed back from the table and stood. "You lied to me."

He stood also and lifted his hands. "I'm sorry. I…"

She grabbed a bottle of water, wanting nothing more than to throw it at his lying face. Instead, she hurled it against the wall. "You lying bastard. Get out."

"Hey!" someone yelled from the hall.

The door opened and Josh grabbed her arm. "Stop it."

She twisted viciously out of his grasp. Any sense lost. The urge to strike back was overwhelming. He'd spied on her crew. Lied to them. They'd welcomed him and he'd lied to them. The fury boiled over. He made no move to defend himself.

"You don't get to quit! You're fired. Get off my property right now."

He raised his hands. "Sadie, let me explain."

The sight of her company shirt on him sparked her fury higher. She grabbed a fistful of his shirt and twisted hard enough to pull him off balance. "Get this off. Take it off and get out before I call the police."

She was yelling—she knew this. She could feel the rasp of it in her throat and hear the echoes of it. Saw the stunned faces of the guys in her peripheral vision as they rushed to the room, but she couldn't stop. The idea of him and Marcus Canard working together enraged her. Laughing at her. Laughing at her stupidity. Strong arms came from behind her, enclosing her.

"Let go of him." Josh's voice was calm and commanding in her ear. His cheek pressed to hers broke the fury and she slumped back in his arms.

"What is going on in here?" Molly demanded from the door.

Josh pulled back on Sadie, and she let him. When he had her out of attack distance, he let go but kept one hand firmly on her upper arm. The guilt on Wyatt's face stirred the embers of her anger.

"You guys get out of here," Josh ordered. "Go home. Wyatt, you stay with us."

"No! He leaves. Right now."

Josh didn't answer. He shut the door on Molly. When the three of them were behind the closed door, against which everybody else probably had ears pressed, Josh let go of her with a push.

"Tell me what's going on."

"I can explain," Wyatt said.

"Explain what? You're a spy." Sadie took a

step forward but Josh put out an arm to block her. She turned to Josh and pointed at Wyatt. "He's a private investigator. Hired by Marcus Canard to spy on us."

"Is this true?" Josh asked Wyatt.

"Yes."

Sadie leaned back on the edge of the desk, her legs suddenly unable to support her. Her stomach contracted painfully as if she'd been punched. She stared at Wyatt. *How? How had he so completely fooled her?* When he turned to her, she looked away. Her throat hurt. Her head hurt. Her heart. Her poor heart hurt.

"What did you tell him?"

Josh's tone only seemed calm. While the effect was soothing, Sadie knew Josh didn't yell when angry. The quieter he got, the more dangerous his anger was. As much as she'd like to slap Wyatt upside the face, she didn't want Josh to beat him up.

"Only what he hired me to find out."

"Which was?"

Wyatt brought a hand up to rub at his chest. He took a step toward Sadie but stopped at her glare. He held out both hands. "I'm sorry."

"Doesn't matter. You lied."

"What did you tell him?"

They both turned back to Josh. Wyatt let out a breath and ran a hand through his hair. "It doesn't really matter. He told me he thought there was something illegal going on. Like some sort of male prostitution ring. But it was just him being vindictive, looking for revenge."

"What did you tell him?" Josh asked. His tone had lost some of its deadly quiet.

"He wanted more information. How you operate, how you train, client information. I told him I didn't do industrial espionage. He didn't like my answer. So I walked out."

Sadie crossed her arms. She fixed her gaze on the window and tried to focus on the traffic whizzing past. He needed to go away. Her heart was about to break. The only thing that could make this worse was if he saw her cry. She remembered her giddy anticipation of that morning and shame burned through her. *I'm a complete fool.*

Josh put his hands in the air. "Go. Get out."

"Sadie," Wyatt said. "I never lied to you about anything but why I was here."

A harsh bark of a laugh tore from her throat.

After he left, an insane urge to call him back tore through her. *How could you?* she wanted to ask. *How could you make love to me? How could you lie to me? How could you?* But the real question was how could *she*? How could she have believed any of this—love, happiness—was real?

She covered her face. When Josh's hand came down warm on her back, she twisted away from it.

"You go, too. I don't want to talk to anyone."

"Are you okay?"

"No, Josh. I'm not okay. Not one little bit okay. Go away."

SADIE SAT WITH her back against the arm of the couch later that evening. In her lap was a bowl of jelly beans. In her hand was an industrial-size glass of white wine. Because jelly beans and red wine were a bad combination. She chose a flavor. Chewed slowly. Stared at the still-empty bookshelf. Rage and loss washed over her. Half of her wanted to rip it apart with her bare hands. The other half wanted to crawl back into bed and cry.

The bed was currently unmade because once she'd convinced Molly and Josh she wasn't going to kill Wyatt Anderson, she'd come upstairs to hide and lick her wounds. She'd fallen face-first into her bed. And smelled him. In that long moment, with the scent of his skin filling her senses, her heart had broken. She'd cried long enough to get angry at herself. So the only logical course of action was to manically rip every bit of bedding from the mattress and burn it in a sacrificial fire in the backyard. She'd opted for the washing machine instead. Because what a great headline that would have been.

She chose another flavor. With the light white wines such as the vinho verde she was currently drinking, the fruit flavors were the best. The toffee and cream flavors were better with a smooth buttery chardonnay. Then she stared at the bookshelf. She should get rid of it. Every time she looked at it, it would remind her. She thought back over the evening for about the thousandth time and still came up blank. Not one clue, not one hint, not one thing had stood out or raised any alarms. Even in hindsight. He'd been good, to completely slip through her defenses.

Her phone vibrated on the coffee table and she glared at it. If it were Molly or Josh calling to check on her again, she was going to beat the phone to death with a hammer. It was Lena. She stretched for it, sloshing wine down her arm. It was a little after eight and Lena was supposed to be out on a date with a new guy.

"You okay?"

"I'm at your back door."

"I thought you were on a date."

A rapid-fire burst of Spanish filled Sadie's ear. Too fast for her to catch any of it except the *pronto* at the end. She moved the bowl and rolled to her feet.

"Come on, Jack. Pee time."

She made her way down the stairs a little unsteadily. Sheesh, how much wine had she drunk?

Maybe a food group other than jelly beans was in order. Jack pushed past Lena as she opened the door.

"What's the matter?" Sadie asked.

"Nothing's the matter. Not with me." Lena lifted the bags in her hands. "I've brought sustenance and sisterhood."

"Who told you?"

"Molly at first. I ignored her. You know how sappy and sentimental she gets. Everything is a drama. But when Josh called, I knew it was serious."

"I don't need you guys talking about me behind my back. I'm fine."

"Oh, please. Get your dog. I'm going upstairs."

Sadie whistled for Jack, but he was too busy inspecting the perimeter of his territory to come right away. She leaned against the doorjamb and watched him. The last of the light hadn't been gone for long and the air held an unusual hint of coolness as if spring was reluctant to give way to summer. The night symphony of crickets was beginning to stir. Soon enough it would be sticky hot even in the darkest of the night. She looked up at the sky. *Star light, star bright, first star I see tonight. I wish I may, I wish I might. What would you wish for if wishes were real?* She clapped her hands to tell Jack she wasn't kidding. She would wish she had never let herself believe any of this love shit was real. That's what.

Upstairs, Jack made a beeline for the coffee table where Lena had set out an assortment of take-out boxes. Sadie's own nose identified Thai food and her stomach grumbled. Lena walked in from the hall. She had changed into yoga pants and a T-shirt and her hands swept her heavy dark hair up into a ponytail.

"What's all this?" Sadie asked.

"Jelly beans, sushi, pad thai and cinnamon whiskey."

"Sounds like a *Chopped* basket."

Lena flopped on the couch and reached for the whiskey. "Appetizer, entrée or dessert?" she asked. She twisted the bottle open and poured two healthy shots.

Sadie sat beside her and took the offered shot glass. "Dessert."

They clinked glasses and downed the shots.

"Hoo-whee!" Lena cried and shook her head.

Sadie enjoyed the burn of the whiskey down her throat. Happy to have a physical reason for the pain lodged there. She slipped off the couch to sit on the floor and began to open packages.

"Salmon avocado rolls. You remembered!"

"You are a boring stick in the mud." Lena sat beside her and gave her a sisterly bump as they made their way through the sushi.

"What happened to your date? The mythical living-room beta and bedroom alpha?" Sadie asked after she'd put away three pieces of sushi and life began to return to her poor protein-starved body.

"He's a loser. Thought he'd alpha me into bed before we even went out on our first date. He'll never make the same mistake again with any other female on the planet, I can guarantee you that."

Sadie spooned half the pad Thai into a bowl and leaned back against the couch. "Josh told you?"

"I'm sorry, honey. I know he hurt you."

The lump was back. She pushed it down with a swallow of noodles.

"I can't believe he lied to me. I can't believe that scumbag Canard. Telling Wyatt I was some sort of backward madam."

"Seriously! What ridiculous sexism. Men can't clean so they must be providing sex? Or women wouldn't hire men to clean, but would for sex? Or a woman couldn't soundly beat out a business competitor unless she's using sex? He's such a stupid pig."

Sadie poured another round of shots. "To Marcus. May he get boils on his ass!"

They clinked and swallowed. Sadie put the bowl of noodles down and eyed the giant bag of jelly beans Lena had brought. She'd been eating her own stash. Perfectly good. But these were fresher. Yum.

"No jelly beans until you've had real food."

"I had real food."

Lena reached for the remote and flicked on the television. "Food. *Chopped*. And then dessert."

After they'd finished off the takeout and cleaned up the mess, and after Lena had won the make-up-a-*Chopped*-basket contest with catnip, octopus tentacles and Cheerios for the appetizer round, they stood facing the bookshelf.

"Looks good."

Sadie sat on the arm of the couch. "He helped me."

"He who? Oh, him?"

Sadie hugged herself. The wave of sadness and regret washing over her left her breathless. Lena's hand, warm and tender, rubbed across her shoulders.

"Yeah," she said in a whisper. "He came over to tell me he was going to resign, and I had it spread out in here and he stayed and helped me put it together."

"Well. Seems like a nice thing to do."

Sadie snorted out a laugh. "I want to smash it to splinters."

"That's extreme. It's a gorgeous piece. Fits

perfectly. It's going to look awesome once you fill it with books and knickknacks. Pictures."

"I slept with him."

The hand on her back froze. "What?"

She fell over backward onto the couch, legs dangling over the arm, and covered her face. "I don't know what happened. We were putting it together, and...that smile. And those eyes. That body. I couldn't stop."

Lena pried her hands from her eyes to stare down at her. "You what?"

"I slept with him."

She let herself go limp and stared up at the ceiling. *There.* She'd said it out loud to another human being. She was so stupid. Had slept with the enemy and hadn't even known it. Like the simpering idiot who's the first to die in a horror movie, she'd been oblivious to any warning signs and gone down into the basement alone. Tears rolled down into her ears. The pain in her heart was back.

"Was it good, at least?"

"Freaking amazing. Best ever."

"Up."

Lena tugged on her hand and she swung into a sitting position, but in the form of a ball in the corner of the couch. A shot glass full of whiskey appeared before her eyes. She took it.

"Truth time."

She brought the glass to her lips and held it there. Truth time was serious stuff. To drink on it would commit her to telling things she might not want to tell. Stuff maybe she should tell her best friend. She downed the shot. It was her third. On top of the wine, Lena really hadn't had to invoke the oath of truth telling. She was probably drunk enough to spill her guts to Marcus himself by now.

"What happened?"

She opened her mouth to say she didn't know. But she did. She knew. She told Lena everything. Jules's curls. The almost kiss. The first kiss. The absolute loss of any sort of sense she had in his presence. If only she could say it was just that she wanted his body. Because then she could dismiss the sex as meaningless. Then the betrayal wouldn't sting quite as sharply. A drunken sob tore at her throat. Lena pulled her into a hug and held on while she cried.

"I can't," she said, pushing away and standing up. "I can't sit around and weep over this. I'm not wasting my time on him. Not even going to feel bad about it. He's the one who lied. He's the bad guy here. He's the one who should be crying."

Brilliant! He needed to be told. "Where's my phone? I've got a few things to say to Mr. Private Investig... Investi-liar Man."

"Time out. Enough is enough." Lena snatched

Sadie's phone from the table and stuffed it in her bra. "Friends don't let friends dial drunk."

"I'm not drunk! How dare he act like he cares about me and make me think..."

She stopped and rubbed at the center of her chest. The ache was back. There was the tipping point of this entire mess. She didn't think he'd pretended to care about her. Not unless he was the most skilled actor on the planet. But she couldn't reconcile those feelings with the lie.

"Made you think what, honey?"

She didn't answer. She dropped to the couch and pulled open the bag of jelly beans. Sweet jelly beans. Tiny little jewels of sugary goodness. She jiggled the pack and wondered what flavor pairing would work best with the whiskey.

"Did you fall in love with him, Sadie?"

The softly spoken words cut through her. Her lips quivered and she pressed them together to hide the emotion. She'd promised truth.

"I was trying not to. I'd told him I didn't think I was cut out for the whole relationship thing, but I was going to talk to him. See if maybe we could try. If we took it slow."

She ate more jelly beans. Complete humiliation burned through her like the whiskey. "And the whole time he was lying. I feel like such a complete fool."

"You haven't made a bigger fool of yourself

than any other woman has done at some point in her life, Sades. We all have. The smart ones only once. Most of us do it a few times."

"Well, I'm not doing it again."

Sadie curled up in the corner of the couch again. "There's something else."

"You're pregnant!"

"Of course not! Go wash your mouth out with Lysol! What a horrible thing to say!"

Lena laughed and held up the whiskey bottle. Sadie nodded. "Double."

"I ain't cleaning up puke."

"I won't puke."

Lena handed her the almost-full shot glass and she held it up. Her eyes met Lena's. "Sister truth."

"Sister truth."

Sadie waited for the burning to fade and for the rush of alcohol to hit her brain. She was seriously going to regret this tomorrow. She sat forward, cross-legged, and leaned sideways to put the glass down with a deliberate clunk. Taking a deep breath, she faced Lena.

"I talked to Grant."

It took a moment. Sadie watched her friend's face move from *Who?* to *Oh, my God!* in a matter of seconds. Lena's hands, warm and strong, grasped Sadie's.

"Digame."

She told her. How he'd had suspicions. How

he'd confronted their mother with the evidence. His letter. "He wants to have a relationship. To get to know each other."

"How do you feel about it?"

"Terrified."

"What did you tell him?"

"That I needed some time. He was okay with that. Seems like a nice enough guy. Just graduated from Wofford College and got a job at a medical research company in Raleigh."

"But?"

"I feel like I can't. I wouldn't mind getting to know him. But I can't have anything to do with my mother. I can't. I've thought about it and thought about it until I want to scream."

"One doesn't necessarily mean you have to have the other."

Sadie flopped back on the couch cushions. "He said that. The problem for me is that he'd have to lie to her. At the very least it'd be a lie of omission. I don't want to put him in that position."

She considered the whiskey bottle. *No. Not a good idea.* She settled for more jelly beans. She took three. *Three is a good number.*

"He said he thought she'd want to meet me. But he could tell her that I don't want to."

She stopped. Her head was pounding from more than the incipient hangover. She had no words for the feelings slithering like a basket of snakes within her at the idea of seeing her mother.

She felt Lena's gentle squeeze on her hand. "I hate her, Lena," she whispered. "I hate her so much. And I hate her more now that I know she was a good mother to Grant and the others."

"Then get to know only Grant. The sisters, too, if you want. You don't owe your mother anything, Sadie."

"I know. But I keep thinking about Lito. I told him about the letter. I promised him that I would give my blood family a chance. And I'm not very good with this relationship stuff."

"No!" Lena gasped mockingly.

"You noticed? Seriously, I think if I face my past maybe I can do better in the future. Is that dumb?"

"No. I think it's exactly what you need to do. Doesn't mean you have to meet her. Unless that's what you want."

"I know what I want. I want all this pain to be gone. I'm tired of being the abandoned foster kid. I just want to be me now. But I don't know how. If I met with her, if I faced her, would the pain go away? Or would it make things worse?"

Lena's voice was soft and warm. "I don't know, sister. Only you know that."

Her heart pounded against her ribs at a sick-

ening pace. She couldn't seem to pull in a normal breath.

"What if she says she just didn't want *me*?"

"Oh, Sadie." Lena pulled her close, a hand
brushing through her hair. "That's impossible."

CHAPTER EIGHTEEN

"GOT ENOUGH DIRT THERE, you think?"

Wyatt swiped at the sweat beading on his forehead and turned. Charlie and Shiloh walked through the backyard. Jules squealed at the sight of her friend and ran to her. Wyatt watched the two girls greet each other as if they hadn't seen each other in years rather than one day.

"We're building a garden," he said to Charlie as she toed the small mountain of garden soil.

She put her hands on her hips. White capri pants and a white blouse glowed against her booth-tanned skin. Approximately ten pounds of gold jewelry was draped around her neck and wrists. Bright gold eye shadow. He could appreciate her unique style now that she'd stopped hitting on him. He certainly appreciated the friendship growing between them.

"You get my little Prissy McPrincess to put her hands in dirt, mister, you better be getting me a picture."

That made him laugh, which felt good. Ever since he'd left the Crew's office the day before, he hadn't had much to laugh about. The rage Sadie had rained down on him was nothing compared to the betrayed pain in her eyes. The anger was deserved. He knew she'd be angry. The pain was salt in the wound.

"I think they'll be okay. I've got an art project for them."

He walked her over to the picnic table under the spreading arms of the live oak at the rear of the yard. Jules was already showing everything to Shiloh. Construction paper, crayons, glitter, glue, stickers. A hard lesson learned: never set an eight-year-old girl free in the craft aisle at Walmart. The first basket had totaled out at over fifty bucks. The paring down had been brutal.

"Hi, Ms. Charlie. We're making the signs for the plants."

"Well, sounds like fun. I'm going to want some of these veggies once the garden comes in, okay?"

"Okay!"

The girls turned their attention back to picking out a color scheme for the garden signs. Charlie nudged Wyatt. "You up for this? Two of 'em are worse than ten, I swear."

"I was a squad leader in Afghanistan. I think I got this."

Charlie laughed. "Okay, tough guy. We'll see how you feel about it later. But for now, here's an emergency kit."

Wyatt looked into the tote bag Charlie handed him. An assortment of Disney movies and a box of Little Debbie swiss roll cakes. He might have to confiscate those. Charlie patted at her non-existent hip.

"I got my phone. You good with the plan?"

"Call at noon. If you answer, make up an emergency. If you don't, all is well."

"Perfect. Thank you. Damn. I don't know why I even bother with this dating stuff. Ain't no good men my age. If they were any good, they'd've made their marriages work."

Wyatt draped his arm across her bony shoulders and gave little squeeze. "You are going to be fine. If he doesn't appreciate you, he's not worth your time."

"Honey, ain't that the truth. Okay. Call me. As planned or just if you need me."

Wyatt saluted her and was rewarded with an amused laugh.

"Okay, girls. I'm going to finish putting the raised beds together. Then we'll put the dirt in."

Two little faces stared up at him. Sun and moon. Shiloh with her corn-silk blond hair and blue eyes and Jules with her black hair and dark brown eyes could not have been more different. But their expressions of disgust were identical.

"Are there bugs in the dirt, Uncle Wyatt?"

"No."

"Or worms? I hate worms, Mr. Wyatt."

"No bugs or worms. I promise."

The girls exchanged skeptical looks.

"You two work on those signs. I'll deal with the dirt."

Which was what he'd had in mind with the project: dealing with dirt. Get out in the sun and work until he was exhausted. Maybe then he could sleep. Charlie's emergency babysitting request had thrown a tiny wrench into the plan, but not much. It would give Jules someone to talk to. He wasn't much good for company right now.

Leaving the girls to the mysteries of glitter and glue sticks, he returned to the frame for the raised garden bed. It was simple enough. A four-foot by eight-foot rectangle of cedar planks, notched to fit together and held in place with a steel pin. Set it up, put the liner in, dump in the garden soil, plant the veggies, water and watch it grow. Or watch the raccoons eat it.

As he worked, the sounds of the neighborhood washed over him. Early May in the suburbs meant the air was full of sound. Lawnmowers, weed whackers, kids on bikes calling out to each other. The sound of the breeze through the limbs of the oaks and the quiet chatter of the girls should have been soothing. But it wasn't. Guilt nibbled along the edges of his peace of mind. More than guilt. He finished smoothing out the liner and stepped back to double-check his choice of location. Good morning sun exposure with the shade from the oak in the afternoon. Should do well. Some manual labor was the thing he needed.

"Okay girls, we ready to start spreading dirt?"

"We're still making the signs!"

He grinned. If it had only been him and Jules, she would help him. But she wasn't going to get dirty in front of her friend. He started tossing the forty-pound bags of garden soil into the rectangle. Probably should have had a load of topsoil delivered, but too late now.

One thing he'd forgotten about this kind of work: it allowed the mind to wander. And it wandered, like the tongue seeking the sore tooth, right to the core of his pain. It wasn't that he'd been undercover. It was that he had slept with her without telling her the truth. His gut twisted unpleasantly. He straightened from spreading the soil and stretched his back. More than dishonest, it was dishonorable.

He viciously rammed the shovel blade through the plastic bags of soil and bent to tear the plastic, spilling the contents of the bags. He thought back to the moment. He'd been hoping for another kiss. A kiss she couldn't blame on grief or escape or anything other than her desire to kiss him. She'd upped the ante by slipping her hands beneath his shirt, setting fire to his desire. He sunk the shovel head into the ground and picked up the rake to spread the soil.

Still. You should have said no. You should have put the brakes on the entire situation. She hadn't known the entire truth at that point. She deserved the truth. Casual sex was one thing. Sex under false pretenses was another. Even with her hands on his chest and that delicious mouth of hers working its way up the column of his neck, he'd been ready to push her back. To stop. But then she'd slipped her hand beneath the waistband of his pants and her fingers had closed around him. Her touch, the assertiveness of it, had stirred more than his body. It had stirred his hope. Were her feelings more than physical? Did she care about him? Could this be more?

"Uncle Wyatt?"

He startled and turned. "What's up, Jujube? You ready to help?"

"Can we go inside? It's too hot. All the signs are done."

"Sure. You can watch the movies Miss Charlie brought. Are you hungry?"

Shiloh held up the tote bag. "Can we eat the snack cakes?"

"One each."

He watched them go inside with an odd wrench

of disappointment. How quickly you become used to situations. He and Jules had depended on each other so much the past six months, he'd become accustomed to spending all his time with her. Now she had a friend. He'd been demoted. But he'd take it if it meant she was happy and doing things little girls should be doing.

He moved more bags to the frame. Almost done. He kept moving. It didn't take long once he had the soil in place. He set out the plants. He hadn't tried to be too ambitious. A couple tomato plants, cucumbers, pole beans, yellow squash and red peppers. Once he had them in the ground and a sprinkler watering them in, he went to sit at the picnic table. The girls had done a good job packing everything up before going inside. He smiled. Jules was so much like her mother, who had been a precociously organized little girl. He picked up the signs they'd made for the vegetables. Maybe he should get them laminated first.

He found the bottle of water he'd left in the shade under the table and drank without stopping. It was getting warmer. The capricious May weather that teetered between perfection and hints of the Southern heat to come was tilting toward summer. He leaned back on his elbows and watched a squirrel watching him from the limb of the oak. He should apologize. *That's what you do. When you mess up, you admit it, apologize and make it right if you can.* He huffed out a humorless laugh. He'd braced himself for yelling. For tears. But not for her furious outrage on behalf of her crew. In her eyes, he'd not only betrayed her, but her guys.

He picked up the signs and sorted through them. He'd get cleaned up and take the girls up to the Office Depot and have them laminated. He checked the time on his phone and spun it around on the table top. Maybe he should call her. Apologize over the phone. Be safer. A little frisson of anger popped in his gut. Woman had thrown a damn bottle. Picked it up and for a second looked as if she wanted to cave his face in before she hurled it against the wall. Maybe he should let it go. She had issues. What if she lost her cool like that in front of Jules? Part of him pushed back against that. *You know she wouldn't,* it told him.

But what if she does? He needed to walk away. Hell, she'd already sent him away. *Stay away, man. You did a job. The end. Nothing personal in it. If she can't understand, then forget her.* That was better. He started gathering the art supplies.

"Abandoned already?"

He turned. Charlie walked across the yard to sit beside him.

"Date over already?"

"Damn straight. First question he asked was how often Shiloh went to stay with her daddy. You don't want my kid around, I don't want you around."

"Sorry."

"Get used to it. Might be different for guys, though. A single dad seems like he'd make a good family man."

He leaned back against the table. "My fiancée broke up with me when I decided to take custody of Jules."

Charlie's eyes met his. "Better off. Anyone who can turn their back on a child has something wrong with them."

"That's what I've come to believe."

She sat beside him. "We don't know each other very well, so I'm going to come out and ask this. Feel free to tell me to mind my own business. I won't take offense."

"Shoot."

"Are you okay? I mean, you seemed like something was bothering you this morning. And you look, I don't know, a little down."

He hesitated. He didn't want to become the latest bit of mommy gossip. But he was pretty sure Charlie wouldn't talk about him. He sat forward and propped his forearms on his knees, staring down at the grass between his feet.

"I thought I'd met someone. But it's complicated."

"She married?"

"No."

"Then what's complicated?"

"I did something wrong. There was a lie and I made it worse."

"Oh. Yeah. I see. Clear as mud now, mister."

He laughed. "Like I said. Complicated. She was the subject of my last investigation. Completely innocent. But we got…close…and I didn't tell her."

Charlie leaned back and gave him the look. That female how-could-you-be-so-stupid look. "Am I hearing this wrong? You slept with her while investigating her and then told her the truth?"

"Sounds even worse when another person says it. Yeah. I feel like a giant pile of crap. I tried to apologize."

"Did she go upside your head? Because I sure would have."

"Thought she was going to throw a bottle at me."

"Good for her."

"So you think it's a lost cause?"

"Do you care about her?"

"Yeah, I do. And Jules likes her. She was awesome with Jules, too. I just think now I don't deserve her. What I did was so wrong."

"Give her a little time to cool off. Try 'sorry' again. Maybe she'll want to talk, maybe not."

"Yeah. Maybe."

CHAPTER NINETEEN

"OH, DEAR GOD," Sadie moaned. She turned her face back into the black depths of her pillow. To hell with breathing. "Close the curtains. Please, Lena. If you ever loved me."

"Stop whining. No one forced all those shots down your throat. Sit up. I have medicine."

"No."

"Get up. It's after noon."

Sadie sat up and her head punished her with a walloping pain that seemed to roll through each brain cell one by one. "Jack?"

"I let him out already. Here. Drink this water. Take these pills."

"I hope those pills are morphine."

"Better. Vitamin B. Do it and you'll get coffee."

Sadie took the glass of water and drank. As the first drops of water hit her tongue, her thirst raged up and she gulped it down quickly. No other water had ever tasted so good. She paused to take the vitamins and held out the empty glass. "Coffee."

She propped the pillows behind her and leaned

back against them while sipping the very strong, very black, very large cup of coffee. "God bless you, Lena. You're a saint."

Lena snorted out a laugh. "Wait until I make you get out of bed."

"Why aren't you hungover?"

Two fingers appeared before Sadie's eyes. "How many fingers am I holding up?"

"Two."

"Because that's how many shots I did last night."

"How many did I do?"

"Four, five. I lost count."

Sadie wrapped her hands around the coffee mug and slurped greedily. Now that she was starting to come to life, other regions began to complain. Her eyes felt like ground glass. Her stomach was accepting the coffee under protest. Her bladder was stretched to maximum capacity. No wonder she'd been desperately searching for a bathroom in her dreams. Her back was stiff and sore. *Awesome.* She finished the coffee and threw back the covers.

"I wouldn't jump right up if I were you."

"I've gotta go."

She got in the shower after taking care of her bladder. She stood under the blast until the hot water gave out. As she toweled off, the delicious scent of bacon and eggs drifted down the hall. Her body threw off the vague sense of nausea and clamored for food. She dressed quickly in jeans and a T-shirt.

As they ate, Jack came up to the table with his harness in his mouth. Sadie shook her head. "I dunno about that, Jack."

"What's he want?"

"To go to the dog park and throw tennis balls. We do it every Saturday morning."

"Let's do it, then. I need to make sure you are fully functional before I leave you alone."

A prickly feeling made its way along Sadie's arms and settled in her gut. A feeling she couldn't blame on her hangover. She pushed the plate away. "I don't want to."

"Why not? It'll be fun. Get some fresh air. Move around a bit."

"Every time I go, I run into Wyatt and his niece."

"Oh. Awkward."

Lena reached out a gorgeously manicured hand and Jack lifted his head into her palm for ear scratches. Sadie held up her hands and studied her own nails. Short, unpolished and rough cuticles. At least none were broken today. She'd never be a girly girl.

"So," Lena said, turning those dark eyes back to Sadie. "You're going to hide the rest of your life? Maybe take Jack to a different doggie playground?"

"Yes." Sadie stood and began clearing the table. Nice try. "That's exactly what I'm going to do. Hide."

"Oh, this is a beautiful park."

"Shut up."

Sadie sat back against the oak tree and adjusted her sunglasses. Her head and body were getting better, but her eyes still felt as though they were rolling around on a bed of jagged glass. How Lena had talked her into this, she wasn't sure. As Jack ran for the tennis balls—Lena had quite a good throwing arm, Sadie discovered— she tried to keep from glancing around. She was in no condition or mood to meet up with Wyatt. Especially if he had Jules with him. Her feelings were a jumbled-up mess of regret and anger.

"Stop looking for him."

"I'm not. I'm… Stop nagging me."

Lena sat beside her and continued to throw the ball in lobs that arced through the air high enough for Jack to jump for. His favorite. "Are you relatively back to normal now?"

"I suppose."

"Then let's continue the conversation about meeting with your mother."

The water bottle in Sadie's hand jerked, sloshing water down the front of her shirt. Her brain gave a corresponding jerk, reminding her that the pounding headache was only sleeping, not gone. That old, familiar feeling of slimy fear and hatred rose up and it did not mesh well with hangover mode.

"I'm not meeting with her."

"Do you remember what we talked about?"

"Yes. I remember perfectly. I'm not a blackout drunk."

"Don't growl at me."

"Don't…"

Don't what? Make me face my fears? She turned her face away. How many times had she fantasized about running into her mother? Angrily demanding to be told why she'd been thrown aside like a piece of trash? Too many to count. The problem was the fantasy always ended there. She never had to hear the answers. She didn't know if she wanted to know them. She drew up her knees and hid her face against them.

"You brought this up. It may have been the liquor talking, but what you said deserves to be considered. These feelings you have. They aren't hurting her. They're hurting you. You said this yourself. Facing the past is the only way you can move forward."

Lena's voice was soft, and she could hear the love and concern in it. But still her jaw clenched. She struggled to keep from jumping up and running away. Tears welled up and her throat ached in a flood of self-pity and loathing.

"I think you have a chance here to face it. I think you'll walk away stronger, Sadie. No matter how it comes out."

Silence spun out between them. She could hear a softball game going on in a distant part of the park. Cheers, the crack of the bat. Jack was nearby, she could hear his doggy breathing. *Stare the devil in the face.* Lena was right, last night had been the liquor talking. But it was only talking out loud. She'd thought those things for a long time before Grant. Before Wyatt. She'd just never had the will—or the opportunity—to do anything about it.

She lifted her head and took off the sunglasses to wipe at her face. She reached out and took Lena's hand. "I know I need to do this. I know I have issues with trust. I'm just all jumbled up because I wanted to face her so I could try to make it work with Wyatt. So I might not mess up a relationship with him and Jules. Now I don't know why I should bother."

"So you were only going to do it for Wyatt? Not for yourself at all?"

Sadie dropped her head to her knees. "No. Yes. I was. I don't know."

"Sadie, look at me."

Lena's voice was soft but commanding. Sadie

turned her head and peeked up at her best friend. "I know, Lena. Don't say anything. I'll do it. And I'll do it so I don't have to feel like this anymore."

Lena grinned. "It would be nice if that hot bod of his could be a bonus prize, though, right?"

She felt her resolve returning. Maybe things were over with Wyatt, but she still had other issues to resolve. The walls she'd built against the pain and fear had become second nature. Pushing people away was like slipping into an old pair of jeans: easy, comfortable. But there was a second wall. The one she'd put between her heart and her feelings. She was getting lonely, trapped between the two. But did she have the courage to tear them down? Would she ever be able to simply offer her love to others? Love people because she loved them and not because they'd proven themselves worthy?

She felt adrift at the thought. It was scary, but she found a part of her yearning for it to be over. She was tired of struggling.

"Will you come with me?"

Lena draped an arm around her shoulders and pulled her tight. "Of course I will."

Sadie pressed her lips together. "I need to tell Josh. I'd want him to be there."

"Are you sure?"

"Yes. Both of you. You give me courage, Lena. But Josh? He's my strength."

"ARE YOU KIDDING ME?"

Her insides crumbled. The tenuous grip she had on her feelings began to slip. Josh's eyes burned with an anger she could see clearly from across the desk. His body language remained calm and he hadn't changed his lazy, slumped position in his chair. But his eyes. They bore a hole through her. This wasn't the reaction she'd expected to her decision to meet her mother.

"No. I'm not. I think it'll be a good thing if I can…"

"Lena put this in your head, didn't she? I knew I shouldn't have called her. What'd she do? Get you drunk and talk you into it?"

"No, that isn't how it was. I have been thinking about it ever since I got Grant's letter. Damn it, Josh! You know me. You know I walk around pushing people away. You know I've ruined every relationship I've ever had. I'm tired of it. I want to be normal. I need to face her. Yes, I talked it over with Lena before I told you. That doesn't mean it's her fault."

"Don't do it. Lena doesn't understand. In her world, family means rainbows and sunshine and unicorn shit. It's a fairy tale you and I know doesn't exist. Name one member of your family who was there for you. None. Zero. Why are you going to suck up to her? You think she's going to

be sorry? Going to love you now? You're going to
bake cookies and exchange Christmas presents?"

"Of course not."

Her temper stirred to life. Josh's words dove-
tailed perfectly with what she'd believed about
her mother all these years. It was how they both
felt about the families who had abandoned them.
She didn't even know who her father was. Or if
she had any family other than her mother, Grant
and his sisters.

"I am not expecting a happily-ever-after here.
I'm expecting to look mommy dearest in the eye
and watch her squirm in her own guilt. I want her
to have to say her pathetic rationalizations out
loud. Then maybe I can stop feeling as though
it's my fault. Maybe I can leave her behind.
Leave it behind. Maybe I can stop being afraid."

Her throat closed up tight with unshed tears
and anger. Of all people, Josh should be the one
who understood this. This need to ask why. *Why
did you leave me? Why wasn't I good enough?*
Jack whined quietly and put his head in her lap.

"You know it isn't going to happen, right?
Whatever story she's been telling herself all this
time is so real, so strong in her mind that nothing
is going to shake it out. She didn't care about you
then and she's not going to care about you now.
I get that you want her to feel bad. You want to
rub her face in it and make her hurt the way you

hurt. But she isn't going to feel it. If she was capable of feeling guilty about what she did to you, she wouldn't have been able to live with it. But she's done quite fine, hasn't she? Raised three kids without a hint of regret."

Her hands curled into fists on the desk and the palms burned as her nails cut into them. She pressed her lips together against the tide of words wanting to rush from her tongue. Because he was right. But so was she. And now she was so confused she didn't know what to think.

"Sadie..."

"Shut up! Shut up! Josh, I know these things. I know she doesn't care. I know this isn't going to make anything with her better. I know I'm not going to get a groveling apology I can kick down her throat and make her choke on. I know it. This isn't about any of that."

"Then what is it about?"

"It's about me looking her in the eye. Making her see me. So I'm not afraid anymore. So I don't wonder anymore. So I don't feel invisible anymore. So I can move past this, finally."

"You know that already."

"No, I don't!"

A tearing burn scorched its way down her throat and she realized she was yelling at him. She sank back in the chair and put a hand over her mouth. Her eyes met his. The anger was gone from his gaze and in its place was a distance more frightening to her than the anger. He had these same fears and doubts and carried the same anger. She knew this. They'd spent too many nights talking until dawn about the devastation of their childhoods for her not to know this. She was ready to take a step beyond survival and into healing. And he was not. Because she'd found her family. And he had not.

"Josh…"

There was a single rap on the door before it swung open and Molly leaned in. "The guys are here for the staff meeting. Everyone can hear you."

The door didn't slam shut, but Molly closed it with clear irritation. Sadie covered her face. Josh's chair scraped against the floor as he stood.

"Don't be mad, Josh. I couldn't bear it. I love you. You're my brother. More of a brother than Grant. I understand why you think this is wrong, but I need to do this. Please."

He pushed the chair back in place and stood for a moment, his head bowed. When he lifted his eyes, her stomach lurched at the sad, haunted look in them. *No, please no.* If this was going to cost her Josh, she'd cancel the whole thing.

"It's a mistake."

With those words, he walked out. Through the door he left open, Sadie could hear the guys talking. Waiting for her to start the Monday morning staff meeting. A meeting she couldn't shove off on Josh. One, because now he was pissed at her and wouldn't do it. And two, she had to address the Wyatt issue and her appalling lack of professionalism in dealing with it. She crossed her arms on the desk and put her head down. How had her entire life gone completely down the toilet so quickly?

The conference room went silent when she walked in. Josh sat in his usual place, to the right of her chair at the head of the table, but he kept his eyes glued to the pen he spun around and around in circles. Sadie put her coffee cup down and lifted her gaze to the gathered group. All of them young guys. College age. All looking at her. Waiting for her to give them a direction in which to take their reaction to the revelation about Wyatt. Her gut churned with shame. She certainly hadn't set a good example.

"Good morning."

It was a start. She cleared her throat. What would she expect from one of them if they'd screwed up big-time? Honesty. She'd want them to own up to the mistake. She owed them that. She glanced around the table.

"Morning, guys." She made eye contact with each of them. She left Josh out on purpose. She glanced over at the door to the waiting room where Molly stood. "I owe all of you an apology for my behavior the other day. I lost my temper and behaved improperly. I'm sorry."

"But…" Noah began.

She held up a hand. "Doesn't matter. My reaction was unprofessional and not an example I should be setting for you." She glanced around the table. "I'm sure you have heard. Wyatt Anderson was a private investigator hired by Marcus Canard to spy on us. Canard thought we were doing something illegal. Wyatt says he told Marcus there was nothing illegal going on. The end. What we do from here is continue to beat the pants off Marcus Canard."

A jumble of voices rose up. Angry. Outraged. Betrayed. Emotions she was well acquainted with. She lifted her hands. When everyone went silent, she lowered them.

"The best thing we can do is continue to earn his business away from him. He is hemorrhaging clients. We're not picking up all of them, but we are getting some. Now, I lost my cool, this is true. But I'm asking you not to discuss this in public. In public, we don't bother with the competition. We focus on doing the best we can. If you want to talk privately, come to me anytime."

She went on to the regular business. She read through her notes without the usual joking and banter. She wanted this over with. She wanted everything to go back to normal but knew normal was gone forever. Things were changing. As the guys got up to leave, she caught Josh by the hand.

"Have time for a word before you leave?"

He hesitated. She'd framed it as a question so he could refuse her if he wanted. Her heart seemed to freeze in her chest as she waited. She needed Josh. Not only for the business, but for her.

"Sure, boss."

Relief warmed her when his fingers tightened against her palm for a brief moment They walked back to her office. She shut the door and turned to him.

"I know you don't understand why I need to do this. I'm not sure I understand it myself. I feel in my gut it's the right thing to do. If it's a mistake, you can be the first to say I told you so. But if this is going to cause real trouble between us, tell me and I won't do it."

He seemed to sag beneath her words. His shoulders drooped and his head dipped. He shook it slowly. With a deep breath, he straightened and put his hands on her shoulders. His eyes met hers. "Nothing will ever cause real trouble between us, Saff. I just don't want you hurt worse than you are now."

"I'm not hurt."

She turned to move away but his hands held her in place. "You are. This thing with Wyatt. Was something else going on there?"

"No."

She twisted out of his grasp and moved to her desk. "How's the Columbia project going?"

He looked at her carefully. "It's going fine. I'm going up there next week. I've got three client interviews to do. But I told you this last week."

"I remember. Sorry."

"Are you okay?"

"Yes. I'm… It's been a stressful week, okay?"

"No shit. You falling apart?"

A sad little laugh escaped her lips. "Maybe a little."

He came around to kiss the top of her head. "I've got glue. Whenever you need."

She leaned back in her chair after Josh left and considered the jelly-bean jar. She closed her hands around the little blob of her belly. Maybe she should find a healthier stress-management technique. *Sit-ups or running. Boxing.* That sounded good. A long sigh drew Jack to her side. She let her fingers run through his shaggy fur. Trouble was, she wasn't angry anymore. Anger took too much energy to maintain. Now she was merely sad. Abuelito was gone. And the first man she'd had feelings for in way too many years had turned out to be a rat fink.

She rubbed the pain squeezing at her heart. Sad. Because really he was a nice guy who was doing a job. Maybe the attraction had snuck up on him also. He did come clean at the end. She sat forward and shook her head. The time to tell her had been before he slept with her. The fresh pile of paperwork on her desk made her sigh.

"What do you say, Jack? If we finish this, we can take the afternoon off? Go for a walk on the beach? Is it a deal?"

He seemed to think so and returned to his doggy bed for a nap. She wished she could do the same. Not even nine in the morning and she was exhausted. A single tap on the door announced Molly's entrance. She closed the door behind her.

"Are you okay?"

"Yes. I'm fine."

Molly slipped into the chair, sitting on the very edge. Her warm green eyes examined Sadie's face. Her hands were clasped together on her lap. Her lips pressed together, then pursed, pressed and pursed as if she were struggling with the words she so wanted to speak.

"Spit it out, Molly."

"Josh and I are worried about you."

"You and Josh need to stop talking about me behind my back. I am fine. I was angry. I'm over it now. The end."

"But…"

Sadie slapped her palm on the desktop. Not loudly, but enough to fully express her irritation. "Enough. Stop it. This is not a couch, and you are not Dr. Phil."

She regretted her words once Molly was gone. *But damn.* How was she supposed to get anything done when these two kept at her? She didn't discuss her feelings. She shoved them down deep and ignored them until they went away.

Except now she knew that they never really go away. Now she knew it was time to clean house. She picked up the phone. Voice mail. Even better.

"Hey Grant, it's Sadie. Call me later when you get a chance. I want to meet with you and our mother."

She ended the call and put the phone down with a trembling hand.

HER CAR WAS THERE. Wyatt could see it clearly from his vantage point in the parking lot next door. He sat in his truck, mulling over his options. He had the Crew shirts he'd been given on the seat beside him. Tucked between their folds was an envelope with a check reimbursing Sadie for the salary paid to him. He'd charged Marcus for it and had been a little shocked when the money came through without complaint. He suspected Marcus had tried to pull something with

Henry Moody and had been shut down. *Whatever.* He was glad to be rid of the man.

He rubbed a hand across his jaw. He wasn't so glad to be rid of Sadie. No matter how he looked at it, it was a mess. Every reasonable thought he had told him to walk away. *Don't Boy Scout this. You apologized already. You don't owe her anything else. Walk away.*

He knew this but couldn't quite let it go. Sure, he'd said he was sorry after she'd found out. But he hadn't been able to sit her down, alone, and apologize for not telling her before they'd had sex. Josh had been there. Molly. He couldn't let it go. He'd not done the right thing by her. *Dude. She nearly threw a bottle at your head. How rational a discussion do you think you're going to have? Walk away. Mail this to her.* He scooped up the shirts and popped open the truck door.

You are so going to regret this.

He had too many regrets already to worry about another one tossed on the pile. He braced himself as he opened the door. Molly showed about a millisecond of confusion before her head started shaking vigorously back and forth. *No. Duh.* He held up the shirts but she was heading around the desk with an expression that was frighteningly similar to the one Sadie had the day she found out. He stopped in the doorway.

"Give them to me and go," Molly said.

He handed them to her and plucked the envelope out. "I'd like to give this to Sadie. And talk to her."

She pulled the envelope from his grasp. "Not a good idea. In fact, the worst idea I've ever heard. You've added enough to the grief she's carrying."

Molly's words caused a spasm of guilt and shame to stab through him. Added to her grief. The man she considered a grandfather had passed away. And he'd slept with her, toyed with her emotions.

"I never lied about my feelings for her," he said. It was true. It didn't help. It sounded like a self-serving lie.

"Go away."

So he left. Hopefully, he'd get better news at Henry Moody's office.

Henry's secretary was happy to see him. It was a small comfort after the reception at the Crew. Not that he deserved any better from Molly. He should be glad Josh hadn't been there instead. He didn't want to have to explain any bruises to Jules.

Jules. She was the reason he was cooling his heels here in Henry's inner sanctum. He'd come to discuss the job proposal Henry was offering. Insurance Fraud Investigator. The exact same job he'd been doing except he'd be on a payroll instead of self-employed. Running his own business had been fine with him for years. But things were different now. And honestly? The paperwork involved in running your own business would kill you.

It was one of the many things he admired about Sadie. How she'd built the Cleaning Crew from nothing and made it such a success. Not only a success, but created a feeling of family among her employees. That was rare.

Hell. He shifted on the uncomfortable couch. Picked up a *Field & Stream* magazine and thumbed blindly through the pages. *No. She's too unstable a person to be around Jules.* He tossed the magazine back on the table. *Can't have it both ways, dude.* He rubbed at his sternum.

"Wyatt? Mr. Moody is ready to see you now."

As he crossed the reception area, she smiled at him. "How's that sweet little niece of yours?"

He stopped. "She's wonderful. Doing better every day."

And he needed to focus on her. Taking a regular job wasn't a sacrifice to him, it was the right thing to do.

Henry greeted him with a smile and a handshake. "I'm going to have to make good on my joke about the sign-on bonus."

"Why's that?"

"Marcus called me. Tried to smear you like you said he would. Said I shouldn't trust you.

The conversation was…unpleasant. But in the end, Marcus decided to darken some other insurance company's door, and I've got you all to myself. A complete win-win situation."

Two hours later, he sat in his truck, a full-time employee of Moody Insurance Company. Lead fraud investigator. He skimmed through the papers again, trying to force his brain to accept the numbers there. He'd known he provided a valuable service, but the almost six-figure number of his salary seemed insanely high. Henry had been right. He should have been charging more. He leaned his head back and let the elated sense of relief fill him. The work was the same. The hours were his to make as long as he provided results. He had an office. A secretary to help with paperwork.

Most importantly, he had financial security for Jules. Now he needed to make sure he kept her emotionally secure. And if it meant no relationships for a while, so be it. He and Jules were a package deal. He'd not risk her heart. Not unless he was sure. And he wasn't sure about Sadie Martin. Not that it mattered now anyway.

CHAPTER TWENTY

A BRIGHT SUNNY Thursday afternoon seemed wrong for the occasion. It should be gloomy and overcast. Perhaps with rumbles of thunder in the distance.

The only other time Sadie had been to Azalea Park in Summerville had been for the Flowertown Festival when the park was bursting with flowers and people in an orgy of relentlessly cheerful springtime celebration. It didn't seem right without the dozen shades of pink flowers assaulting the senses at every turn.

"You don't have to do this if you've changed your mind," Lena said quietly.

Sadie unhooked the seat belt and shook her head. "If I don't do it now, I'll never do it."

"Nothing wrong with never," Josh said from the backseat.

The look Lena gave him in the rearview mirror was so murderous that even in her advanced state of anxiety, Sadie didn't miss it.

"We are here to support Sadie's decisions."

"I am supporting her decisions."

"No. You aren't."

"Yes—"

"Shut up, both of you."

Sadie pressed her palms together, carefully lining up her fingers, and touched the index fingers to her lips. If only she could stop trembling. It would be so much easier. She scanned the bit of the park she could see from the parking spot. Grant and her mother were waiting for her by the gazebo. Her heart galloped wildly in her chest as if it were seeking an escape. She dropped her hands to her lap.

"What am I going to say?"

"I can think of a strong opening."

"Josh." Lena twisted in her seat. "Shut up if you aren't going to even try to be helpful. See, you made her cry. Happy now?"

Sadie lifted her head from the dashboard. She wasn't crying, she was laughing. This was why she had wanted him to come. Lena, with her warm motherly support, was going to be most helpful in the aftermath. Josh knew she needed armor to face the demon. She couldn't walk up to her mother naked. She needed her shell.

"Maybe something along the lines of 'So, how's your life been while I was passed around from home to home?'"

Josh leaned over the car seat. "That's good.

Or, 'Hey, did you really think an eight-year-old was adoptable?'"

"Stop it, both of you." Lena popped her door open and turned to Sadie. "Ready?"

The fear came back, slick and slippery along her limbs, making her clumsy as she fumbled for the door handle. The sunshine and warm air seemed wrong against her clammy skin. Josh climbed out of the backseat and put an arm around her shoulders as Lena walked around to her. She took Lena's hand and lingered for a moment in the shelter of their love.

"Remind me why I'm doing this."

"Beats me."

"To face her. To face your fears. To move on. To be free."

"Oh, yeah."

She seemed unable to move. She wanted to walk into the park with her head held high. A confident, successful, happy woman. She wanted to prove her mother's lies and abandonment hadn't meant a thing. Hadn't stopped her from achieving what she wanted in life. But it had. It had colored every relationship she'd ever had. Josh walked Sadie away from Lena. He turned her to face him and gripped her upper arms. He bent to look into her eyes. "Head up. Shoulders back. You do this, Saff, you do it right. You walk up to her weak, she's going to be able to excuse her own weakness. She is here to explain herself to you. You walk up. You listen. You walk away. Deal with what she says later."

"Stop trying to talk her out of this." Lena was next to them.

He held up a finger. "Stop it. You don't know what you are dealing with here. I do. She's going to do this. But she's going to do it on her terms. Not yours. Not her mother's. Hers."

"And you know what those terms are?"

"Better than you do."

"It doesn't matter. This is about Sadie."

"Will you both shut up? Like this isn't hard enough?"

The irritation helped. She clung to it. Clung to the heat of it, the energy that pushed her to action. She drew in a deep breath and lifted her hands to the sky. "I'm going in."

Suck it up and deal. But her old standby was failing her as she walked alone down the path toward the gazebo. The fear crept back in, nibbling along the edges of her confidence. The anger that had burned out the fear began to fade. Neither her heart nor her lungs seemed to want to function normally. Both stuttered and flailed in her chest like fish on dry land. She wondered if her decision to meet her mother alone was a mistake.

Grant stood and lifted his hand. A tall young man with dark hair. The joints of her body seemed strangely loose and she paused along the path, unsure if her hips and knees would follow the proper sequence for walking or if she was about to fall face forward into the crushed oyster shell.

The woman sitting on the bench rose. Her mother. *No. Never mind. This was a massive mistake.* The rush of emotion paralyzed her. Her mind seemed to float free of her body. *Leave. Turn around and walk away. Now.* Her body was no longer accepting commands from her brain. She could only watch, every color and movement hyperexaggerated, as Grant gently squeezed the hand of the woman and walked toward Sadie. And now her mother was turning, turning in torturous slow motion. If this were a horror movie, this would be the moment where the monster hidden inside the human would reveal itself. Slimy, scaly. Razor sharp teeth. A sound startled Sadie out of her runaway thoughts and she realized it had come from her own throat. Half moan, half whimper, it served its purpose of slamming steel back into her spine. She pulled her gaze away as Grant approached her.

"Hey," he said.

"Hi," she squeaked out. She studied his face, looking for herself there, but found nothing.

"Emmie looks like you," he said with a smile. A warm hand squeezed her shoulder. "I'm going to let you talk to her. We'll meet up again another day."

"Okay."

She couldn't seem to spit out more than one word at a time. Grant walked away and she turned back to her mother. *Show no weakness. Show no fear.* The two women stared at each other. Grant had said she resembled her mother, and she supposed she could see why. The same dark hair. Hers was cut so short it was impossible to tell if they shared the wild curls. Same fair skin. Same height and slim build. A smile bloomed and died on the woman's—her mother's—lips, and her hands clasped at each other. *How does it feel? To look upon your living past? Am I your worst nightmare?*

Soon she was close enough to see they shared the same cheekbones. But not Sadie's Cupid's bow lips and dark blue eyes. Good. She wanted to be her own person. Like Athena, she wanted to have sprung fully formed into this life.

She stopped and the silence spun out as they stared at each other. The fear she could see in her mother's eyes helped calm her own fear. Fear meant she knew she'd done wrong. Now seemed a very bad time to try to suss out exactly what she wanted from this meeting, but only now did her mind find a moment of detached clarity. She knew exactly what she wanted. As a child, she'd assumed, as children do, that everything was her fault. Her mother stopped coming to see her, turned her back on her, because there was something wrong with her. As an adult, she knew this wasn't true. Intellectually. But the rejection had stained her very soul. She didn't need anything from this woman. The child she'd been did. She needed to hear the words spoken aloud.

"Hi." It was a stupid, lame opening, but better than staring at each other until dark. She stuffed her hands in her pockets and resisted the urge to scuff her foot through the oyster shell gravel. "I don't even know what to call you." *Womb donor?*

"You can call me Dawn. Grant says you go by Sadie?"

"No good nicknames for Sapphire."

A rueful smile crossed Dawn's lips. "Can we sit down?" After they'd sat—as far apart as possible—on the bench, she shook her head. "Sorry about the name. I think I did better with the others. Although only Ruby uses her real name."

Sadie shrugged. Dawn turned with one knee drawn up on the bench and her arm stretched along the back. An open, inviting position. Sadie didn't feel invited.

"Why exactly are you here?" Dawn asked.

"Grant wants to know me. I'd like to know him. But I didn't want him to have to lie to you or his sisters."

"And you want nothing for yourself?"

Sadie turned a hard gaze on the woman beside her. "I think I was three when I learned to expect nothing from you."

Dawn's relaxed, confident pose crumbled. She turned her head. Her jaw clenched and her throat worked. She drew in a deep breath and let it out. "I deserve that."

Sadie remained silent. She was not going to ask for it. It was going to be offered freely or Dawn could go to hell. An unexpected calm settled over her.

"I guess you want to know why. That's what I'd want to know."

Dawn reached out to take Sadie's hand and Sadie pulled hers away. *No.*

"I was young. Stupid. Too stupid to have a baby. I should have given you up right away. But my parents—I was a saint compared to them. I thought I could do better."

Sadie looked around the park. Josh and Lena were sitting on a bench on the other side of the expanse of lawn. They were watching.

"I was drinking and drugging. I wanted to get it together and get you back. But I never could. And when I finally understood and faced what drove me to use, I found out I was pregnant again. I panicked. I thought they'd take Grant away, too. I thought if I said they could put you up for adoption and I moved away, they wouldn't come for him."

Sadie let the words sink in. She tried to imagine it. Young, stupid, addicted. She'd known plenty of people like that in her life. Statistically, she should have been one of them. So that's what it came down to. Immature stupidity. Josh turned on the bench and she could feel his careful watchfulness. She kept her eyes on him.

"How old was I when they took me away?"

"Six months. I owed a drug dealer money. I didn't have it. He said he'd take sex instead and I said no. He turned me in for revenge."

Sadie tried to imagine life if she'd been left in the care of a woman running up tabs with drug dealers. Wouldn't have been a pretty childhood. *So, lovely, a scumbag drug dealer got you out of a horrible situation and into a bad one. Awesome.* She leaned forward, propping her forearms along the length of her thighs, and stared down at the ground.

"Who's my father?"

The long pause following the question was the only answer Sadie needed, but she let it play out. She was going to force Dawn to say these things out loud.

"I'm not sure. I was so messed up, Sapph... Sadie. I'm sorry. It was a guy I met at a party. I can't even remember his name."

"What are you sorry about?"

"Looking back on it now? I'm sorry I was so selfish. I'm sorry I wasn't ready to get myself straight. I'm sorry I couldn't admit it to myself and let you go. I'm sorry I didn't sign you up for adoption right away. I'm sorry I lied to you and made you promises that were only meant to make me feel better."

Sadie straightened. That was it. That was all she could stand to hear. She stood to leave but Dawn caught her hand.

"Can you forgive me?"

"Not right now. Tell me something else. Did you really sign me away because you were afraid of Social Services? Or did your new baby daddy not know about me?"

Dawn's fingers went cold against her palm before her hand fell away. Her face went even paler and a desperate fear and pain filled her eyes. *Ah. There it was. The truth.*

"He didn't know. He didn't want kids. But I was pregnant, and we were going to try to work it out. And we did. He loved Grant, and has been a great father. I wanted to tell him. After I saw what a great dad he was going to be, I thought about telling him and seeing if we could get you back if you hadn't been adopted already. But I was afraid."

"Because you didn't want to jeopardize your new life."

Dawn looked away, twin streams of tears running down her cheeks. The tears didn't move her. She'd cried her share. She waited.

"Say it, Dawn."

Dawn shook her head slowly and wiped at the wetness on her cheeks. "I thought about you every day," she said in a choked, hoarse whisper.

A harsh laugh rolled out of her throat. "Well, that makes everything better, doesn't it? *Say it!*"

From the periphery of her vision, she saw Josh stand and take a step in her direction. She lifted a hand to signal him to stop. He stopped but remained standing.

"Yes," Dawn hissed out, turning her head away. "I was finally sober. I had a good man. I had a job and a home and a new baby I could take care of properly. I couldn't risk it."

Thank you danced on her tongue, but Sadie bit it down. While she was grateful for the raw truth, she wasn't going to thank this woman for giving her what she'd deserved all her life. She walked away. She needed no more from this woman. Now she could stop looking back. Concentrate on the future. Maybe she could try to talk to Wyatt again. See if a spark could be stirred from the ashes. If he even wanted anything to do with her after the mess she'd made of everything.

THE CAR RIDE home was quiet. Sadie pressed her forehead against the window, watching without seeing the landscape roll by. She could feel Lena's worried glances. Josh sat unmoving in the backseat. It wasn't what they thought, she wanted to say. It wasn't her mother. She wasn't sure what it was, but she felt a languid sort of exhaustion oozing through her. In the Crew parking lot, Lena wrapped her fingers around Sadie's wrist. "Are you really okay?"

Sadie scooted across the expensive leather seat to hug her friend. Her best friend. The sister of her heart. "Yes. I am. This was good. Thank you. I just need to decompress. Process it all."

"You'll call me if you need me?"

"Promise."

She kissed Lena's cheek and climbed out of the car. Josh got out of the back, his eyes dark and suspicious. He leaned down to look at Lena through the car window. "I know we don't always get along, but thanks for this. Thanks for being there. You're a good friend."

Sadie would have given anything to see the look on Lena's face right then, and she suppressed a smile. "You, too," Lena said. They watched as the BMW pulled out onto Savannah Highway, heading toward downtown and Lena's luxury condo overlooking Charleston Harbor. Sadie slipped her hand into Josh's and tilted her head at his vintage Harley. "You have the spare helmet with you?"

"You want to take a ride?"

"If you've got something else going on…"

"Nothing. Where you want to go?"

She lifted her shoulders and let them drop. "Don't know. Somewhere. Anywhere."

Thirty minutes later, Jack had been let out to do his business, Sadie had slathered herself with sunblock and put on boots, jeans and a long-sleeve T-shirt, and she clung to Josh as he guided the bike through traffic, heading south. She'd ridden with him a few times before. Short rides around the block. Today she felt the need to escape. Sitting on the back of a powerful machine, feeling the rumble of it beneath her, the sound of the engine filling her ears and the feel of the wind they created rushing over her washed away her tension and fear and anger.

They stopped at the last traffic light before hitting the long stretches of country roads leading to marshes and quiet barrier islands. Sadie undid the straps on her helmet and put it between her thighs. Josh looked over his shoulder at her. "Just for a minute," she yelled in his ear.

He must have understood because when the light turned green, he gunned the bike in an explosion of sound and speed. Sadie tilted her head back, feeling the wind lift her hair and the sun on her face. Traffic was light and Josh continued to increase their speed. She pressed forward against him. "Keep it steady," she yelled.

She sat back, trailing her hands from the death grip she kept around his waist up to his shoulder blades and let go. The bike wobbled a bit with the change in her position as she held her arms up over her head. The wind rushed over her, beating at her arms, making her work to keep them aloft. Her hair flew up and back, strands whipping against her face. A deep, primal scream rolled up out of her lungs only to be snatched away by the wind. It felt good. So good. Josh gunned the bike and the speed, the hint of danger, the rush of it all sparked something vital and alive in her. She screamed again. Screamed out her fury at her mother. Her anger at herself. Her grief for Lito. Her confusion over Wyatt Anderson. Her throat felt raw but her heart beat strong. The scream turned into laughter and she leaned forward to hug Josh around the waist and press her cheek against his back.

He slowed as the bike passed from the bright sunlit fields into a dark corridor of oaks that formed a tunnel over the narrow country road. Josh pulled the bike over at a small picnic area.

"Feel better?" he asked as they sat on the picnic table. There was a short, low dock over the creek where a couple of old men tossed out shrimp nets with practiced grace.

"Yeah. Much better. Thanks."

"You going to tell me about today?"

She shook her head. Not that she wouldn't tell him, but that she wasn't sure she had the words.

"She was so pathetic, Josh. I wanted to be mad at her, but she was small and pathetic. Her excuses were stupid. Her admission was petulant, like I was supposed to understand. It was still all about her. Her problems. Her life. Her needs. Her wants."

"Did you expect different?" His voice was soft, warm.

A long sigh escaped her lips. "No. I guess not. She wasn't as scary as I thought. Just a person."

"So that's good, right?"

"Yeah."

"So what's the problem?"

"I don't know."

Silence spun out. Josh threaded his fingers through hers. "Are you sure it's just your mother?"

Her mouth opened to deny his implication but the words dried up in her throat. She shook her head and took Josh's hand. "I remembered something. Well, *remember* isn't quite right. I'd never forgotten, I'd just never let myself think about it."

"Tell me."

A bitter bark of laughter accompanied the sting

of tears in her eyes. Shame burned through her gut. "I feel ashamed, Josh. Why am I ashamed of myself about something I did when I was a stupid kid?"

"And how old were you?" he asked. His body relaxed and he bumped his shoulder to hers.

How he could do that, she'd like to know. Turn it off. Shut it down. Or maybe he didn't. Maybe he walked around with the same fears and pain she did. "You know I love you, right, Josh? No matter what? Anything you need, anytime."

He pressed back. "I know, sis. Just…let's not go there right now. Tell me what you think you have to be ashamed about. It helps me to help you."

She sighed. "It's so stupid. When Dawn signed away her parental rights, I was eight. I was living with a family in Mount Pleasant. I was the only foster and they had two other kids older than me. I don't know why, maybe something my social worker said, but I thought they had adopted me."

Josh's sharp intake of breath revealed his instant understanding. This is why she could only say these things to him. Why he could only talk to her.

"How long?" Josh asked.

"A year. They moved me the summer before

I went to middle school. I was so shocked. And angry."

And betrayed. The howling pain and humiliation had been too much for her at age nine. That's when she'd shut down. That's when she'd stopped letting people get close. That's when she'd stopped believing anyone. Josh put an arm around her and she turned to him, burying her face against his shoulder. But there were no tears. The pain was too big for tears. She hung on to Josh.

"Poor baby," Josh crooned in her ear. "You had your trust destroyed." She nodded against his shoulder. "But you've rebuilt it pretty well, don't you think?"

She pushed back. "No! God, no. I don't trust anyone. I think everyone is lying to me."

"Do you think I'm lying to you?"

"No!"

"Lena? Molly? Lito? Was Lito lying to you?"

"No, but that's different."

"It's not." She started to get up but Josh grabbed her hand.

"It's *you* you don't trust." She went still. "You don't trust your ability to know when a person is worth your trust. Or your love. And given what you just told me, that's understandable."

"But it's ruining my life."

"How? You have great friends, a family you've

gathered around you, a successful career. Doesn't seem so ruined to me." He reached out and caught her chin in his hand, turning her to face him. "Wyatt Anderson." She tried to turn her face away but he held on tight. "You fell in love with him, didn't you?"

"I didn't mean to."

Josh laughed and let her pull away. "We're a couple of messes. You know that, right?"

"Speak for yourself," she said, stung. "And why haven't you ever tried it?"

"What? Falling in love? You know that's something I can't risk." He pushed off the table and pulled his helmet back on. "Let's get back before it starts getting dark."

Sadie climbed down and took his hand. "I'm sorry."

"I'm not mad, Sadie. Are you okay for real now? Did any of this help?"

"I think so. I think it's going to take a while to work through it all, but I know everything I need to know. I'm not keeping secrets from myself anymore."

CHAPTER TWENTY-ONE

SHE COULDN'T CONCENTRATE. Every time she tried, she would drift away to the single thought that had been circling her mind since the motorcycle ride with Josh. Why didn't she feel any better? In fact, she felt worse.

A little before noon, she pushed the remaining paperwork—mostly business permits and related governmental nonsense for the Columbia expansion—into a pile. She picked up her purse and walked to the reception area. "I'm going out."

Molly spun around in her chair and pushed her reading glasses into her hair. "Are you available or not?"

Sadie hesitated. She wasn't sure where she was going. She needed to go. The idea of getting in her car and driving until she didn't feel like driving anymore was appealing. She rubbed at her forehead. Being a responsible adult sucked sometimes. "Not. Well, unless it's a real emergency. You know."

"I know, honey. Do you?"

"Do I what?"

"Do you know if you have a real emergency, we're here for you? Like you'd be for us?"

She pressed her lips together and blinked against the tears stinging at her eyes. A warm feeling spread through her. She nodded. "Yes. Thank you."

The day was a little too warm to be termed perfect, but the sun was shining and the sky was blue and that was good enough for her. She put the windows down and enjoyed the warm breeze as she navigated up Highway 17. She turned at 171 and made her way to the Earth Fare parking lot. Because if you ate a healthy, organic, hormone- and antibiotic-free lunch, the jelly-bean binges were canceled out. Certainly, this was a proven fact in some universe.

She took her pasta salad and bottled water back to the car. A strange combination of restlessness and exhaustion battled within her, making her unsure what to do with herself. While she ate, she considered Molly's words. Usually she bristled when someone offered her help or indicated she might need it. She took care of herself, thank you very much. But she hadn't been defensive. Not at all. She'd been grateful. Maybe she was losing her mind.

She laughed out loud in the empty car. After the past few weeks? Grant showing up. Meeting her mother. The entire Wyatt fiasco. And, starting it off, losing Abuelito. Her throat contracted painfully. She wished he was still here. What would he have said about her meeting with her mother? Packing away the remains of her lunch, she remembered what he'd told her the day she visited. *Don't let her failure be your legacy.*

How? How do I do that? She took a sip of water and her gaze went out to the road, to the traffic on Folly Road. She put the bottle down and cranked up the engine.

Less than ten minutes later, she had left the Explorer parked near the entrance and was slowly walking along the shady paths of Holy Cross Cemetery.

She walked directly to the spot. She stood for a while at the edge of the grave. On the bright white marble headstone, his name and dates had been added to those of his late wife, a woman Sadie had never met. The grass was green but had a yellow tint to it as if it hadn't quite recovered from being removed and replaced. Sadie sat down at the edge of the grass. She picked out a few leaves and brushed the grass with her hand.

"Hey, Lito," she said. It seemed silly saying it out loud, but at the same time her voice broke. She pressed her hands against her eyes. *Selfish.* That's what she was being with her tears. He was free of pain. Happily reunited with the love of his life. Her wanting him back because she needed him was selfish.

"I don't know much about how this heaven stuff works so I don't know if you can hear me or not. But I think I'll pretend you can."

She looked up into the arms of the oak tree and listened to a mockingbird sing his song for her.

"I met with my mother. Maybe you know that. Or maybe it's only God who can see everything. But you were right. I knew you were, but I guess as a kid, I'd always felt like it was my fault and the feeling was stronger than the knowing."

She stopped and closed her eyes. She could see him. Not the sick, frail Lito, but the smiling, healthy man who had made her sit with him on the ground in the backyard as he lured wild kittens to the edge of the blanket they sat on. They never talked much but she got used to sitting in his presence. She smiled. He'd used the very same techniques on her that he had used on the feral cats. Feed them. Gain their trust by being with them. Teach them through words and touch that humans aren't so bad. She saw him in her mind's eye, simply nodding at her revelation.

"She admitted it. Everything. How she didn't try because she was using drugs. How she gave me up for adoption because she was afraid I'd mess up her new life. She left me behind for her own selfish reasons."

Her fingers played with the grass as she told him everything. About meeting her mother and the things they had said. A hitching sigh slipped out and she covered her eyes.

"It didn't help," she whispered. "I thought it would make it better. But it didn't. It didn't change a thing."

When at last the tears had washed away most of the pain, but none of the disappointment, she wiped at her face with the hem of her shirt.

You have to forgive her.

The words sounded in her ear as surely as if Lito himself had been there sitting beside her. Her body flinched away from them. *Forgive? No. Forgive her? Tell her it was okay? No.* That wasn't going to happen. Never. *She should feel guilty about it every second of her life.*

Sadie lifted a hand to her chest and took stock. The anger was back. Her jaw was clenched, her heart beating fast, her gut twisting and tight. *What are you angry about? What Dawn did or the idea of forgiving her?* She wished for a couple of shots of cinnamon whiskey so she could demand the truth from herself.

"Truth time," she whispered.

Why don't you want to forgive her? Because it lets her off the hook for what she did? Is that what forgiveness is? Or is it understanding that humans are fallible? Spectacularly fallible at times. She remembered herself at fifteen. Angry. Lonely. Scared. Starved for love. She'd done her share of acting out. Drinking. Smoking pot. Lost her virginity to a boy she didn't even like because she craved the warmth of his arms around her. What if she'd gotten pregnant? What if the drugs had taken over?

She found she could understand and forgive the stupid teenager her mother had been. It was her conscious decision to abandon her child so she could keep a better life for herself that Sadie was having trouble with. She couldn't forgive that part. The anger crept back in. She stood and brushed the bits of dirt and grass from her hands.

You don't forgive her for her sake, but for yours.

She froze, staring down at the gravestone. In spite of the warmth of the day, she shivered as a breeze brushed by her. A tiny trickle of fear flowed through her as the knowledge became clear in her mind. Her anger wouldn't go away until she let go of it. And she had to somehow forgive her mother to let go. Because it was no longer her mother's abandonment impacting her life, it was her anger about it. Her shame about it.

The idea rocked her to her core and she sat down with an ungainly thud at the foot of the grave. *Let it go. She messed up. She was stupid and scared and made poor decision after poor decision. That's her shame to bear, Sadie, not yours.* A strange, light feeling washed through her and she drew in what seemed like the first unhampered breath of her life.

"Oh, Lito," she whispered. "Is that all? That's all I ever needed to do?"

Her thoughts turned from her mother to herself. If she could forgive Dawn, let go of the anger, could she forgive herself? Forgive a desperate, scared little girl who misunderstood a grown-up? Who wanted so badly to have a home and a family that she leaped to a comforting conclusion? Because it wasn't really that social worker's fault, nor the family's. She'd never said anything out loud. She had convinced herself that it was true. Like a child. Julietta's face rose in her mind's eye. She was the same age. Would she judge Jules if she'd thought something like that? As her naive way of trying to find normalcy after such a loss? She wouldn't. Her heart would break for the little girl.

So she let her heart break for the little girl she'd been. All she had wanted was a home. A family. Maybe a kitten.

After the tears faded away, she felt a sense of lightness. She didn't want to move. Didn't want to do anything to jeopardize this new feeling. She knew someday she would have to forgive her mother in person but today was not that day.

She was free.

"Thank you," she whispered.

Walking back to her car, her thoughts turned to Wyatt Anderson. As with her mother, she held two sins against him. She could forgive him the fact that he had been hired to investigate her and the crew; it was his job and he couldn't have known coming in they would be attracted to each other. But that he'd slept with her without telling her the truth—she didn't know how to get around that one. She couldn't quite be angry because, if she were honest, she had known some part of him hadn't wanted things to go that far, but the part of him she had had in her hand sure did. So they'd both made a mistake that night. They'd both given in to their desire for each other before either of them should have.

She climbed into the car and sat for a moment, letting the air conditioner chase out the hot air. He'd snuck into her heart without her noticing. He and Jules both. Nothing to be done about it. She'd messed it up. Maybe the next guy who dared to try to love her would have better luck.

Except she didn't want another guy. She wanted him. Them.

"Enough, Sadie," she said out loud. She put the car in gear and drove out of the parking lot. "One life crisis solved is enough for today."

Sᴀᴅɪᴇ ʟᴏʙʙᴇᴅ ᴛʜᴇ tennis ball high and hard and watched as Jack took off after it. His impressive leap into the air made her smile. He ran back to her, and she took a moment to ruffle his fur. "You getting tired yet, Jackie Boy?"

"I don't think he ever gets tired."

Sadie looked over her shoulder at a pair of denim-clad knees. She tilted her head. Wyatt. A dart of nervous hope stabbed her, and she couldn't deny she'd come to the park hoping this very thing would happen. She looked around. "Where's Jules?"

"Having a spa day with her friend."

"Oh."

She didn't know what to say. So many thoughts were colliding in her head. Why was he here? What did he want? Did she even dare hope?

"Can I sit down?"

"Sure." She busied herself with pouring some water for Jack while he sat beside her. "I'm glad to run into you. I wanted to apologize."

"That's what I'm here for."

"To get an apology?"

"No, to make one myself." He reached out and touched her hand. "I shouldn't have slept with you before I told you the truth. I didn't plan on it ending up like that."

"I know. I remember you pulling away. I remember you trying to put the brakes on things..."

He let out a breath and scrubbed a hand through his hair. "No. I could have stepped back. I'm the one in the wrong here, not you. I should have told you the truth right then and there or walked away. I was more than deceitful. I was dishonorable."

His eyes were on hers, dark and troubled. She shook her head. "Not dishonorable, Wyatt. You wouldn't be here if you were. You wouldn't feel bad about it."

"But deceitful."

She pet Jack and let the word hang there between them. "Maybe a little. Are there degrees of deceit? Because I know you weren't just trying to get into my bed."

"That doesn't make me feel any better about it."

"I accept your apology. I'm not holding anything against you about it, if that helps. And I do want to apologize for my outburst. The way I reacted was unforgivable. Immature and stupid."

"You had every right to be angry."

"But not to scream and throw things."

"Accepted."

Sadie could feel the distance growing between them. She bowed her head. *Don't cry. Try to keep some dignity.* "Okay. Well. Then I guess that's that." He smiled. Not enough to pop those dimples, but it was a smile, so she took it. "So, we're good?"

"We're good."

She looked into his eyes, trying to find the courage to say the words. *Can we start over? Try this for real? Do you still have any feelings for me? Because I'm in love with you. You and your funny, funky little niece both.* The words wouldn't come. His eyes, while warm, held a bit of polite distance and his smile seemed strained.

She looked away. and took a sip of her bottle of water. *What did you expect? That he'd ask you out? Just because you've reached an epiphany in your life doesn't erase the hot mess of a woman you've shown him. Get back to basics. Suck it up and deal.*

"Sadie, I wish things could be different. But I've got Jules to consider."

She looked away, screwing the cap back on her water bottle. "I understand. You certainly didn't see me at my best."

"I understand. Losing your grandfather. My lies."

"I met with my mother."

"Your mother? Had you never known her?"

"Sort of. I remember a few visitations when I was little. But she gave up her parental rights when I was eight. Doomed me to foster care for the rest of my childhood."

"Jesus, Sadie. Are you okay?"

"Mostly. It was some pretty ugly truth facing, but I feel better."

He took her hand. She wanted to pull away. Didn't want the reminder of the warmth and comfort of his touch. She couldn't, though. If this was the last time he touched her, she wanted to remember it. She let her fingers intertwine with his.

"I know I push people away," she said in a rushed whisper. She hadn't planned on saying anything, but her heart had other ideas. "I know I'm prickly and difficult. I know I have a hard time trusting people. I don't want to do that anymore. That's why I met her. To face the past. To try to let it go and move on with my life."

"I'm glad. You're a good person, Sadie. Good things should happen to you. I wish…"

She squeezed his hand. "What do you wish?"

His gaze met hers. The sad longing she saw there hurt her heart. She couldn't let the words out. She wouldn't beg him to love her.

"I wish I knew what to do."

"What do you want to do?"

His hand came up and gently cupped her cheek. A thumb gently caressed her bottom lip. She couldn't hold back a sigh.

"What I want doesn't matter anymore. That's

what I've realized. Everything I do impacts Jules. She's still at a delicate stage."

"I know. I understand." She took his hand, pressing her lips to the back of it before clasping it between both her hands. "When the social worker told me my mother had signed me over for adoption, I misunderstood her. I thought the family I was with had adopted me. For the first time in my whole life, I felt safe. I felt like I had a home. I stopped worrying. I started breathing. Called the fosters Mom and Dad."

She let go of his hand and crossed her arms. "Then I was moved to another home. I know exactly how Jules feels. Like her entire world has collapsed. But she has you. That alone is going to save her."

He shifted so he was closer and put his arm around her. "I'm sorry."

"Me, too."

She leaned into his strength and felt comfort and peace. Saved it up to remember on cold lonely days.

"I have to go," he whispered.

"I know."

And that was it. He walked away. No final kiss. No goodbyes. Just walked right out of her life. Jack sensed her mood and pressed close. She looped her arms around him. "Yeah, Jackie, we need another place to play."

CHAPTER TWENTY-TWO

HE CAME AWAKE IMMEDIATELY. A roll of fading thunder rattled the windows. A flicker of lightning lit up the room a millisecond before a sizzling, crackling boom crashed overhead. Almost lost in the sound was a small cry. Jules. He threw back the covers and fumbled for the T-shirt he'd thrown at the end of the bed.

"I'm right here, Jules," he called as he went to her room. Nothing happened when he flipped the switch. Great. "Hey, baby girl, it's all right."

He made his way to her bed, stubbing his toes on and stumbling over books and toys. He reached for her and she leaped from the bed, attaching herself to him. Her legs locked around his waist and her arms crisscrossed around his neck, almost choking him. Her cheek was wet with tears as it pressed against his. He brought his hands up to hold her tight.

"It's okay, baby, I've got you."

"Make it stop."

Another earsplitting crack of lightning rattled

the windows, and she pressed her face against his neck.

"I can't make it stop. But I won't let go until it's gone."

He reached down and pulled the comforter from her bed and draped it over her. As he made his way down the hall to the living room, the storm continued to rage overhead. It was a doozy. *Hopefully a fast-moving doozy.* He sat on the sofa and she burrowed into him, pulling the blanket around her and over her head. The sounds of thunder and lightning continued to fill the room. If Jules hadn't been so afraid, he might have enjoyed the display of Mother Nature's power. He tightened his arms around her.

"It's okay. It won't last for long. It's going away now."

She went still in his arms. "How do you know?"

"Easy. You count the time between the flash and the thunder. If the time is getting longer, the storm is moving away."

"Really?"

"Let's test it out. Wait for the lightning."

When the flash came, he began to count. "One. Two. Three."

Boom!

Jules squealed, but it had more of a startled tone to it than the terror she'd shown earlier.

"So, three that time. Now, when the next one comes, we'll see. You count with me."

When the flash came, she whispered along with him. "One. Two. Three. Four."

"A little more that time," he said.

By the time they were getting up to ten, Jules was drifting back to sleep. On the next flash, she didn't even count. He could feel her breathing, deep and relaxed. He didn't want to wake her so he tried to shift around to a more comfortable spot. Pretty early, he guessed, as his eyes drifted closed. Too early to be waking up.

"Uncle Wyatt?"

He jerked out of his doze. The light in the room had changed. Brightened. The storm had passed and morning was closer than he thought. Or he'd overslept. "Yeah?"

Jules squirmed until she was splayed out over his chest, half lying, half sitting on him. Her face was serious.

"What's wrong, Jujube?"

"Nothing." She fidgeted with the edges of the blanket. "I had a question. But I'm not sure."

He shifted so he was sitting more upright and rubbed a hand across his face. "You can ask me anything, Jules. Anything. I'll never be mad at you for asking a question."

Her eyes met his, dark and thoughtful. *Are all eight-year-olds this smart?* She snuggled down against him, her cheek pressed to his chest, and he put his arms around her.

"I don't think you'll be mad," she said as her fingers plucked at the fabric of his shirt. "I just don't know if I should."

Stay with the original plan.

"You can always ask me anything, Jules."

Her hand went still, and she took a deep breath.

"Would it be okay if I called you Daddy?"

Everything went still. For a brief second all was numb, then an overwhelming feeling welled up in him. His heart seemed to expand until surely it would explode out of his chest. This must be how it feels to hold your newborn child for the first time. This must be the sudden, blinding, overwhelming love he'd heard others speak of. It took a moment to answer.

He gave her a gentle hug. "Yes. It would be very okay. If that's what you want."

She pushed up. "'Cause you sort of are, right? I mean, I don't have a real daddy, but you and me, we're our own family now, right?"

"That's right. You and me. We're a family. I love you like a daddy would, Jules."

She smiled and leaned forward to give him a smacking kiss before snuggling into his arms again. "I love you, too, Unc... Daddy."

She said the word slowly as if testing it out. Wyatt wiped at his eyes and stared up at the ceiling. A smile crossed his lips. *You're a daddy. Congratulations.* He found her hand and held it in his. She'd already drifted back to sleep. He remembered when she was a baby. She'd seemed so tiny then, but even now, at eight, she seemed so small and fragile.

Eight years old. He brushed the hair back from Jules's face as the realization washed over him. *Jesus.* She was the same age Sadie had been when her mother left her. He imagined Jules with no family, nobody willing to take her in, moved from home to home. The thought of it made him sick.

Sadie had lived it. Been in foster care all her life. He tried to picture an eight-year-old Sadie. Had she been a tiny bird of a girl like Jules? All dark hair and skinny arms? His heart, which had moments ago been so jubilant and full of love, now almost broke.

The return of electricity was heralded by the beeping of various devices. The microwave was the loudest and most obnoxious. He slid out from under Jules and went to silence the noise before it woke her. He found his cell. Six o'clock. Way too early. He carried her back to her bed and tucked the blanket around her. She mumbled something and rolled over, already deep asleep. The easy sleep of a child. He stood and watched her. *Daddy.* How much courage had it taken for her to ask him that? He only hoped he could live up to the honor. He nodded. Yes. It was time to make that phone call. Get the adoption process going and make her his daughter.

He tiptoed out but left the door open a crack in case she woke up. In case she was scared again. He leaned against the kitchen counter as the coffeemaker hissed and spit, looking out at the garden. The storm didn't seem to have damaged the seedlings, but he'd check it out later. His mind kept circling back to the vision in his mind's eye of an eight-year-old Sadie, awake and terrified in her bed with no one to come and tell her it would be okay. It explained quite a lot.

Her prickly exterior. The anger. The way she kept her thoughts and feelings wrapped up tight and wouldn't admit to anything resembling want or need. Growing up like that must have messed her up. He ran a hand through his hair and across his face. More proof that walking away had been the right thing to do. He might understand the emotional damage done to her, but Jules wouldn't. Jules shouldn't have to. It was enough that she had learned the hard fact that parents sometimes die; she didn't need to know some parents walked away from their kids. She didn't need to wonder if he would walk away from her.

He poured coffee and sat at the kitchen table. No. For Jules he needed to find a woman who knew what family was. Who knew what a child needed in terms of love and support. Who knew how to show and accept love. Not someone like Sadie, who kept her heart locked away from the world.

Except.

She didn't. Not really. She and Josh were as close, if not closer than he and Maddie had been. She'd taken him in and given him the chance to build a good life for himself. And Molly. Molly was the grandmother who looked out for them both. She'd built a little family and he knew there was nothing she wouldn't do for them.

And the guys. She felt responsible for them all. She worried over them like a mother.

He moved restlessly around the kitchen, pulling out ingredients to make pancakes with when Jules woke up. It'd become their Sunday morning routine.

So, sure, okay, she was capable of caring. Once you get beyond the razor wire she kept strung around her heart. He turned the mug around in circles on the table and replayed the evening they'd spent together. She might claim it was only sex, but it hadn't been. She'd let down her guard. She'd told him secrets and he'd told her his. He'd been under the razor wire that night. And it had been good. The sex had been incredible. The shared confidences in the dark had made it even better.

Until Jules's phone call had interrupted. And she'd sent him off without a word, without a complaint, without any resentment. She knew Jules came first. She expected Jules to come first. *Damn, man. It's been there all along.* Since the first meeting in the park, she'd asked about Jules. Asked if she would be comfortable at the dinner. When he'd come to tell her he was quitting, her first response was that he had to do what was best for his family. For him and Jules.

A sinking feeling filled him. He was under the wire. He and Jules both. Sadie had let down her guard and taken them both in. Quietly. Without expectations. She'd loved them both. He'd been the one pushing away. He'd been the one holding his emotions back. He'd been the one who didn't know what a family could look like. He put his hands to his face.

Jules wandered into the kitchen. Her hair was a snarled mess and she dragged the comforter behind her. "What's the matter, Unc... Daddy?"

He held out his arms and she came to him.

He lifted her up on his lap. "Nothing. You want blueberry pancakes this morning?"

She leaned back and put her hands on his cheeks to tip his head down. "You looked sad."

"I'm not sad. I realized I believed something about someone that wasn't true."

"So you're sorry, not sad?"

"Exactly. How'd you get to be so smart?"

She shrugged. "Shiloh's mom makes chocolate chip pancakes. Can we make those?"

"I don't think we have any chocolate chips."

She jumped down to go into the pantry. Wyatt watched her. She'd seen it more clearly than he. He was sorry. He was sorry he'd let his own fears for Jules color how he saw Sadie. He was sorry that he'd slipped so effortlessly in love with her that he never even noticed she might feel the same. And he'd walked away from her. He hadn't even tried to trust her.

Jules came out of the pantry with a bag of peanut butter chips that were supposed to have become cookies. "What about these? We can chop up a banana on top, too. Does that sound good?"

"Can I ask you a serious question, Jules?"

She climbed on the chair next to him, kneeling in the seat so they were eye to eye. "Like a grown-up question?"

"No. It's about something you did."

"Am I in trouble?"

"No. I'm curious. When you met Ms. Sadie for the first time, you told her how your mother used to curl your hair. Remember that?"

Her little face went serious and she nodded. "Uh-huh."

"Why? Why did you talk to Sadie about your mother when you hadn't talked to anyone else about her?"

Jules pushed her messy hair out of her face. "I knew she cared."

"How did you know?"

Jules sat down and her face crunched up in concentration. "I think it's like—it's like you can tell. Most people treat you like a kid. But some treat you like you're you."

He tried to decipher that. *Treat you like you're you.* "Like a person?"

"Yes. A lot of people act like they want to talk to a kid, but they're faking. Ms. Sadie doesn't fake it. She likes me."

No, he thought as he kissed the top of Jules's head and thanked her, Sadie didn't fake anything. Especially about the people she cared about. He was a fool. Worse than a fool. He'd walked away from a woman who cared about Jules as much as she cared about him.

"Are we making pancakes?"

He stood. "Sure are. Peanut butter and banana pancakes. Get the flour, Jujube."

He turned the griddle on and pulled down a mixing bowl, remembering the first couple of pancake disasters they'd had before he got the hang of it. He'd made a mess of things with Sadie while trying to figure out this single-father thing. He had a choice. He could leave it as it was and pretend it'd been a "wrong place, wrong time" kind of thing. Or he could try again.

CHAPTER TWENTY-THREE

SADIE DIDN'T WANT to get out of bed. She didn't want to face the new week. Everything had changed. Lito was gone. Wyatt was gone. She'd faced down her mother. She'd found the secret to letting go of the anger and fear that had colored every aspect of her life. She'd talked with Grant again. They had a long journey ahead of them, but they both agreed to take it slow.

Jack's doggy breath in her face got her up. She should be happy. She should feel a million pounds lighter without her past weighing her down, not slow and sad. She brushed her teeth, unable to meet her eyes in the mirror. *It's because you screwed everything up with Wyatt.*

Duh. She spit into the sink. *You didn't even have the guts to try.* Not that it would have done any good. He thought she was damaged goods. Way too damaged to be trusted around Jules. That hurt. The idea that she would hurt a child after all the hurt she'd been subjected to in her life cut deep. But she understood. More than understood, she approved. He put Jules and her welfare above anything else. Above anyone else. As he should.

"Okay, Jack. We're going. Settle down."

She let him out the back door and sat on the step as he went through his routine. She heard a car pull into the front parking lot and checked the time. A few minutes before eight. She whistled for Jack. The guys would be getting here soon. Maybe Josh would take over the staff meeting. She didn't have the energy to talk today.

Footprints crunched on the gravel path that led around the side of the house. Jack barked ferociously as the gate opened. "Jack! Hush."

"Stupid mutt. Like you didn't know it was me."

Josh shut the gate behind him and came to sit beside Sadie. He shoulder bumped her. "How you holding up, sis?"

"Good. Okay. Getting there."

"Did you figure out your valuable life lesson?"

She elbowed him lightly in the ribs. "Don't be a smart-ass. Yes. I learned it wasn't what she did that ruined my life. My anger and resentment is the problem."

"So you're better now?"

There was a tone underlying his teasing words. The fearful tone of one who'd been abandoned. She hooked her arm around his waist and pressed her cheek against his shoulder. "Not by a long shot. I still need you, brother. I'll always need you."

"Touching. And we need you to start this meeting so we can get to work," Noah said from behind them.

"Be right there."

She got coffee and settled at the head of the conference table. "All right. Let's get going." She flipped open her notebook. "First up, Josh has interviewed and accepted four new clients in Columbia. He'll need a team willing to travel there for cleanings. Travel, hotel and meals will be paid for. There will be a five-dollar-an-hour bonus."

She paused to let Josh add more but he only nodded.

"We've been running through supplies at an increased pace and I want to ask…"

She stopped as Molly appeared at the open doorway between the conference and waiting rooms.

"Sorry, Sadie. There's someone here to see you."

"I'm in a meeting."

Molly moved aside and Wyatt Anderson stepped into the room. The shock of seeing him there froze her in her seat, and she struggled to remember how to breathe. She stared at him until she realized her mouth was hanging open and snapped it shut. Why was he here? She blinked and resisted the urge to pinch her arm. Was she still in bed? Dreaming?

"What the…" one of the guys said. A low chorus of angry mutters rose behind his words.

Josh lifted a hand and silence returned. Sadie's heartbeat also returned, slamming out a reverberating percussion that she could feel through to her bones.

Wyatt's gaze moved briefly from Sadie to Josh and he gave the barest nods. He lifted the bouquet of roses in his hands. Pink roses. A wild, light feeling rose inside her. She looked into his eyes. A small smile turned up one corner of his mouth. He made his way around the table to her and held out a hand.

"Your grandfather wasn't the only man who loved you, Sadie. I love you. I know I came here under false pretenses, but that was the only thing I ever lied to you about. How I feel about you was never a lie."

Around the table, the guys had turned to stone. She could hear Molly sniffling at the doorway. *This is it, Sadie. Take his hand. Reach out and put your hand in his.* Fear, her old friend, elbowed aside the light feeling she realized was hope. Fear was used to this moment. This was where it lived. Between her and the people who tried to care about her. She was afraid to look into his eyes. His hand remained outstretched. Steady, strong and unwavering. Waiting for her.

"I know I've screwed up with you," he continued. "Especially where Jules is concerned."

She looked up then and was captivated by the emotion in his eyes. Love.

"I'd convinced myself that Jules was the reason I needed to walk away from you. But she's actually the very reason I shouldn't walk away. Who is ever going to understand her better? Who is going to know exactly how she feels? Who is going to be dedicated to protecting her the way I want her to be protected? You will, Sadie. You've lived it. You know her pain. And you would never add to it."

Tears stung her eyes, and a blink sent one tracing down her cheek. Her lips pressed together. That alone was a balm on her soul. That he knew she'd never hurt Jules. The hand he held out to her moved slowly to catch the teardrop against his thumb.

"I love you, Sadie. I want us to be together. I don't want to walk away. I don't want you to push me away. Take my hand."

Reach out. Take his hand. Her hand twitched on the desktop. *Do it. Trust him. Trust yourself.* He smiled patiently at her, waiting for her. Her hand lifted from the desk. *Jump, Sadie. Jump.* Her fingers closed around his and her jumbled up emotions quieted. He tugged her gently to her feet and pressed the flowers into her arms. She bent her head to take in the sweet scent. Lito's roses. She reached out and touched his chest. Swallowed down the fear that was trying for another go at it. *Next leap—say it.*

"I love you, too."

Wyatt smiled and those dimples popped and almost made her sink back to the chair with relief. He took the flowers from her and put his arms around her. She threw her arms around his neck as his mouth came down to hers, and she held on as his arm moved to her waist and he dipped her deep without breaking the kiss. Now the guys were hooting and catcalling. She didn't care.

"And that, guys, is how you do it," Josh said as he stood. "Come on, meeting's adjourned."

"Yeah," Sadie said as the guys began to leave the room. "Get to work. And don't call me today. I'll be busy."

* * * * *

LARGER-PRINT BOOKS!

HARLEQUIN

Presents

GET 2 FREE LARGER-PRINT NOVELS PLUS 2 FREE GIFTS!

PASSION GUARANTEED SEDUCTION

YES! Please send me 2 FREE LARGER-PRINT Harlequin Presents® novels and my 2 FREE gifts (gifts are worth about $10). After receiving them, if I don't wish to receive any more books, I can return the shipping statement marked "cancel." If I don't cancel, I will receive 6 brand-new novels every month and be billed just $5.30 per book in the U.S. or $5.74 per book in Canada. That's a saving of at least 12% off the cover price! It's quite a bargain! Shipping and handling is just 50¢ per book in the U.S. and 75¢ per book in Canada.* I understand that accepting the 2 free books and gifts places me under no obligation to buy anything. I can always return a shipment and cancel at any time. Even if I never buy another book, the two free books and gifts are mine to keep forever.

176/376 HDN GHVY

Name _____ (PLEASE PRINT)

Address _____ Apt. #

City _____ State/Prov. _____ Zip/Postal Code

Signature (if under 18, a parent or guardian must sign)

Mail to the **Reader Service**:
IN U.S.A.: P.O. Box 1867, Buffalo, NY 14240-1867
IN CANADA: P.O. Box 609, Fort Erie, Ontario L2A 5X3

Are you a subscriber to Harlequin Presents® books and want to receive the larger-print edition?
Call 1-800-873-8635 today or visit us at www.ReaderService.com.

* Terms and prices subject to change without notice. Prices do not include applicable taxes. Sales tax applicable in N.Y. Canadian residents will be charged applicable taxes. Offer not valid in Quebec. This offer is limited to one order per household. Not valid for current subscribers to Harlequin Presents Larger-Print books. All orders subject to credit approval. Credit or debit balances in a customer's account(s) may be offset by any other outstanding balance owed by or to the customer. Please allow 4 to 6 weeks for delivery. Offer available while quantities last.

Your Privacy—The Reader Service is committed to protecting your privacy. Our Privacy Policy is available online at www.ReaderService.com or upon request from the Reader Service.

We make a portion of our mailing list available to reputable third parties that offer products we believe may interest you. If you prefer that we not exchange your name with third parties, or if you wish to clarify or modify your communication preferences, please visit us at www.ReaderService.com/consumerchoice or write to us at Reader Service Preference Service, P.O. Box 9062, Buffalo, NY 14240-9062. Include your complete name and address.

HPLP15